MIDNIGHT KISSES

Shifter Island Book One

LEIA STONE
RAYE WAGNER

Copyright © 2020 by Leia Stone and Raye Wagner

All rights reserved.

Cover by KD Richie (Story Wrappers)

No part of this book may be reproduced in any form or by any electronic or mechanical means, including information storage and retrieval systems, without written permission from the author, except for the use of brief quotations in a book review.

This is a work of fiction. Names, characters, places, and incidents either are the product of the author's imagination or are used fictitiously. Any resemblance to actual persons, live or dead are purely coincidental.

To contact the authors please use the contact form on their websites.

LeiaStone.com

RayeWagner.com

To the mothers and fathers who raise their children to believe in themselves.

Chapter 1

THE LATE SUMMER BREEZE, unusually hot and dry for Montana, washed over me, bending the tall grass. Mixed with the scent of lavender and lilac, my father's musky scent hit me, followed by the sound of his heavy footfalls. I'd shifted back to human after a run in the woods, and my skin still tingled; my wolf close to the surface.

Smiling, I sat up and turned toward him. "Hello, Father."

The moment I saw his somber expression, my heart tumbled into my stomach. "What's wrong?" Without waiting for an answer, I sprang to my feet and sent out my alpha heir power, trying to sense if anyone in the pack had been mortally injured or killed.

Nothing felt out of the ordinary, so why did he look so ... stricken? "Father?"

He plastered on a fake smile, but the expression

never touched his eyes. "The alpha king has called for you. It's time."

My gaze dropped to the stiff white paper in his hand. Embossed lettering danced on the page, moving in golden swirls, and there was no mistaking the logo: a capital A above an island, its snow-capped tip surrounded by rippling waves. We all knew that symbol at the top of the paper, an official declaration from the alpha king. I tried to steady my breathing while my heart made an attempt to escape my chest.

"Already?"

Swallowing the lump at the back of my throat, I blinked, determined not to cry. Tears were not befitting an alpha's daughter. No one wanted a leader whose first instinct was emotion. I needed to be strong for me and my pack.

But before I could stop myself, words tumbled out: "I thought I had another year at home."

"So did I," my father said, his nostrils flaring. His eyes blazed with emotion. Was it fear? Rage? As quickly as I saw it, he reined it in. Of course, a shifter must control their feelings at all times lest they lose themselves to their animal instinct. "But you're of age."

He extended the letter as if he couldn't stand to touch it any longer, and a sob formed in my throat.

These mountains, this blue sky, the trees covering our land ... the pain of leaving home tore through me. I was born of this place, connected to the earth here like all of our pack. To go to Alpha Island, to leave my pack

... the thought made my stomach churn. I wouldn't be permitted to see or speak to anyone from home for four years, only letters—and only if I could find someone to bring them here, to the mortal realm where our pack was exiled. Judging by the frequency of visitors, the odds didn't fall in my favor.

I yanked the paper from his hand, angry with the injustice of the system. "They don't even like our clan. We all know it! I hate that we have to play by their rules."

My father frowned at my outburst. "It is the way of the alpha, and our pack needs *you* to lead. Without training your magic, you won't be ready to take over when I die."

I grimaced, knowing the other option. Those who refused the summons to Alpha Island were sentenced to death, traitors to their pack and their alpha heir blood. One hundred percent not going to happen.

My father cleared his throat. "The pack will need a strong leader when I'm gone. You must train. Show the other packs we have sufficient power to deserve their respect."

I wanted to protest or pout, but at nineteen winters old, and as the alpha's daughter, I needed to act like I had my crap together.

So I took a deep breath, shoving my emotions away to deal with later, and nodded. "I'll make Crescent Clan proud."

He opened his arms, and it took me an awkward

moment before I understood the gesture. My father was not one for unnecessary affection. He taught me to be strong, to never show weakness unless it served a purpose. While I struggled at times with adhering to his strict doctrine, having him fold me into a stiff hug meant this was a big deal for him. As his arms wrapped around me, I felt the lump in my throat grow. Peering up, I looked into his eyes, the same pale blue as mine—the only part of him I'd inherited. Only, my eyes burned with unshed tears while his glittered like crystal, hard and sharp.

"Do you wish you had a son?" I whispered.

He pushed my silver-white hair away from my face, shaking his head. "Never. You've been your mother's greatest gift to me."

Before I could blink them away this time, the tears spilled down my cheeks. I thought of the stories my father had told me about the woman who died giving birth to me and gave him a small smile. My father rarely talked about my mother. It must've upset him too much. I was the only piece left of her. My father's commanders had urged him to take a breeding companion after her death and try to have a male heir, but he refused. It was just me. Me and Dad.

"Show them what you're made of, Nai." He bopped my chin, and just like that, I was brought back to my sparring lessons as a child. He'd said the same to me before every match.

Reaching up, I traced the white crescent moon, our

clan's alpha mark, on his forehead, and my fingers thrummed with energy. His link to our clan's magic always gave me little zaps when I touched it. His mark was an exact match for the one on my head.

I needed to be strong like he'd raised me, regardless of the rumors about the other packs and the stories of what happened on Alpha Island, regardless of the fact that I wouldn't see him for *four years*.

"Hold down the fort while I'm gone," I said, pulling away. "I'll be back before you know it—an alpha heir, ready to serve." I saluted him with a silly grin, hoping to keep things light.

Pursing his lips, he cleared his throat. "Just be safe, Nai. The other heirs won't like another Crescent Clan wolf on the island."

I waved him off, feigning confidence I didn't feel. "I'll be fine."

But we both knew the island was dangerous as were the trials.

We walked over the packed dirt path toward the main lodge together, and for the first time, my father checked his long stride and paced beside me, indicating we were equals. Members of the pack stopped what they were doing and tipped their heads in respect as we passed. I held my chin high, clutching the paper in my fist while pretending *not* to be nervous when all I felt was worming trepidation.

We rounded the corner of the log-style lodge that served as the pack's headquarters, and I stumbled when

I spotted four Alpha Academy guards wearing matching black shirts with the island symbol embroidered on the left side like some stupid fraternity. They stood beside a shiny black SUV.

I skittered to a stop, staring nearly open-mouthed at their hulking figures. Men didn't grow this big unless they were dominants. All four of them stood well over six feet tall and wore black baseball caps. That was shady … especially if they were covering marks on their foreheads. They might even be from Midnight Pack. The thought sent fiery tendrils of anger through my chest. The ruling pack could bite me, but…

My pace slowed as I compared my fraying cutoffs and tank-top to their swanky threads. I didn't need to arrive looking like a Montana farm girl even if I was one.

All of the guards stood as still as statues. None of them spoke as my dad and I approached.

"I need to leave now? Like, right this minute?" I mumbled under my breath, hoping I was wrong. My gaze dipped to my pale feet, the skin dusty all the way up to my ankles. Sadly, I wasn't Cinderella; I wasn't going to a ball, and those beefy dudes were definitely *not* my Fairy Godmother. An outfit change definitely wouldn't hurt.

My father gave a curt nod, eyeing the guards with disdain. "Lona is packing your things and will be out shortly."

Damn. Damn. Damn.

They should've given us a day at least. How was I going to say goodbye to Callie and Mack? They were out hunting and wouldn't hear the news until I was long gone.

I huffed. "Fine."

"Remember, your cousin is there," Dad whispered. "He'll be looking to expose your weaknesses."

I grunted and shook my head at the unnecessary reminder. Nolan had always looked out for Nolan, except when he was chasing some female around like it was breeding season. His mother and my father didn't speak after a falling out, but she still carried alpha blood, so she could technically take over the pack and so could her son.

"It'll be fine," I said, not wanting my dad to worry.

Lona came out the door with my worn duffle; the faded green bag was almost as big as her body. Tears tracked down her wrinkled face as she crossed the porch and descended the stairs.

"Lon." I ran to my childhood nanny, a surge of protective instinct for the petite woman welling within. "We all knew this was coming. I'll be fine."

Apparently, "fine" was the word of the day.

She nodded, sniffling as she handed me my things. "They used to give notice—at least a couple weeks. I could've made a nice dinner..."

Lona displayed her love through food, and no one, including my father, complained about that. She was an amazing cook.

She pulled me in for a long hug, forcing me to drop the huge duffle I'd just taken. With her affection, the mixture of fear and sadness swelled within my chest, bubbling up into my throat. If I didn't leave ASAP, I was one hundred percent going to bawl—in front of everyone. Through the bond, I could feel the clan approaching, and sure enough, when I spun toward the SUV, a Land Rover no less, the entire pack stood there, crowded in the grassy clearing among the old pickups and dirt bikes. As one, Crescent Clan all dropped to one knee, holding their right fists over their chests.

Something they'd only done for my father, in times of great respect.

I was totally going to lose my cool.

Swallowing hard, I bowed to my people. "It'll be my honor to serve you."

My father was the alpha link for our people's magic; his fire magic could keep them alive in the bitter Montana cold. When he died, Crescent Pack's link would transfer to me—if I graduated Alpha Island. I wasn't ready for the responsibility or respect that came with being alpha, not yet. It was something that had to be earned.

My father leaned in and whispered into my ear. "Beware the alpha king and his heirs. All they want is to retain power, and they'll stoop to *anything* to get it."

As if I needed those reminders. Midnight Clan was the reason my pack was cast out from the magic realm into the mortal world. They were dirty, high mage suck-ups. I would never get involved with them. I gritted my teeth and nodded as fierce determination filled me.

I was the only child of the alpha of Crescent Clan. I'd go to the island and fight for my place, fight for my people, fight to keep our magic strong.

I hefted the canvas bag over my shoulder and marched toward the guards waiting to take me away. As I approached, I studied them. They looked identical. Legit. The four dudes were practically carbon copies of each other... quads, or whatever four people who looked exactly alike were called. Brothers? Obviously. Same height, build, even the same pinched expression of disgust, which their matchy-match sunglasses didn't hide. What was their deal? They glowered as if I were the offensive one.

Yeah, I hate you too.

Their outfits designated them as royal guards to the king, and anything related to the Midnight Pack I hated with passion just out of principle.

Dark hair peeked out from beneath their caps as my gaze ran over their chiseled jaws and then to their muscled arms. Of course, they were beautiful. The assholes always were.

The closer I got, the more my ire rose until irritation prickled my skin, and I had to grit my teeth to keep from snapping at them. Who did they think they were? Sending four guards to collect me like a criminal!

Nolan only had one. This was disrespect through and through.

Obviously, they weren't too high on the food chain or they wouldn't be here in the mortal realm escorting me. But why four? That wasn't normal. Did they think I was a flight risk? I inhaled through my nose and growled when I smelled their dominance—all four of them. This close, their earthy musk blended, and the scent both burned the inside of my nose and lured me. At least one of them smelled *really* good, but I pressed that thought down and tried to ignore it.

One of them cocked his head to the side, the side of his mouth curled in what might be a conspiratorial smirk. He peeled away from his clone brothers and circled to the driver's side. The one standing next to Driver Dude's vacated space looked ready to explode with anger; his muscles were so taut. His nostrils flared, and he dropped his sunglasses just long enough to level me with a green-eyed vitriolic glower.

What the hell? How dare he challenge me on my land?

Punch him in the face? Or let it slide?

"Rage, stop," the driver snapped and chucked a half-empty water bottle, hitting the one who glared at me square in the chest.

Dude didn't move, just kept his evil glare fixed on me.

Hah! His actual name was *Rage*? How fitting.

The guard on his right bumped him with an elbow

and then climbed into the passenger seat. After he closed the door, Rage stepped to the side and opened the rear passenger door while keeping his head turned toward my clan. Never look away from a threat ... it was like he didn't trust us.

He stood there, a silent sentinel, waiting for me to get into the car, and I growled. The final clone brother limped around the back before getting inside, favoring his right leg.

I took one last look at my father and Lon and the rest of my pack and nodded. There would be no big goodbye; it just wasn't the way.

See you guys in four years ... if I survive.

"I need to put my bag in the back," I growled at Rage. "Especially if you expect me to sit between two of you brutes." I circled my hand to encompass the big dudes already in the car. Why did I have to smash in with four giants?

One of them grunted, and the hatch rose, probably activated by Shotgun Dude.

I tossed my bag into the cargo area and then climbed in, sliding into the center of the leather bench seat, and then got smooshed into Clone #3 as *Rage* got in on the other side. He closed the door with a shoulder-check to my side that forced me to bump the mute dude on my left.

"Excuse you," I growled at Rage, glaring at him from the corner of my eye.

Someone needed anger management.

He raised his eyebrows over his mirrored shades and said, "Oops."

His deep voice was gravelly and did something weird to my insides. Not butterflies, definitely not butterflies. More like murder hornets.

As soon as the giant douche on my right settled into his seat, I popped him in the ribs with my elbow. "Oops," I shot back.

"That's enough," Shotgun said.

The scent of leather and car freshener swirled in the vehicle, but the smell was quickly overwhelmed by eau de male wolf. The worst thing you could do to a dominant wolf like me was to trap her in a vehicle with a bunch of other dominants. I'd be lucky to get through this drive without ripping off someone's head.

Ignoring my annoying escorts, I steeled my heart and leaned forward to stare out the window. My gaze landed solely on my father, but his stoic expression, combined with the knowledge he couldn't see me, kept me from waving.

The engine of the SUV purred to life, so quiet compared to the rumbling old truck we owned, and I wondered if the disparity of wealth had anything to do with our pack's banishment from the magic realm. I closed my eyes and rested my head against the back of the seat, feigning sleep.

Mother Mage, help me get through this drive without becoming a murderer.

With my eyes closed, I let my thoughts wander.

What was I getting into? The magical vow my father took as a young teen before entering the island—decades ago—kept him from telling me exactly what to expect. I'd prepared my entire life for battle, propriety, and the way of the alpha. But having been banished from the shifter realm when I was just a baby, I didn't have the advantage of knowing what lay beyond the veil. Pretty sure Amazon didn't deliver there. Nerves churned and twisted my insides. If I puked, I'd definitely be aiming for Rage.

Driver Dude drove down the winding road, the only way in or out of Crescent Valley, while I drummed my fingers on my bare knees. The vehicle was clearly built for luxury, or at least, I'd heard such from the young men in my clan who dreamed of lavishness. But the pothole-ridden path was meant to discourage visitors, so I relaxed and let the movement rock me, lulling me into semi-lucidity.

As soon as we hit the paved street, my heart lurched.

"Have you eaten yet today, cub?" asked the brother who sat shotgun.

Rage, the grouchy one to my right, snorted. "She's hardly a cub, Justice."

Justice? Rage? What kind of names were these?

I ignored their domineering question and peeled my eyes open, staring at the heads of the two in front. Not really identical. Driver Dude's hair was straight; only the ends curled around the collar of his shirt. But Shotgun's hair was wavy—Shotgun, aka Justice. I glanced at the silent brother on my left, but he was staring out the window.

Forcing a dry swallow, I faced Rage.

The dark curls poking out from his cap strained against whatever product he'd used to try to tame it. His profile was like his personality, all hard angles ... except for his lips. Blushing, I forced my attention down ... to his neck, where his pulse feathered between tense muscles. His arms were jacked, the muscles curved and dipped, straining against the confines of his shirt. He clearly had a standing date with the gym. Probably where he burned off the steroids.

Driver Dude angled his head and muttered, "I don't remember her name."

Nice. I had Tweedledee, Tweedledum, Rage, and Justice as escorts. I hated to have a pity party so early on, but *why me?* I let the thought bounce around my head and then realized it was useless. No one else could take my place. As much as I hated our system, I'd known this was coming. I just thought I had more time with my father and our pack.

"Who cares what her name is, Noble? Why does it matter if she's hungry, Justice? *She's* Crescent Clan." Rage's voice was more animal than human by the time he was done.

Oh, hell no.

"Fewer words, buddy. You're annoying me." I glared

at the one named Rage and was rewarded with an absolute feral look.

Rage growled, his canines elongating.

What is his deal?

"Reel it in, Rage," the brother on my left snapped, stretching his arm around my back to smack king d-bag on the arm. "If you shift in here, we're all going with you."

My mouth dried, but before I could contemplate the horror of five dominant wolves trapped in an SUV, the brother on my left poked me in the ribs.

"My brother asked you a question, and it's rude not to answer. Have. You. Eaten?"

I knew they were brothers; they looked insanely too much alike.

"Well?" he demanded, his jaw snapping shut with a click.

"I'm not hungry," I muttered, returning his glare. Not true, and my stomach promptly rumbled loudly, declaring my lie. Male wolves and their need to feed a female wolf was beyond sexist and annoying. I'd starve before accepting food from them. It was a move for power, and I wouldn't play into it.

The brother to my left sighed, and I rolled my eyes to the roof of the car. My attention was captured by the knobs and buttons; I wondered what they all did. Was that a television screen? I was going to ignore these jerks all the way to the island!

The driver shook his head. "Listen, cub, I can't bring

a hungry wolf to the island. We have an hour drive before we hit civilization."

A green and gold package landed in my lap.

"There's a granola bar to tide you over," Justice said from his shotgun seat.

Rage smacked Justice in the back of the head. "Why are you being nice to her? Let her starve."

"Calm down." Driver dude's voice was softer than the others; he was clearly the voice of reason.

The brother to my left looked at the driver next. "Noble, would you like to offer her a refreshment as well?"

The driver's hands clenched the steering wheel until his knuckles turned white. "Piss off, Honor!"

Noble? Rage? Justice? Honor? What kind of freaking names were these?

I glared at Rage beside me and leaned into him. Placing the food bar in his lap, "Thanks for the offer, but I'll decline—on all counts."

The driver, Noble, chuckled. "I think this cub has claws."

I liked them better when they were mute.

"What's your name, cub?" Noble asked as he maneuvered around the potholes on the road leading out of town.

Oh, *now* they were going to be friendly?

I stared at my reflection in his glasses through the rearview mirror, wishing I could rip them off. "Not a *cub.*"

I was nineteen, and they couldn't be a day older than twenty-one. Was this a joke?

"Then *what*?" Rage growled.

"*Alpha heir* to you, buddy." Might as well put these douchebags in their place right now. No island guard would talk down to me like this; I didn't care how dominant they were.

All four of them laughed at that, and a blast of cold air hit me as the air conditioner came on. "Be nice, *cub*," Justice growled. "Or the next four years will really suck for you."

Was that a threat?

Fuming, I leaned forward and angled the vents away from me, blasting Rage and Honor with frigid air. How dare they?

Calm down, Nai. Don't show weakness unless there's a reason. Recalling my father's teachings, I closed my eyes and took a deep breath.

"What's with the names? You guys named after virtues or something?" I glared at Rage, who clearly wasn't named after a virtue. More like his personality. But the others were Honor, Noble, Justice.

Justice grunted, but that was the only response I got.

"What's your story?" Rage asked, his lip curling. "Didn't Crescent Clan already send their heir last year?"

Nolan.

I tipped my chin up. "Nolan is the *spare*."

Before Rage could reply, the Land Rover swerved, and I was thrown forward as Noble slammed on the brakes.

What the...?

"Get down! Rogues!" Noble snapped.

That one word sent ice water through my veins.

Rage grabbed my head and forced me down by the back of the neck so I could no longer see out the front windshield.

Patches of fur rippled down my arms as I tried to control my wolf. She wanted to come out now? With a snarl, I twisted and snapped at Rage's wrist, fully intending to bite him. He yanked his hand back just in time, and I bolted upright, peering out the window. "Dammit!"

McCain and his crew.

Rogue wolves were akin to feral cats. They'd left their packs, usually forced out after repeated offenses. They had zero social skills and were more wolf than human. McCain was the worst. Stripped of pack and magic, he *always* wanted blood—the only way to steal the mage-bestowed magic running through our veins.

What the hell was Noble waiting for? A peace talk?

"Run him over!" I shouted.

McCain stood in the road with his scrappy pseudo-pack of six wolves, blocking our way.

"I ... can't," Noble faltered. "It's against wolf shifter law. They must strike first."

Was he kidding? I chortled at the lunacy of his

statement. "Screw the code! I've seen this guy gnaw the flesh off a grown man faster than a royal betrayal. Run the rogue over before we—"

A heavy thump on the roof stole my breath, and I froze. I longed to shift into my wolf form, but my wolf was shy in times of stress. A really lame trait to have as an alpha heir.

Spinning to my right, I stared at a fully shifted werewolf standing just outside our window.

"Noble, go!" Justice shouted from shotgun, and the more tolerable of the brothers gunned the gas.

A loud scraping sound grated across the metal above, reverberating through the car. I looked up to see three inches of werewolf claws piercing the ceiling.

Before I could formulate a course of action, Rage launched into me, his face connecting with my chest as he forced me down across Honor's lap with a headbutt.

"Get off—" I grunted.

Rage rolled to the side, and I gaped in awe as he held a sleek black gun up to the roof of the car.

A small snapping noise rang out, a burst of light exiting the barrel with each silver bullet, followed by two more. Good thing they had silencers or all four of us would be deaf for the next hour. My ears just rang a little.

A thud rocked the car as Noble plowed through the group of rogues, and a faint keening registered before it was gone.

My attention went from the holes in the roof to the giant dominant draped over me.

I blinked at him, and my lips parted.

Those eyes!

His glasses had come off, and my thoughts derailed as I stared. Fire danced across my skin, its heat soaking deep into my chest and melting my insides.

His startling green eyes, the color of spring grass, held me captive for one long breath. That warmth in my belly was *not* attraction. *Nope.* So, I pushed it down and reminded myself that this guy was an idiot … and an ass. But … I wasn't prepared for how hot a total douche could be. Striking and unique seemed inadequate adjectives—

What the hell?

My nostrils flared, and I closed my mouth with a snap. His baseball cap had flown off in the scuffle, and peeking out from under his tousled hair, the outline of a full moon shimmered across the surface of his skin. The mark of Midnight royalty was on his forehead.

These weren't regular guards. Of all the packs, they belonged to my sworn enemy.

Midnight.

Chapter 2

SNARLING, I shoved at Rage, trying to wiggle the rest of my way out from underneath him.

"Get off me, *Midnight*!" I hissed.

I should have known it would be them. Of course, the alpha king would send Midnight Clan to retrieve me. To rub it in my face.

But royalty?

Sending one of their heirs—or four of them to be exact—that wasn't done. Most clans had at least ten to twenty heirs to ensure someone would be bred strong enough to take over the pack when the alpha died. I didn't know much about Midnight Pack other than they were the ones who drove our clan out of the magic lands. If the king sent his heirs to retrieve me, they must be distant spares, not even worthy enough to enroll in Alpha Academy.

His eyes widened as if I'd slapped him, and he growled back. "I said stay ... down!" His gaze darted to my lips, and then he licked his own.

My mouth dried, and I blinked up at him stupidly.

"Hey, Rage," Honor said, his voice drifting down to me from above. "We're all good here. Safe and sound." He cleared his throat. "Get off her so she can get off me. Please."

I was basically lying in Honor's lap.

Awkward.

Rage pushed up, his right arm caging me in on one side and his brother's chest on the other.

My gaze bounced, trying to escape the dominant over me, and I sagged with relief when all I could see was the mangled ceiling ... and Honor staring down at me.

He raised his brows, and I noted his eyes were hazel —not spring-grass green.

"You should sit up—and wipe the drool off your chin," he said with a cheeky grin.

I shot up so fast my hair tumbled into my face as I bounced off Honor and smacked into Rage by accident.

This damn car was too small for these giants!

"Oww," I muttered between clenched teeth, pushing my hair back.

Honor chuckled, and without thinking, I swung my right elbow back, twisting my body with the strike to give it extra power. I felt my elbow connect with his collarbone, and he released a muffled grunt, making me grin.

He *deserved* it, and it wasn't anything more than I'd do with Mack when he was out of line.

A blur of brown hair flew into my face, and I came face-to-face with Rage once again.

"*Don't* hit my brother," he snapped.

Sucking in a sharp breath, I tried to swallow as my retort caught in my throat. The other three spoke all at once.

"Ease up, Rage."

"I'm fine," Honor said.

"Give the cub a break," Noble spoke from the driver's seat. "She's just asserting dominance."

Justice managed to get out "Seriously, Rage—"

And then I lost it. "Get the hell out of my face unless you want to lose one of those pretty green eyes!"

I planted my hands on his chest, splayed out fingers over rock hard muscle, and then shoved him against the door with a snarl. Climbing onto my knees, I leaned forward—into his personal space. "The next time you decide to play *alpha*, remember which clan you belong to—and which one you don't." I shoved him one more time and added, "I don't answer to you, so stop with the pissing match."

My heart thrummed with adrenaline as my actions caught up to my consciousness.

Not smart, Nai.

Rage's expression was pure murder. His eyes glowed orange, and I could *feel* how close his wolf was. A pelt of black fur swam down his arm before disappearing beneath his skin.

Forcing a tight smile, I smoothed his shirt. "Uh, so yeah, this car is small, and that ... might've been a little more than necessary."

I yanked my hands back, realizing that I was practically feeling him up. With my cheeks burning, I took my seat and fastened my belt.

The other three men all stared at me.

Closing my eyes to them, I tamped down the urge to run—not that there was anywhere to go.

"Maybe we should ... uh ... start over," Noble said. "My name is Noble, from Midnight Clan."

I blinked my eyes open.

Before I could ask, he pointed to the guy riding shotgun. "This is my brother Justice." Then he pointed to the dude on my left. "And Honor."

Yeah, I'd caught the names before, but I'd play along for nicety sake.

I turned to Rage. "Is your name really Rage?" Unsurprisingly, he curled his lip in a non-answer, so I glanced back to Honor. "Is it?"

Because if their mom named three of them after virtues and one after a vice—

"His name is Courage, but..." Noble faced forward

and put the car in gear before merging back onto the road.

Shaking my head, I snorted and then muttered, "But clearly, Rage suits him better."

Noble and Honor chuckled, and Justice grunted, but it wasn't lost on me that none of them bothered to contradict me.

I continued playing nice. "I'm Nai."

They all just nodded but stayed silent.

Awesome.

The next hour crawled.

The strain between me and three of the Virtue brothers waned—a little. At least enough for me to ask a few questions and listen in on their good-natured teasing. The other one, Rage, just sat next to me like a tightly-coiled snake ready to strike. I'd learned they'd been raised on the island and pried for more info.

"Do all three clans live on the island or just Midnight?" I asked. The magic lands were as big as the United States and host to all types of shifters and mages. But Alpha Island, where the school was, held the royal heirs of each line while they went through school. Yet, I wondered where the rest of the packs resided. I heard Midnight Pack held over a thousand wolves. Could they all live on one island? If so, how big was it?

Justice flattened his lips and shook his head. "Seriously, you don't know this?"

"All of the wolf packs live on Alpha Island—except

those from Crescent Clan and the rogues," Noble interjected before his brother and I could start a fight.

I knew my father's pack had been excommunicated for some reason, but I didn't know whether our pack lived in the magic lands or on actual Alpha Island prior to being kicked out and forced to live among humans.

"Do any other shifters live there?" I heard a long time ago they all did.

"Alpha Island is for werewolves only," Justice growled.

I frowned. "Yeah?"

From what my father was able to tell me, I'd learned the island, in the past, was for all royals whose magic allowed them to shapeshift. Not just werewolves.

"When did that happen again? That it became werewolves only?" I asked, pressing my luck.

"Do you always talk this much?" Rage growled, plugging his ears.

I ignored the idiot on my right, but when no one answered my previous question, I decided to try another vein.

"So, can you tell me anything about what happens at the school?" I tried to shift the conversation to different waters.

"Alpha Academy is guarded by high mage magic," Honor said.

"And that magic binds you so you can't reveal what happens while you're there," Noble said, wagging his brows at me in the rearview mirror. "It's very secretive."

"I knew about the binding." Everyone did, but I was hoping maybe these dudes could give me a tiny bread crumb.

"If you knew, then why are you asking?" Justice groaned from the front seat.

Ugh, these douchebags were rude!

The hulking mass on my right moved, and the seat dipped, making me bump him.

"Sorry," I muttered.

Sorry not sorry, jerk.

Tugging at the frayed hem of my cutoffs, I tried to pinpoint why I was feeling so irritated. Being a dominant female close to such dominant males from a rival clan ... it had my wolf so riled I felt like crawling out of my skin.

I was done playing nice. New goal: ask as many annoying questions as possible, and see how long it would take to set Rage off again.

"My cousin didn't get four Midnight Clan escorts. What gives?" Last year when Nolan left, they'd sent one skinny dude to pick him up. Was I seen as that much of a threat? Because if so, that was badass.

Rage muttered under his breath, unintelligible except for the explitive and the undercut strike punctuating his sentiment.

Noble, the peacemaker, shook his head and growled, "Rein it in, Rage."

Justice suddenly turned in his seat to face me, meeting my eyes with his green gaze, identical to Rage's. "We're not the usual heir collection team. We received a summons to go pick up the heir from Crescent Clan today, and we follow orders without question, understand?"

Huh. Why would someone from the academy want the A-team picking me up?

"Sure, I understand English just fine. Thanks for asking." I ignored his huff and laid on another question. "Who sent the summons?"

That adage about curiosity killing the cat had no bearing on wolves. I was as curious as they came and not afraid of death.

Rage grabbed his ears. "Holy mage, woman, do you *ever* stop talking?"

What a baby! The last time I'd covered my ears like that was when I was five. Maybe he had issues; like eating paint chips as a kid or wasn't loved by his mother enough. Whatever it was, it wasn't my problem. With the sweetest smile I could muster, I pried one of his meaty fists away from his head.

"Nope." I popped the "p" and let go of his hand. Every single wolf in the car grinned—well, almost everyone.

"I like her," Noble declared.

Justice spoke up from the front seat: "Well, don't. She's not in our pack."

I crossed my arms, secretly grateful for the

reminder. I couldn't let my guard down. "Damn straight, and I'll never forget Midnight's betrayal."

All four of their eyebrows furrowed. *"OUR betrayal?"*

Rage grinned for the first time, and holy-mage-of-everything-beautiful, he just got hotter.

Bastard.

"She's been lied to." Rage shook his head, and his voice held a bit of pity.

My vision turned crimson, and I gasped. "Have not! The king ordered your clan to attack. They murdered half of my pack, including *my uncle*, before casting the rest of us out—and for what? No solid reason was ever given!"

My wolf pounded against my skin, demanding to be freed. Whose bright idea was it to put us all together in one small space? And why was my wolf so anxious to come out *here and now*? Maybe someone was trying to get me killed.

"Nai." Honor patted my thigh tenderly as he spoke, and Rage's gaze flicked to his hand, nostrils flaring. "Your uncle was convicted of a high crime by the High Mage Council. Our alpha was merely following orders from them."

Shock ripped through me, and my mind blanked. *High crime?* There's no way anyone in my pack would deliberately offend the high mages...

Dad never told me what his brother had done, just that it had brought trouble to our pack. He would've told me if it was a high crime though ... right? The five high mages ruled *everything*, both in the mortal realm as well as that of the magic one. Most of the time, they left our kind, werewolves, alone to be governed by the alpha king. Even so, we all knew no one, including the alpha king, could refuse an order from the high mages.

The fact that my uncle committed a high crime couldn't be true. They had to be lying—of course they were lying. This was Midnight clan. I wouldn't let them drive a wedge between me and my dad, let alone my clan.

Nice try.

"Whatever. You're the ones who've been lied to." I crossed my arms and fell silent.

Damn, this ride was boring and never-ending. I leaned forward and glanced at the clock. Ten minutes? Ugh. Better keep on with my questioning.

"So, what are your jobs on the island? Let me guess. Security?" If they were last in line for the throne among ten or twenty siblings, they wouldn't even go to school. They'd just be used for cushy jobs around the alpha king like security, war advisor, or breeding companion to females of good lineage.

Useless, basically.

All four boys shared a look I couldn't interpret.

"Something like that," Justice said, and the car went quiet.

The Virtues carried on between themselves, talking about random guy crap, and I tuned them out, resting my head against the back of the seat once again. I did my best to ignore Rage too. But that was easier said than done. Every time he moved, the seat dipped, and I slid into him. Eighteen times in sixty minutes, but who was counting. The guy must have werewolf ADHD.

I must've dozed off. One minute, my eyes were closed and my head against the leather headrest; and the next thing I knew, I jerked awake, all nuzzled up to the most lickable-male a she-wolf could hope to mate with. If said male wasn't a member of the most traitorous clan in the world.

Oh. My. Flippin'. Mage.

I inhaled and nearly moaned before thinking. My mouth watered, and my wolf wanted to see if Rage tasted as good as he smelled. This wasn't right. Rival packs were supposed to smell revolting. Not this bottle of pheromone yum.

My wolf and I needed to get on the same page—pronto. I yanked my head off of his shoulder and murmured, "Mmffttstff ... sorry."

Yikes.

I turned the color of a tomato but bit my tongue. The end of my incoherent babble was an apology, so it should count.

He looked down at me, and heat pooled in my abdomen.

No.

With a stony expression that could cut diamonds,

he said, "No worries. This isn't the first time a girl's fallen asleep on me."

My cheeks burned as his brothers chuckled.

"Won't be the last." Justice reached out for a fist bump, and I smacked his hand out of the way.

"Grow up," I snapped. "You're more likely to put a girl to sleep out of boredom—not exhaustion."

"She's like the sister we never had," Noble declared, laughing as he pulled the car into a canopy of trees.

"Eww." I crossed my arms. "I'd rather die."

I sat up straighter. This wasn't just any canopy of trees. An iridescent shimmer flickered within the opening, and anxiety tightened my gut.

This was the portal to the magic lands.

"Five dollars says she pukes," Justice said, narrowing his eyes. "The weak ones always do."

I flipped him off. Glare away, pretty boys. I was *not* going to puke.

The car crept forward, and a rainbow mist appeared between the trees.

My anxiety gave way to excitement, and the feeling thrummed through me. I squealed, bouncing up and down in my seat like a lunatic. "It's the portal! It's real."

As soon as I realized we weren't moving, I glanced at the guys—who were all staring at me.

Honor's frown was filled with pity. "You really have been stuck in the human world your whole life, huh?"

Bless his heart.

"Yeah, because of your Al—"

Rage clamped a hand around my mouth. "Stop talking."

Rage was too manhandly for my liking. He needed to be taught a lesson. Wrenching away from his hand, I then reached up and clamped my hand over *his* mouth with a sneer.

Oops.

His lips were still parted, and the second his tongue hit my skin, an electric current zipped up my spine. My thoughts fritzed—gone. What had I been saying?

I'd forgotten what I'd been doing.

Why did he *lick* me?

Oh yeah.

"Doesn't feel so nice, does it?" I asked, ripping my hand away.

Ugh. Why did my voice sound so breathy?

Rage's green eyes were wide, mirroring my shock. He swallowed hard, but his rough voice held a note of warning. "I meant for you to stop talking ... so you can focus." He swallowed again. "Or you could be ripped in two."

What the what?

My eyes bugged. How did my father not cover *that* in his brief chat on portals? "How do I not get ripped in two? That seems like something important you should tell me."

"Just calm down and focus on your breathing,"

Honor shared with a snicker, and I suddenly felt like I was going to faint.

Noble reached back toward me. "Alpha Island invitation."

Oh, the swirly thing my father had handed me this morning. Was that a part of this portal process?

I pulled it out of my back pocket and unfolded the paper. Noble then looked at Rage. "Crescent Clan heir summons."

Rage held another thick piece of paper out to his brother, and I craned my neck to try and read it. Too late. All I saw were more magical swirly letters and the same embossed emblem.

Noble rolled down the window.

"What's next—? Whoa!" I stared opened-mouthed as a man materialized out of freaking nowhere. *Boom*. One second, nothing; and the next, the guy was ten feet in front of the car … floating in the air. I looked closer. Not a man. A high mage.

My body froze and skin tingled. I'd never seen one before.

Honor tapped my chin. "It's rude to stare."

Holy crap.

I shrank down, half-hiding my face in Rage's arm but also keeping one eye out to see the race who ruled us all.

Pretty much … scary as hell. At least, I couldn't imagine anyone more so.

The high mage was close to seven feet tall, thin

and wiry, wearing dark robes with swirling galaxies of stars that moved on the cloak. He didn't walk so much as float, and the closer he got, the more his presence crawled through the car. The air charged with electricity, and I had to tamp down my fear. His eyes were the most unsettling because ... eyes shouldn't look like that. Like his robes, his eyes were dark with small universes swirling in slow circles within. My legs went weak. I wanted to ask about them, but I also wanted to live, so I kept my questions to myself.

His gaze flickered to the papers held before him.

"Another heir from Crescent?" The mage's voice sounded like a blend of French horn and wind chimes. More contrasts that were freaky when put together.

"Unfortunately," Rage offered, making the high mage grin, "Rules are rules. If the council sends the summons, we'll respectfully fetch."

I didn't know Rage well, but that sounded like sarcasm, and I didn't appreciate the dog reference.

"Their last heir, sir." Noble looked slightly less terrified than I felt.

"Well, thank goodness for that." The high mage pinned me with a glare, and I dropped my gaze to Rage's knees.

I could feel the galaxy dude looking at me, assessing me like spiders crawling over my body. Was that magic? It felt like he was touching me, and my wolf didn't like it. I could feel her cowering. Breathing in deeply through my nose, I felt my wolf suddenly lurch to the surface.

Now?

I'd struggled with control over my wolf form since I was a young pup. In a fight, when instinct should take over, my wolf mostly stayed inside, so I was forced to fight in my human form. Other times, like this, she was too eager to come to the surface. She had it backward … and was wildly unpredictable.

She was *not* happy.

A small patch of fur bristled on the top of my hand, and Rage immediately reached out and clamped down on it. The contact was so sudden that it stopped my shift. Clutching my fist firmly in his, he pressed against me and nodded to the high mage.

"All set?" Rage's voice held something I couldn't place.

Protection?

I felt the high mage's energy leave the car then, no longer creeping over my skin and stirring my wolf.

"Go ahead." The high mage handed the papers back, and the portal started to swirl—like a rainbow inside of a washing machine. Then, he disappeared. Poof.

Gone.

I let out the breath I'd been holding. And Rage released my hand.

"*Their last heir, sir,*" Justice teased, mocking Noble's voice far too well.

"Screw you, dude. They legit give me nightmares. I

heard a high mage could make it so you shoot blanks—or even that you couldn't get it up—"

"You can come out of my armpit now," Rage muttered, shoving his elbow into my side.

Blushing, I straightened, not realizing until now how much I'd tucked into him. "What? I was ... looking for my earring."

I didn't even have pierced ears.

A sly grin played at the edges of his mouth. "Mmm-hmm."

Noble threw the car in drive and, as we inched forward, glanced at me through the rearview mirror. "No more talking. Focus on your breath. Got it?"

"Wait, I—"

He gunned the gas, and the tires squealed as the car beelined for the shimmering portal.

Blessed High Mage Council, don't let me die.

As my breathing grew short and shallow, I pinched my eyes shut and then opened them because I didn't want to miss a thing. I was going to Alpha Island, to the magic lands. Going through a *portal*. This was epic even if I was about to die.

The car got closer, and I sucked in my breath, tensing my thighs with an iron grip.

Rage reached over, grabbed my forearms, and slid his hands down to mine, stroking my skin.

Holy mage...

Threading our fingers together, he leaned into me and whispered, "Relax."

Everything inside of me melted. That voice was almost as good as his lickable-pheromone-yumminess. Any witty response I might've had evaporated as we entered the rainbow washing machine.

The entire car lit up like the aurora borealis, colors splashing across the seats, ceiling, and walls. Not to mention me and the quads. With a flash of agony, my vision turned white as it felt like my skin was ripped away. My stomach flipped, but Rage's grip on my fingers clamped down, keeping me steady. When I thought I couldn't take the feeling of being spun any longer, the car shot out of the portal and to the other side. Rage dropped my hands as quickly as he'd grabbed them, and like a mist of cool water on a hot day, relief washed over me, followed by a sense of rightness. I took a deep breath, but my smile faded as I looked out the window.

What the heck? Where was the magic?

I blinked and shook my head. Staring at the trees, I nudged Rage with my elbow. "It looks exactly the same as before we went through the veil."

Rage grunted. "What did you expect? Faeries?"

Well, clearly the hand holding was to keep me alive, not because he enjoyed my presence.

"You okay?" Noble asked.

I nodded. "Never better. I think someone owes you money, right?"

He grinned and held his hand out to Justice. "A fiver, please."

"Is this seriously happening right now?" Justice groaned. "She's like the scrawniest wolf ever. How did she not puke?"

I looked at Noble, and he winked.

Hah! I had an ally in these brothers.

Now that we were in the magic lands, that meant we'd be to Alpha Island shortly and then on Academy grounds ... an academy I knew nothing about.

"So ... first day of school..." I said, tipping my chin high. "Do I get one of those Alpha Academy shirts like you guys?"

Justice just growled at me.

Clearly, he was a poor loser. Note to self: don't be on Justice's team.

Noble shot me a look of pity, and my confidence disappeared as fast as it had come. "Yeah ... about that. I think you'll find things here on the island are a bit more formal than what you are used to."

Rage's gaze went to the hem of my cut-off shorts. I played with the frayed ends and shrugged. I didn't do formal; I was from Montana. When I wasn't training with my father, I milked goats and lay in the cornfields with Callie and Mack, talking about pack stuff. Not a single dress in my entire wardrobe.

I was about to ask another question when we drove up to a normalish quaint town that resembled something out of a Harry Potter movie. Over the next ten minutes, I inched closer and closer to the window on my right, not because Rage smelled good but the view was better. I think.

A red barn stood on a hilltop, and my jaw unhinged as I stared out the window at a huge black bear, ignoring Rage's groan of frustration.

"Holy crap, is that a shifter or a regular bear?" I pressed my face to the glass, ignoring Rage as he pushed me back.

As if answering my question, the bear started to contort and shift, losing fur and mass until he was a naked male staring out at our passing car with stony eyes. My cheeks went red as I averted my gaze.

"Listen, if you want to keep your head attached, don't stare at them," Rage said. "Bear shifters have nasty tempers."

I had no idea if he was joking or lying, so I reeled back and took it in with the buffer zone he provided.

I'd only ever grown up around wolf shifters, but my father said there were bird, seal, panther, bear, coyote, deer, and countless others living in the magic lands. Along with the mages…

The mages had nothing on humans, numbers-wise, but a mage lived anywhere from two to ten times longer than humans. A couple thousand mages could do a lot of damage in a mortal war—which was why they mostly stayed here, in the magic lands with the shifters.

Whether shifter or mage, all magical creatures were ordered to stay in the magic lands unless given permission to leave or were exiled, sometimes with their power stripped.

The Crescent Clan's exile was instituted by the alpha king, confining us to a few hundred acres and limited access to town. If we did anything in Montana without the alpha king's approval, there could be hell to pay. Thankfully, Amazon delivered. Eventually.

"Are there really fifty different kinds of shifter?" I asked Noble now that we were buddies. Why did everyone else need a throat punch? Maybe they didn't. A lobotomy might work instead. But in either case, I was saved by the noble Noble.

He nodded. "But the high mages, alpha wolf shifters, and vampires are the most powerful."

My blood ran cold. *Vampires?*

"I ... I thought all the vampires died out in the last war?" I hated that my voice shook a little.

A creature that sucked blood from your veins to become more powerful? A shiver ran down my spine. Nightmareville.

Rage groaned and shoved his fingers into his ears.

Legit baby.

"Someone forgot their happy pills this morning," I muttered. "Maybe you should see a healing mage for that. Or get therapy for life skills."

He glared at me, and I glared back, unwavering. Take that, bully.

Breaking my glare-off with Rage, I turned as Honor said: "A few vampire nobility are still around, but they live off in the cliffs and don't come to the island."

Thank the mages for that!

"We're here." Noble pulled the car into a parking space, and I looked up to see a ferry sitting on a shore of deep blue water that lapped onto a black sandy beach —just like the colors of the night sky.

Whoa. *Is that…?*

Just beyond the misty shore loomed Alpha Island. From here, all I could see was the highest tip of the snow-covered mountain in the center of the island.

Without another word, Justice grabbed my duffle while Rage hooked a hand under my armpit, and then I was being hauled toward the boat like a criminal.

"Hey! What's with the manhandling? I'm a willing participant here." I jerked away from him.

He tucked close to me. "I don't want you getting scared and running off. I have a package to deliver."

I'm a package now? *Great.*

I stepped onto the boat while the boys chatted up the mage captain. He wore a long thick cloak and bore the mark of a mage on his forehead. The triangle with a single dot inside always fascinated me. I'd only met a handful of lower-level mages in my life, ones who came to trade on our farm, but they all bore this mark.

The man was tall and lanky as most mages were, but this one looked more powerful than a simple boat captain should. There was intelligence in his deep brown gaze, one that washed over me and gave me chills. The mages had a hierarchy: novice, adept, advanced, master, and then, of course, high mage, but there were only five of those in existence at any given time. I didn't understand it much, but if I had to guess, I'd say this guy was advanced or master.

He stepped over to me, pulling a small, black palm stone from his cloak.

"Summons." He held his hand out to Rage.

Rage produced the papers once again as my heart kicked up about a hundred notches. Any time someone asked for that summons, weird things happened.

His gaze bored into me. "Nai of Crescent Clan. Alpha heir?"

"Yes, sir." I gulped. Hey, I wasn't about to piss off an advanced magic-user. My own magic was piddly-diddly compared to this guy. As a wolf heir, we only had access to one of the elemental magics: usually earth or fire, and only once we went to Alpha Academy and learned to use it, but this guy … he could probably turn me into a toad.

He held out his palm, facing up, and the black stone began to glow.

"Upon entering this island, you are magically bound from speaking about your experiences at Alpha Academy. Do you accept?"

The hairs raised on my arms, and I swallowed hard.

This was it. This was the magical binding everyone talked about. For some reason, I looked at Rage as if asking his permission, which was stupid. He simply gave a curt nod, and my gaze flicked back to the advanced mage.

"I accept."

He raised an eyebrow. "Then, touch the stone."

Oh. Right.

I took a breath and steeled myself, reaching out to lay my hand over the stone. The second my skin touched the cool black surface, an electric jolt ran the length of my arm, exploding at my shoulder blade. I yanked my hand back with a yelp and grimaced at the mage.

Oww. He could have warned me.

"Interesting." He narrowed his gaze at me.

Justice griped, "Come on, you big baby. I want to get back in time for dinner."

Interesting? Why did the mage say that? Interesting meant strange, and I didn't need to be any more strange than I already was—or am. Before I could dwell further on it, I was shuffled onto the boat.

After a few moments, the boat took off from the dock, and I gripped the sides, peering over into the water at something black swirling in its depths.

"Selkies. Don't make eye contact, or they might sing for us," Noble said. "They're still pissed about Shifter Island becoming Alpha Island."

So, what my father told me was true. Of course, they were pissed. The alpha king kicked out all other shifter species from the island and claimed it for wolves only. This forced other shifters to the fringe areas of the magic lands to mingle with the mage folk and live in less desirable conditions. I wanted to tell him being driven from your home sucked, but the consequence of dealing with Rage and Justice's tempers and/or sarcasm was one hundred percent not worth it. Also, I'd heard selkies' songs could be dangerous, so he was right.

Twenty minutes later, we approached the white crystalline beaches of Alpha Island. A shimmering iridescent barrier hugged the shoreline, stretching as far up and over the horizon as I could see. Nerves churned in my gut as I saw the group of guards standing with their spines erect, each one carrying at least two katana swords.

"Wow, they really guard this place," I mentioned when Rage stood, and I knew from his furrowed brow and tight jaw that something was wrong. The other three Midnight brothers stood as well, and suddenly, I felt like hiding.

As the captain pulled the boat up to the group, over a dozen guards, all huge beefcakes nearly as large as Rage, stormed onto the boat.

"Prince Courage! Your uncle has been very concerned. The island has been on lockdown all day. Where have you been?"

The guard's words registered and then rattled my brain like an electric fence.

Prince Courage. Rage. Rage was ... a prince...

"Oh, mystic mages." I facepalmed. The four brothers of Midnight, they weren't distant heirs of the alpha king. No one carried the title prince unless they were directly in line to the throne. They were *the* heirs. But *uncle*? That meant the king had no children, fascinating considering how valuable heirs were. Maybe he was sterile.

Rage's brow furrowed, and he handed beefcake the summons he'd shown the high mage earlier. "We were following orders to fetch an alpha heir. Surely, my uncle knew that, considering he signed the summons."

That's when Captain Beefcake took one long glance at me, and his lip curled. "Who are you?"

I raised my eyebrows and pointed at the paper in his hand. "Nai, alpha heir to Crescent Clan."

The dude frowned, his gaze bouncing from the summons to me. "Is this a joke?"

I looked at each of the brothers, but none of them were laughing. I wasn't laughing. Beefcake dude wasn't laughing. Not even the captain was laughing. "I'm pretty sure it's not," I said dryly.

Like 99.6% sure. What in the name of the high mages was going on?

A deep crease appeared between his eyebrows. I was 99.7% sure he didn't think I was funny.

"We have a problem." He shoved the paper back toward Rage. "The king didn't sign this; it's counterfeit. We'd better go talk to your uncle."

My stomach dropped. Counterfeit? How did he know that? And why did I feel like I was to blame?

I glanced at the four brothers, my attention

bouncing from one to the next. All four of them wore similar expressions, making my situation clear as Arkansas crystal. Hello there, trouble, we meet again.

With every step, that one word replayed in my mind.

Counterfeit.

If the king didn't send for me ... who did?

Chapter 3

"She wasn't due to start until next year!" the alpha king's dark, gravelly voice raged behind the closed door on my right. Something crashed against the wall, exploding with a rain of breaking glass, and I jumped, gripping the edges of the bench.

Alpha king is an alpha ass.

As we'd approached the alpha king's chambers, Rage had pointed at a wooden bench in the foyer and told me to sit. At the time, I'd been pissed, but as soon as the top dog started yelling, I felt nothing but relief. At least, this way I could assess him without him staring me down or using his alpha mind-control on me. I dreaded the day I had to look that sadistic monster in the eyes, the man who'd ordered the attack on my clan, the man who'd banished us to the human world. My blood boiled just thinking about his vicious cruelty, but as alpha king, he held power over all of us. The king had been yelling ever since Justice closed the door, and now I leaned in to listen.

"How dare you leave the island...?" he seethed. "Do you have any idea how dangerous the mortal realm can be for our kind?"

Silence.

"Sir, we were just following orders—" Noble tried to defend their actions, but Alpha Ass was having none of it.

"If someone delivered an order to cut off your own head, would you do it? Cursed mage, boy—use your brain. Why would I send my only heirs to pick up Crescent trash?" He punctuated his declaration by throwing another heavy object against the door.

Yikes. Homeboy was legit psycho *and* a giant douchebag. Huh, maybe Rage's winning personality was a genetic gift from this guy's side of the family.

"But the summons—" Honor's mild tone was drowned by the king's temper.

"The summons is forged! Did any of you even look at the signature stamp? That is *not* my mark." The king sounded absolutely infuriated. If he stroked out ... I wondered who would take his place...

Somehow, I suspected Rage was first in line to inherit Midnight Pack and the alpha king position.

"Should we take her back?" Justice asked, his voice like smooth whiskey.

Silence. Was he contemplating it? I mean going back to my family sounded amazing, but now that I was here, I kind of wanted to explore. Besides, going through that two-hour drive, the portal, and the magic oath all over again sounded awful.

I leaned forward, waiting for him to reply.

"We can't. The advanced mage already initiated her magic at the boat dock," he growled. "If you take her back, we'd have to explain why to the High Mage Council. I'm not willing to risk our favor over this. No, we'll just have to train her early. However, I do want to find out who the traitor is who forged this summons."

"Traitor?" Rage's voice could cut glass.

"Yes, find out who forged that document and bring me their head," the king growled. "Preferably severed from their body."

Yikes.

"I'll show her to her quarters, then," Noble offered, his voice coming from near the door. He probably wanted to get me out of here.

"No," the king barked. "Rage, you do it. Drop her off, and be done with her. The less you involve yourselves with lowlife Crescent scum, the better."

Scum. Ouch. My throat tightened, and I blinked up at the ceiling. I'd love to go home for another year. The island usually pulled us after our twentieth birthday. I'd just turned nineteen.

Before I could ponder further, the double doors

Midnight Kisses

yanked open. I jerked back as Rage stormed out and grabbed my duffle bag. "Let's go."

I jumped up and followed him, scurrying to keep up with his long stride. We exited the foyer, and after the door to the castle closed behind us, I deemed us far enough away to ask questions.

I leaned into Rage and whispered, "Who do you think sent the summons? That's super shady, right? Got any enemies?"

He stopped walking and faced me, his green eyes blazing. "Yeah." His nostrils flared, and he leaned down to look me in the eye. "You."

His answer sucked the air from my lungs, and my jaw gaped. That was *mean*. Outright mean.

"We're not on the same side, Nai," he said, "You're Crescent; I'm Midnight. Our clans are enemies—and for good reason. Crescent is *shady*. I wouldn't put it past one of your own people to have forged that so you could come to school early. So just learn your magic. Then, go back to your cursed lands, and leave us be."

He marched away, leaving me with my jaw on the ground. We both knew no one from my clan could've done that from the mortal realm. He'd said it just to hurt my feelings.

Any delusion I had that we might've mended our rift during our two-hour drive dissipated in that moment. What he'd said about being enemies was one hundred percent true. So, why did my heart sting?

"You have a personality problem. You know that?" I hurled the words at his back, wishing I had something—anything—else to throw.

He just grunted.

I stood rooted, watching his lithe form stride away. He still carried my heavy bag, and I let my attention drift to the surrounding courtyard dressed in late summer blooms of reds and oranges, mixed with the vibrant shades of green. All that beauty … and my gaze gravitated back to Rage, only this time, my ire flamed the same colors as the flowers—vitriolic red. Hate wasn't even a strong enough word.

This was why the king sent Rage instead of Noble. No chitchat. No friendship. Zero bonding. Rage had no qualms about throwing me to the curb. Like garbage.

I passed a few students out in the courtyard, all between twenty and twenty-four years old. Despite bearing different marks, they mingled—mostly. Or they did until Rage strode by. Conversations dwindled as he passed, and their expressions morphed into mixtures of jealousy, lust, and pride. Mostly *lust*. Pretty sure they all wanted to lick him or be him, both of which pissed me off.

Stupid wolves.

When their attention landed on me, their gazes flicked up to my mark. And then, they scowled.

Judge much, assholes?

Yeah, I hated this place already. A *lot*.

We passed a large fountain at the edge of the courtyard. Then the pathway led through a hedge, a clear demarcation at the far end of matching buildings. As we walked between the two gray stone structures, I noticed the path led to a massive clearing in the middle of four buildings. Each one faced a different direction, north, south, east, or west. And while each structure was the same height and width, and constructed of the same materials, they were not all the same.

I stared at the south-facing building, its gray stone polished and free of vines. Flowerbeds lined the walkway, the dark mulch a stark contrast to the vibrant growth. Engraved into the dark wood door, a full moon declared the residence to be owned by the Midnight Clan.

Shocker.

I pivoted, scanning past the other students until I located Rage.

"Yours is that one," Rage said, dropping my duffle at my feet. He pointed to a dilapidated building facing west. "Your cousin can help you—or not. Just be at the atrium in an hour. Opening ceremony starts at five."

Without giving me an opportunity to ask questions, he pivoted and strode away.

Kicked to the curb—just like I'd thought. Glaring at his back, I wished for air magic so I could force him to kneel before me. Or better yet, fire magic so I could light him up.

Thanks a lot, Prince Asshole.

He froze—which meant I'd probably said that out loud.

Oops.

"That's *Prince Courage* to you," he growled. "Don't make me teach you respect."

Respect?

I laughed maniacally. "Pretty sure you need to know what that is to be able to teach it."

We'd gathered an audience, and while I might not know much about the ins and outs of this place, being an alpha meant not letting others dominate you, Rage included.

I crossed my arms. "If you want my *respect*, you'll need to earn it."

Someone gasped, and someone else snickered.

Maybe I'd find the snickerer later; they might be the only other sane person here. Right now, I needed to leave—pronto. I hefted my bag and marched toward the Crescent Clan's quarters. Hopefully, Nolan would be nicer than I remembered. I was done with asshats for the day.

I stormed toward the building with the crescent moon on its faded door. The grounds on either side of the walkway were overgrown with weeds—not a bloom in sight. Several steps leading up to the door were broken and crumbling, and I grimaced at the vines crawling up the gray stone ... *poison ivy*.

Leaves littered the ground of the portico, and the volume of debris in the corners indicated years without attention—probably ever since our clan's banishment.

Great.

Reaching up to the door, I knocked, but the sensation of attention from behind served as motivation to try the handle. This was my clan's dorm anyway, right? The knob turned, but the wood grated against the jamb as I shoved the door open.

Stepping inside, I noted the afternoon sunlight filtering through the windows, illuminating the layers of dirt and grime. Everything was covered in years of dust, from the chandelier above to the—I dragged my flip-flops through the gray dust and shook my head—marble floor below.

Gross.

After kicking the door closed behind me, I shouted, "Hello?"

Nothing.

The stale air carried the scent of rodent droppings. I saw no evidence that this area had been disturbed recently. Did Nolan even live in this dump? Not that I'd blame him if he didn't. I'd rather camp in a tent then live in this biohazard. I dropped my bag next to the stairs, figuring the bedrooms would at least be one level up, and then set off to find Nolan. Hopefully, I'd find a snack along the way. I was starved.

My flip-flops slapped against the floor as I wandered in and out of the dusty, unkempt rooms. This place was massive. I spied a ballroom, a game room with foosball, pool, *and* air hockey, and a study, all down in the south wing. But the neglect made it all the worse. Seeing a dusty, half-broken foosball table was a crime but less so than the books piled on the floor in the library.

My stomach rumbled in protest of my missed meal, and I closed the door of a musty sitting room and then headed back to the foyer. From there, I moved to the north side of the first floor, getting my bearings around this place.

The sunlight waned, and I flipped the light switch in the kitchen, groaning in dismay. How could we have no electricity? Did that mean no refrigerator?

What little light streaming through the windows illuminated the boxes covering the counter. I knew they were food. I could smell it. Rotten bananas and sour milk—which meant someone had lived here recently enough to spill milk and still have it stink.

Nolan, you filthy pig.

The groan of the door protesting its abuse caught my attention, and I shouted, "Nolan?"

"Eww, this is nasty," a young woman griped, her voice floating down the hall to me. "Effin' alpha king and effin' Midnight Clan."

No idea who she was, but I liked her already.

"Hello," she called in a singsong voice. "I know you're in here, Crescent girl. I've come to save your sorry tail from an alpha heir beatdown."

I chuckled—couldn't help it. Is that what the others thought? That Rage would actually hurt me? I mean he was a total asshole of the highest order but ... beatdown?

No way. She must have been outside just now and caught my little spat with Rage.

A young woman about my age stepped through the doorway, and her expression of disgust melted into a grin. "There you are."

She was several inches shorter than I, maybe five and a half feet, with auburn hair and fair skin dusted with freckles. She wore a green dress, full-on medieval-times attire, and her hair was pulled up into a fancy twist with a crown of flowers. The three-quarter moon mark stood out on her forehead. *Harvest Clan.*

With a smile, she crossed the black and white tiles of the kitchen floor and extended her hand to me. "My name is Kaja. I'm from Harvest Clan." Shaking her head, she added, "Please spare me the farmer jokes."

I snorted. "Wasn't going to go there. I'm Nai."

We shook hands briefly.

I never dreamed I'd actually make a friend here. I thought it was a kill-or-be-killed kind of mentality on the island.

"The way you told Prince Courage off like that ... *epic*. Had to meet you and save you from dying of dust inhalation." She indicated the thick layer of grime that rested on everything.

I chuckled. "Sometimes, men need to be put in their place." Then I pointed to the nasty kitchen. "What's up with this? Does my cousin seriously live like this?"

Her face suddenly became somber, "Well, we all get maids and stuff paid for by the crown. When your pack got ... uh... "

I understood her message, loud and clear. We no longer had the luxuries of a clan that was accepted here.

"Are we supposed to wear a costume?" I asked, indicating her outfit and changing the subject. What had the boys said on the way in? Something about things being more formal...

Kaja laughed and then waved her hand up and down, pointing at my body. "Tonight, we are. Aren't you going to change before the opening ceremony?"

Crap. I'd forgotten. "Yeah, totally—"

"You don't have Alpha Academy-approved dresses, do you?" She flattened her lips and snorted.

"Nope."

She frowned. "Did they send you the supply list and dress code?"

Anger flared between my shoulder blades like a searing poker right through my back. "No. They didn't."

She grabbed my wrist and tugged. "Come on. If we hurry, we might still make it before the High Mage Council arrives. I'm not letting Midnight sabotage you. You and I are going to be bestie-pals, just so we're clear."

A grin pulled at my lips, and I followed along,

letting her drag me out of the kitchen while she chatted me up.

"Why are you being so nice to me?" I asked when she took a breath. "Not that I'm not grateful, but you don't know me." Technically, we were all in competition with each other for the alpha king position. I'm sure it was assumed Rage would take it, but rules stated any one of us could fight for it after we graduated.

She glanced my way with her eyebrows raised high. "First of all, I'm tenth in line to be alpha, and I have eight more siblings at home. So I'm just here to make my mom happy in case my entire family dies overnight."

I snort-laughed. Eighteen heirs! I couldn't imagine that many siblings.

"Second, the Midnight heirs disappeared this morning, and there was a big freak-out. The whole island was locked down—and *you* came back with them, bringing fireworks with you. I don't need to know any more than that."

"Well, I'm grateful to have a friend," I told her honestly. This girl was a bit forward, but I'd take that any day over stuffy and priggish.

"Excellent. Me too. Now, what size dress do you wear?"

The next thing I knew, I was in the north-facing dorm amidst a swarm of Harvest girls. Despite my protests,

Kaja bullied me into an ankle-length blue dress the same color as the sky at dusk. The dark material was a stark contrast to my pale skin, but apparently it met the high mage dress code for formal events by covering my knees.

Who knew?

Most likely everyone—except me.

Chapter 4

KAJA and her elder twin sisters were in first and second years respectively. Then, she had another two sisters in third and fourth years, but they'd stuck to their rooms when I'd come in. Apparently, their mother bore lots of daughters but only one son, who was currently two years old. The poor kid would probably never be alpha of the pack either. That went to the eldest, who was almost always the strongest.

The twins had the same dusting of freckles as my new friend, but their wavy locks were the color of honey, not auburn like Kaja's. The twins also had skills, I had to give them that. They'd done something crazy to my eyelashes that made them look like fans, and I was pretty sure this gunk wasn't ever going to come off. I put my foot down at the body glitter. Allowing only a sprinkle on the braid on the top of my head, which made it look like a crown, especially with the rest of my long blond hair in soft curls. We didn't dress up like this in Montana. *This* felt like wedding dress-up. It was weird ... and fun.

Kaja and I walked along a stone path, our pace hurried so we didn't miss the ceremony. Turning my attention back to my new friend, I asked, "So, seventeen siblings ... what's that like?"

"Fun. Loud. Crazy. I would probably talk to myself all the time and die of boredom if I were an only child." She shrugged, chuckling.

I laughed with her. "Then, good thing that's me being the only child and not you, right?"

Kaja nodded; she had quickly wormed her way into my heart.

"Who's your eldest heir?" I asked.

We weaved in and out of walkways and past buildings, and I, totally lost, was glad Kaja knew the way.

"Nala. She's set to become alpha. Her water bending is probably powerful enough already."

"Cool. I heard—"

A blur leapt from the trees, cutting me off as I stumbled to avoid the collision. "Effin' mage!"

My cousin Nolan popped in front of me, glaring daggers. "Nai, I need a word with you."

He grabbed my arm and yanked me off the path, into the bushes.

My heels sank into the dirt, and I snarled at him. "Let me go."

He dropped my arm just as Kaja peeked through the foliage and frowned at us.

"Nai?"

"Tell me where to go, and I'll meet you there," I told my new friend, jerking my head at my cousin. Whatever Nolan wanted had better be good.

She told me to follow the path, and after she left, I faced Nolan, glaring.

"Don't you ever touch me like that unless you're issuing a direct challenge, in which case I'll happily oblige," I snapped, seething.

How dare he! I was the heir, and *he* was the spare. Apparently, he still thought he was better than me. Totally delusional.

However, Nolan had changed over the last year. Where he'd always been scrawny, he now had the build of an alpha, well over six feet tall with broad shoulders. Yet, if his oily hair and smell were any indication, he was still weak-willed, lazy, and—obviously—quick to anger.

"What the hell is going on, Nai? I heard the Midnight heirs brought you in?" Nolan towered over me, his voice low. His features were furrowed in what appeared to be concern though, something he'd never exhibited on my behalf.

Maybe I didn't know how to read him after all.

"Yeah … well, I started a year early." I crossed my arms, not willing to give him any other intel.

Two other heirs passed by. Nolan glowered at them

before pulling me further away. He swallowed, his eyes widening, making him look almost … *desperate*.

"Our parents didn't prepare us for this place, Nai. We have nothing: no maids, no money … *nothing*. They make us work for food and then give us leftover stuff. We're second class citizens—if that."

My stomach sank, and I frowned, suddenly nervous. My mind went to the rotting box of food on the kitchen table. Surely that wasn't provided by the school? Swallowing, I focused on what I knew. Nolan had always been a pig. Maybe he was complaining as an excuse for the sty-like conditions of our dorm.

"Well, would it kill you to clean up a little? The dorm is disgusting?"

He shook his head as if he knew what I was thinking. "You'll see if you have a spare second after tonight. You're about to become a slave to the alpha king."

With that, he stormed off, leaving me with a tornado of confusion. Slave to the alpha king? What the mage did that even mean?

"Nai? You lost, luv?" a familiar voice called, and I spun to find Noble, hand extended through the bushes. He looked as handsome as sin in a three-piece suit. Behind him stood Honor, Justice, and … *Rage*.

When my gaze fell on the meanest of the four Princes, my mind blanked. Warmth spread through my chest like liquid honey. As if that man could get any hotter, Mr. Lickable-incarnate launched into the stratosphere of hotness in a charcoal gray suit.

Yum. No, wait ... bastard.

Rage said nothing as his gaze traveled over my body, slowly, the heat in his eyes making his attention a tangible caress. My heart flipped.

"Noble, let's go," Rage snapped.

Why were the hot ones always such assholes?

Noble extended his arm to me, and I grinned, taking his outstretched hand. "Thank you, friend."

He tucked my arm into the crook of his, and I let him lead me down the path.

"You clean up good, cub," Honor called out behind me, making my grin spread. "And that dress—"

Rage blasted past and quickly outpaced us. "Focus on the ceremony, you idiots."

"Do they teach anger management here?" I pondered aloud. "Someone might suggest that ... as an elective. Just a thought."

Noble waved my comment off. "He's grouchy because Uncle Declan was pissed we went to fetch you, and he ripped us a new one."

"Again?" I cocked my head. "Wasn't that what he was doing when we first got here?"

It was not lost on me how crazy it was that they casually referred to the alpha king as *Uncle Declan*. I wanted to know more, like why the king appeared to have no children, but I didn't dare ask.

Honor snorted.

"That was just the warmup," Justice muttered.

Yikes. "Do I want to know?"

Noble shook his head. "If you ever get called to have a meeting with him, make sure you let me know before so I can be there with you."

"Why?"

Noble lowered his voice just as Honor stepped up next to his brother. "To help you."

Honor leaned forward to look me in the eye and offered a sad smile. "The alpha king doesn't like mistakes, so do your best to stay under the radar."

Whoa.

I nodded as his words sank in. The king was worse than I'd believed. My attention drifted ahead, to a well-lit atrium, and curiosity seized me.

"So what's this ceremony we're going to, and why is the High Mage Council there?"

The path ended at the entrance of the glass dome. A bunch of older teachers stood at the doorway, welcoming students inside.

"Well," Noble said, smirking, "this is a test to see what your elemental affinity is."

I nodded. Because we were descended from the high mages, albeit watered down and mixed with wolf, we had cool mage powers linked to the elements. This was one of the main reasons we came to the Academy: to learn our elemental affinity and how to harness it. All wolf shifters had greater speed, hearing, sight, smell, and even healing, compared to humans, but alpha heirs also each had an affinity: air, fire, water, or earth power. Our control of the elements, which was only seen in those of royal blood, was extremely limited, compared to the power of the high mages. My dad told me he once saw a high mage drag someone across the room using only his mind. The mages had a whole host of powers.

Elemental magic set us alpha wolves apart from the other shifter breeds and even the rest of the wolves in our pack. My father was a fire elemental. His magic trickled through the pack so that they could also pull on it and use it to a lesser degree at times, including me. If you wanted to see a campfire lit from two feet away, I was your girl. But the power stopped there with the other wolves from our pack.

I assumed I'd be like my father and have fire affinity, which would be great. Then, I'd be able to light Rage on fire with my mind so he didn't know who did it.

"All right," I shrugged. "What kind of test?"

Tests and I didn't usually get along. Like how Rage tested my patience; I was getting a C- there, at best.

Honor chuckled. "This one is easy. You just touch a crystal."

I frowned, thinking back to the crystal I'd touched before getting on the boat and how it had zapped me. "That's it?"

"That's it."

I could do that.

"What's your affinities?" I leaned into Noble. "Or is that rude to ask?"

"Rage is right; she never shuts up," Justice grumbled, stalking off, leaving me with Honor and Noble, the only sane ones.

"Dick!" I shouted at his retreating back, and a few students around us gasped.

Noble's grin stretched from ear to ear. "Not rude to ask. I'm a water elemental."

Whoa. So cool.

"I heard water elementals also have a smidge of healing ability," I said.

He nodded. "Only smaller injuries and cuts, and it doesn't work on myself. It's one of those selfless gifts."

Which explained why I'd want Noble around if I got called in for a "meeting" with the alpha king. Did he torture students? Could he be any more evil? I shook my head, dislodging the disturbing thoughts. "Being selfless must be the pits."

We burst into laughter, only to be shushed by a teacher standing at an open doorway to a glass-domed building.

"Prince Noble…" Her gaze dropped to our hooked arms, and her mouth popped open.

"Madam Sherky." Noble dipped his head to the tall, lithe, Midnight woman.

As we entered the open double-doors, Noble leaned into me. "Sorry, Nai, gotta scram. Enjoy the show. I hope you have a cool affinity."

I let go of him, whispering, "If I'm a water elemental with healing abilities, then I'll help you when you get hurt. I can be selfless too."

I was half kidding, but the tender expression that crossed his face made me think he was touched.

He leaned over and kissed my cheek. "You're too good for this place."

I stared at his retreating back, his words pinging around my head. My stance remained solid: Midnight Pack was a bunch of psycho backstabbers ... *except* Noble. That boy was sweet as honey. Honor was decent too, but I didn't know him well enough to call him a friend yet. He was quieter than Noble.

"Psst!" Kaja hissed.

As I scanned the room for her, my jaw dropped.

Holy mage shifter babies.

This room reminded me of a meadow, only inside. Verdant flora occupied much of the space with white creeping vines growing up the sides of the walls all the way to the glass dome ceiling. Glowing white hummingbirds dipped in and out of the space above our heads. Like a magical wedding venue.

I squeezed in next to Kaja and followed her gaze to a raised platform at the front of the room.

Wearing their swirly magical robes, five high mages stood there. Recognizing the one from the portal, I swallowed hard. He'd allowed me to enter, but his magic felt like an inquisition. His deep blue cloak identified him as the most powerful water elemental.

"That's the high council?" I whispered, staring at the five men.

Rumor was they lived for a millennia before passing

on to whatever upper realm of honor the high mages received—allegedly better than what shifters, vampires, or even the "regular" mages inherited. We lived over a century easily, so I wasn't going to complain. *Much*.

One of the dudes had silvery-white hair like mine, except he was so wrinkled he might've had one foot out of this mortal realm already. The other four were younger, and their scary-as-hell eyes were probably lethal weapons.

Kaja nodded and dropped her voice so low I could barely hear: "My sister told me they possess *all* of the elemental affinities, but each of them is the master of one."

I studied their colored silk cloaks. Orange for fire. Blue for water. Brown for earth. White for air.

But the old dude … he wore an iridescent silver robe. Was he like the king of them all? Or so old he was merely honorific? There were only four elements, so *something* was up with him.

"What about…" I pointed at the old mage. "…that guy? What's his strongest element?"

Kaja shrugged. "I heard he can raise the dead."

Raise the dead…?

Chills skittered over my skin, and I spun toward Kaja, my eyes wide.

"Are you serious?" I hissed.

Her expression gave no indication of humor, but I didn't know her well enough to really have a read on her.

"Just do what they tell you, and you should be fine."

"That's not very reassuring," I muttered.

My attention flitted past the five members of the High Mage Council to the armed soldiers standing behind each of them. Those guys were the epitome of badass—from their modern breastplate armor to the shiny and sharp weapons they carried. Killing machines. One for each. I was admiring their black tactical suits when my gaze fell on the high mage crest patch, and I gasped, realizing who the soldiers were.

"Are those their shields?" I stared at them with hero worship and tried to contain my excitement. Next to the alpha king, these wolf-shifters held the highest positions we could have.

Kaja nodded. "Pretty cool, huh? My second eldest sister is one." My eyes landed on the fierce redheaded shield standing behind the old dude with her hand at the hilt of a blade.

So freaking cool. I wanted to call my dad just to tell him I'd finally seen one. The High Mage Council was so important that they each had a living person bound to protect them, a shield. The shield would absorb any injury inflicted on the high mage—even death, keeping the high mage alive.

The old mage gazed around the room almost as if he was looking for someone. I was about to ask Kaja another question when he approached the podium.

Blood rushed in my ears, my heart hammering so loudly I was sure the entire room could hear it. What or who was he looking for? Did he know I wasn't supposed to be here until next year? He couldn't know that … right?

I squirmed, remembering what Dad told me about the abilities of the High Mage Council—they could do just about anything. Mind reading was definitely in their capabilities … to what degree, I didn't know.

The old high mage held no microphone, and yet his voice amplified so we could all hear. "Welcome to Alpha Island. As is customary, my brethren and I are here to host the elemental affinity ceremony."

I glanced at the four other high mages, none of whom were looking at the old mage or the alpha heirs. One yawned, and another leaned over to say something to the high mage on his left. All four appeared bored at best. Clearly, we weren't their favorite yearly obligation.

A woman, who I assumed was an elemental mage teacher, wheeled out a giant crystal cluster with jutting points of various widths, lengths, and colors. The entire room did a collective ahhh, including me, and we leaned forward.

As a wolf, I loved the earth, and something about natural crystals resonated deep within me. I had an entire row of pretty stones I'd collected over the years in Montana, but I'd never seen a crystal quite like this. The tips were clear quartz, but inside of the crystal where it was a single mass, colors swirled within—wisps of red, blue, green, yellow, orange, purple, and even black. Could such a piece naturally occur?

"The Affinity Stone was gifted to us by the Mother Mage herself. May she rest in peace."

"May she rest in peace," we coursed, giving honor to the woman who created our magical races. It was said she held a multitude of DNA strands within her magic, and she borrowed matter from the mortal realm to construct the first of dozens of magical races: mage, shifters of all kinds, and vampires. The Mother Mage, also known as the High Queen, was the "mother" to us all.

The old man's voice grew reverent. "After the queen created the magical races, she grew weary and rested from her labors. All of her creations left, off to explore the magic lands and seek their fates. All but one. An alpha wolf shifter remained, her most loyal companion. After a century together, he became her mate, and she decided to honor him by bestowing their offspring with elemental magic. And so you were created. A spark of high mage power for those who lead their kindred, a reward for love and loyalty."

I bowed my head in respect. Out of hundreds of Crescent Clan wolves, only Nolan, myself, and my father and aunt would bear any elemental magic, and it was all due to the Queen Mother's love for the alpha wolf she spent her life with. It was a grand love story. It was said not even death parted them. The High Mage Council had since banned interracial breeding—like under penalty of death—but the High Queen's love story showed just how powerful a race could be when combined.

The mage finished his story and cleared his throat. "Her final gift to the alpha heirs was the Affinity stone. Once we know your element, you'll be matched with your mage master teacher."

My gaze ran the length of the wall where a half dozen teachers stood. The elemental mage masters could make or break your education here. I didn't know much, but I knew that. I needed to have a strong affinity and be assigned a powerful mage master. Someday, Nolan could challenge me.

And I'd do all I could to discourage that.

Chapter 5

THE HIGH MAGE at the lectern stepped closer to the Affinity Stone and then continued his address. "When I call your name, you'll come to me. I'll prick your palms with the sword of truth, and then you will place both hands on the crystal."

What—what—what ... the hell is the sword of truth? Prick my palms?

No, no, no...

I glanced around the hall again, but no one else seemed disturbed by his announcement. Not even when he held up the biggest dagger I'd ever seen—at least a foot long. Was that silver?

This whole thing was weird.

I ground my teeth, but my decision was already made. I wanted my elemental power. I needed it. That magic not only set me apart from the other wolves in my pack; it would filter to my pack when I became alpha.

I stood straighter.

The Affinity Stone pulsed, splashing rainbows across the room, and my heart raced.

A hush fell over the crowd, and we waited for the first victim—er ... student.

"Mallory of Daybreak."

The high mage said her name as though reading it from a list, but there was no list. Just a creepy old high mage waiting to impale us with a silver weapon.

I swallowed hard, rising up onto my tiptoes so I could see. A tall willowy young girl with long blond hair stepped forward boldly; she kept her chin cocked up, giving an air of superiority. She reminded me of the Barbie doll my father had given me when I was seven.

Holding out his gnarled hand, the old man dropped his voice so the rest of us couldn't hear. He said something to Mallory, who had placed her palms out in front of him. She nodded, and he grabbed her wrist, driving the tip of the blade into her left palm and then again to her right.

My stomach plummeted. Holy mage. I'd rather join the undead than be stabbed in the palms in front of all my classmates.

So much blood.

"Now, place your hands on the crystal," he said in a soft tone that nevertheless carried to everyone.

Mallory rested her hands over the crystal's tips, and her blood dripped onto the cluster.

Wow!

In an instant, red, orange, and yellow lit the room. The magical live flames climbed up her arms until her entire body was covered by the beautiful iridescent glow. She withdrew her hands, and the magic around her disappeared as she turned, facing us. With a smile of triumph, she held her hands aloft, her palms healed even though the magical fire continued to dance there.

"Ah, how exciting," the high mage exclaimed in a tone that indicated the opposite. "A fire elemental. Thank you, child. You may take your place next to the mage masters and older students of fire."

He called Kaja up next, and when she looked at me hesitantly, I gave her a thumbs-up. Her blood dripped on the crystal. Within seconds, she held glowing gold rocks, indicating she was an earth elemental, and was placed with a mage master of that ability.

There was no predisposition based on pack or lineage, or so it seemed. I now wondered if I would have fire like my father or something else entirely. I looked beside me to see that I was now alone. Everyone else in the room hugged the walls, indicating they were older years, which meant…

"Naima of Crescent Clan," the old high mage said, yanking me from my stupor. My stomach clenched, and my palms slicked with sweat.

Pull it together, Nai!

I met his gaze, and the universes swirled beneath the cloudy depths of his eyes.

Queen Mother, have mercy. I didn't expect to be this terrified. I shouldn't be.

What if I didn't have an elemental affinity? If I had no magic, they'd throw me out. There would be no need to even be taught here—I would go home a failure, leaving Nolan to take my place as heir in the first position. It happened every century or so; they said it was a curse, and if any clan were to be cursed … it would be mine. Then I really would bring shame to my clan.

Please, don't let me be a dud.

The high mage's lips tipped up in what I hoped was a smile. "Please join me."

A few of the alpha heirs snickered, and I heard one of them groan—probably Justice. Or Rage. Someone needed to pull the sticks out of their backsides. How was it that they were brothers with Noble and Honor? Why were they here anyway? They already knew their affinity.

I scooted past the crowd at the edges of the room to the aisle, keeping my head held high. Never let your foe see your fear, my father would say.

As I strode toward the raised dais, I started to wipe my sweaty palms on my skirt before remembering it wasn't my dress—not to mention everyone was staring.

I stepped onto the dais and felt the heat of one of the high mages' gaze—blue cloak, the same one from earlier. I was no genius, but for some reason, that dude had it out for me. I could feel his magic wash over me as if ... scanning me.

Mother Mage, protect me.

I wished he'd stop staring.

Something fizzled in the air, and then it was just me and the older high mage. I blinked and then frowned because the tall high mage standing in front of me was no longer wearing long silver robes with his milky galaxy eyes. He was ... smiling at me kindly, and we were both dressed in shorts and tank-tops, standing outside on a sandy beach.

What the mage was going on? I spun, looking for the crowd in the room but saw only miles and miles of endless shoreline.

"Isn't this your favorite place?" he asked.

My jaw hit the sand, and I shook my head. "I've ... never been here."

I'd always wanted to go to the beach, but since the alpha king banished us to our small lands in Montana, I'd never been able to go. This was absolute confirmation that he could read minds. Right? And teleport people to beaches...

He cocked his head and inhaled deeply through his nose. "You are more powerful than I thought—"

"What? I'm confused..." My heart, which had been lulled into a slower beat because of the crashing waves, picked up its pace again. Nothing about this made any sense. And if no one else was here...

"Where are we?"

He shrugged noncommittally. "That's a conversation for another day. I'm going to need your hands now."

Apparently, we were going forward with the ceremony ... on a beach. Had the other students seen this? Did he take each student to their favorite inner-mental landscape? Maybe it'd be best to get this over with and return my body to the school. I held my palms out, my confusion by this time far greater than my fear of the silver dagger.

Even so, I forced a swallow and then asked, "Will it hurt?"

The high mage chuckled, a legit laugh—which sounded like wind chimes. I was 84.8% sure he didn't laugh with the other students. He wasn't even friendly with them.

"Definitely not," he responded. His expression turned somber then. "But I need you to listen. Before you drip your blood on the crystal, you need to pick an affinity and tell me what it is."

What? I shook my head, trying to dislodge the heaping piles of WTH.

"We get to pick?" I asked, frowning. "Is this what you were discussing with everyone else?" Maybe that's what he whispered to everyone. You want fire? *Okay, done.*

He shook his head. "I need *you* to pick one. We're

running out of time. I cannot hold us in this place much longer without the others knowing—"

What the what?

"Oh-kay. Fire," I said, thinking of my father and the ability to make one's blood boil in their skin. Seemed like a decent affinity.

The high mage grinned, and it was all feral excitement. "Then, think orange—the color of a deep sunset."

Orange. Orange. Orange, I chanted in my head for good measure.

"Close your eyes," the mage whispered.

This dude had me so confused, but I wasn't about to question a high mage during a special ceremony. Closing my eyes, I breathed in and tried to think of the color orange. *Why?* I had no idea. Maybe it helped my element come to the surface?

I felt an icy kiss on my palm like a snowflake brushing warm skin after pulling off my gloves. For some reason, Rage popped into my mind then. I thought of how his gaze dipped to my lips when he was lying on top of me in the car. I wondered what his affinity was. Water? Air?— Ugh, he was such an ass. My lip curled in disgust.

Think Orange, Nai!

Crap!

Orange sunset, illuminating red-rocked mountains...

Cold icy magic bludgeoned me in the solar plexus,

and I gasped, clenching my eyes shut. The biting cold seared my skin like an icicle slicing into me, and I hunched over with a cry.

He said it wouldn't hurt!

"Oww," I muttered between my teeth.

"Holy fecking mage!" one of the students shouted.

My eyes popped open, and my jaw dropped. Gone was the sandy beach. I was back in the atrium of Alpha Island, my hands hovering over the crystal and dripping blood. Colors danced and swirled above us. Gradually, the blues, yellows, and greens faded, and then, there in my palms, a vibrant teal light swirled and twisted, mixed with a deep, beautiful orangey-red. The vermilion became flames, licking my palm as if it were dry wood, and the teal transmuted to a light blue and then swirled in my hand like a mini water tornado. *Yikes*. This didn't look like fire element.

My stomach dropped.

"How many affinities does she have?" someone cried from behind me.

I grimaced. My attention jumped from my hands to the high mage who still held them. He muttered a chant under his breath and opened his eyes, fixing them on me. There was disappointment there and … fear, but then it was gone.

"Sorry," I whispered, guilt wiggling in my gut. Perhaps that was residual discomfort from whatever that pain was. "I tried to pick one." My voice was barely a whisper, meant only for him.

He shook his head. "No matter, Nai. You did fine."

Pride swelled within my chest, and a warm trickle of energy flowed up my arm. The ache over my abdomen waned like putting aloe vera on a sunburn. "Thanks."

"She has two affinities!" the old man told the crowd, which now pushed closer, including the teachers. My gaze scanned the crowd before landing on Rage. He'd pushed off the wall and now stared at me through a slitted, sharp gaze.

"What in the name of the high mage?" a man shouted, his voice raspy and harsh.

I spun on my heel and faced the High Mage Council. The one dressed in royal blue glared at me. "It's been nearly a century since we had a student with two affinities—and that alpha almost destroyed her clan."

I gulped as silence descended over the crowd.

He took one more step toward me, and my entire body stiffened. "We'll be watching you, *wolf*."

Shock ripped through me, and shame burned my cheeks.

My eyes flicked to Kaja, who looked down at her feet. Rumor was that a century ago, a Harvest Clan alpha had two affinities and went mad from it. She had to be put down...

Before I could retort, the high mage at my back cleared his throat. "Calm yourself, Kian. I'll keep an eye on her myself. Now, back down so we can finish." His tone was clear. That was an order, and this badass was clearly in charge of the others. The old man's shield,

Kaja's sister, stepped closer to him as if threatening Kian to refuse.

Kian scowled but said nothing more.

Ha! *Take that, a-hole.*

"Fire is her stronger affinity," the old high mage declared, ignoring me except to hold up my hand as all traces of my affinity test vanished but for a small glowing of my palms. "Water affinity is also present. She'll need to be trained by both the fire and water elemental mages. See to it that she has all things needed for training." He nodded at me and pointed to a mage master teacher dressed in black with purple and gold trimming on his cloak. "Start with Mage Carn, Fire Master."

Whoa. None of the other students got assigned a mage teacher by the High Mage Council.

I nodded, careful not to seem too excited. Especially with Kian still glaring at me.

After closing my palms, I expected the colors to go away, but they didn't. I could still see threads of energy looping and twisting around my finger.

Knock it off. I shook my palms to try and clear them as I stepped down from the stage and walked toward the mage teachers.

A few minutes later, the high mage told a mage teacher to take the crystal back to the safe, and then all of the high mages and their shields left. Gone. No long-winded speeches about how we should live up to our affinity or how those with power should use it for good

—none of that. Kudos to the high mage for doing it right. I was getting sick of the stares—two affinity freak over here. Just my luck. I couldn't even take this test right.

A beautiful older woman, with long dark hair and piercing green eyes, strode over to the podium and rapped on it with a gavel. She looked familiar, but I couldn't place her. "Hello, new students, I'm Elaine, the headmistress of Alpha Academy. I'm sorry the alpha king could not be here tonight to welcome you. He had a pressing matter."

Did her gaze just flick to me?

Oops.

"I'm not one for speeches, but as alpha heirs, you've been entrusted with great power, and all of us here at Alpha Academy expect you to honor the gifts you've been endowed with—and use them wisely."

Well, at least she admitted she wasn't one for speeches. Was there a handbook for bad speeches passed around by people in authority?

"And now, we'll leave you to your festivities. Enjoy tonight..." She scanned over the crowd, her features hardening as she looked at the new heirs. "For tomorrow, the hard work begins."

The bright lights dimmed, and a cacophony erupted.

Chapter 6

"Oh my mage! Did you see the look on Prince Courage's face?" Kaja said, grabbing me around the waist and pulling me toward the door. "I mean, I'm sure you didn't, but he completely freaked out when your affinities showed up. Two!"

I shook my head. "I highly doubt he 'freaked out.'" I used air quotes for good measure.

She stopped and faced me. "Girl, he was two seconds from storming that stage."

Heat crept up my cheeks. There were a couple of ways that could be interpreted. *One*: he was going to protect me from the creepy high mage in the blue robes who complained. Or *two*: he was going to kill me. Based on our past, I was 85.3% sure it was the latter.

I tugged at my borrowed dress. "I can't wait to change out of this thing. No offense."

The small group of about fifteen heirs dispersed

along the paths outside the gazebo, heading back to the dorms.

"Oh, don't think you're changing into sweats, Nai. The night's not over." Kaja smirked, and something about her expression screamed trouble. "My older sisters are going to the after-party, and I got us invites!"

Her voice went up to a legit squeal at the end, and I chuckled. "You're way too peppy for this time of night."

Kaja put her hands on her hips and cocked her head to the side. "Don't tell me you'd rather go back to your dorm."

Dust and rat-infested dorm with psycho Nolan? Or a party? "I'm in."

There'd better be food. I hadn't eaten all day, and someone was going to get killed if I went too much longer without a meal.

Like one hundred percent. I just wanted to eat and forget this day.

AN HOUR LATER, after Kaja graciously fed me snacks, I clutched a delicate blue mask in my hands.

"Tell me again why we have to wear these?" I asked Kaja's older sister, Nell. She'd loaned me a legit ball gown, complete with rhinestone heels, all of which I had yet to try on.

"It's tradition," she said as she touched up my make-up.

The Harvest Clan dorm was opulent and spotlessly clean, and I kinda wished they'd adopt me.

"Some third years started it like a century ago. It's our one night to hang out together without worrying about alpha status, challenge fights, or whatever might befall warring clans. We magically hide our clan marks, change our hair color, wear masks, and live with abandon until the sun comes up."

Warring clans seemed like a bit of an exaggeration, but I understood the concept and shrugged. "Well, I've always wanted baby blue hair."

Nell grinned. "You've got it. I've worked on the hair changing spell all year with my mage teacher."

She held her hands over my head, and I peered down and grinned as my white locks deepened into a soft powdery blue before my eyes. My gaze bounced to the dress, and my grin grew. *Nice*. She'd matched the same blue as the gown, only several shades lighter.

"Holy mage, that's sick! How can a water elemental change my hair color?"

Her lips curled into a smirk. "Your hair has water in it. I'm simply manipulating the properties so light refracts off the strands differently."

My eyes widened while she spoke, and when she finished, I shook my head. "Dude, you do not look like you should be talking about light refraction, but I need you to teach me that. STAT."

Nell snickered, but I was serious. Blue was a good

look for me, and I had both water and fire elements, so it was plausible, right?

"Once you get through your basic water studies, I could probably teach you," she said. "Maybe over the summer?"

"That would be awesome." Suddenly, the next four years didn't seem too bad.

"Is it true people hook up at this thing?" Kaja asked as she fastened her mask. With her new, jet-black hair and half of her face covered, I wouldn't know it was her unless she spoke.

Nell nodded. "It gets a little crazy. When you go in, you'll prick your finger and place a drop of blood into a magical chalice. It keeps you from kissing anyone you're related to."

"Eww," I groaned. Kissing Nolan would legit make me vomit. Just thinking about it was enough to make me declare, "I'm not hooking up with anyone. I'm only going for the food."

Nell grinned. "I said that my first year too. You'll see."

Her words sparked a rush of nervous churning in my gut, but I gritted my teeth and fastened my mask. Naima of Crescent Clan was no wuss. I'd go to this party like a normal socially awkward girl and have fun. If no one but Nell and Kaja knew who I was, then I might even dance.

Kaja bounced on her heels. "Girl, get your dress on so we can go!"

I'd been dreading the dress, or maybe that churning in my stomach was too many pretzels. Was that even possible?

I creased my palms over the opening ceremony dress they had loaned me. "I just got used to this one—"

Nell pointed at the closet. "Get in there and change, or I'm going to do it for you. You'll look fab, so let's get a move on."

Stepping into the large walk-in closet, I slipped out of my earlier dress, and when my gaze landed on my abdomen, I shrieked.

"Nai?" Kaja's concerned voice came through the door.

At the same time, Nell asked, "What's wrong?"

Anxiety crawled up my chest and burned the back of my throat as I stared at the three silvery squiggles several inches above my belly button, right where the icy pain had punched me during the affinity ritual. I traced the lines, and the veins in my hand glowed blue. Then a strange light, the same blue color, ran up my arm. As soon as I yanked my hand away from the peculiar marks, the magic faded.

What the mage does this mean?!

No one said anything about magic tattoos at the ceremony. Did this happen to everyone? The high mage who'd conducted the ceremony said it wouldn't hurt, and no one else doubled over in pain, so my guess was no. *Maybe I'd ask my new friends—*

Dread filled my belly with the thought. Our friendship was too new to trust them with something like this. At least, not yet.

"I'm fine. Just, uh ... saw a spider." It sounded like a question, but I didn't know what to say.

Doing a quick scan of my body, I confirmed there were no more marks.

"Some badass alpha she'll make," Nell said loud enough for me to hear, but the playfulness in her tone took out all the sting.

"Shut up," I called out, deciding to ignore the weird mark and deal with it later. Maybe there would be something about it in my classes—or the library. I pulled the huge sparkly royal blue ball gown up and stepped out of the closet before asking Kaja to lace up the corset-style back.

"Dayum, girl, that looks hot with your blue hair."

I grinned. It didn't matter if I broke my neck and died in these heels. I looked like a freaking magical princess.

Nell beckoned us from the door. "Let's roll, girls. Reality hits tomorrow. This is our one night of stress-free fun."

With that, we followed her outside and slipped into the night.

∽

"FINGER," a tall buff guy with black hair said, holding

out his beefy hand. He wore a black mask covering his clan mark and was poured into an expertly-tailored black tux.

After trekking at least half a mile off-campus, we'd arrived at the open door of a huge mansion, at least five stories tall.

One by one, we held out our fingers, and he pricked them, squeezing a single drop of blood into the chalice.

"This place is obsessed with blood," I muttered to Kaja. However, if the magic kept me from kissing Nolan, I had *zero* protest.

She laughed, and I stepped through the door, only to be stopped by the buff dude.

"Hang on," he said. "You need a voice mod, right?"

"Huh?"

"Yes!" Kaja whisper-yelled. "Do me too."

Before I could ask what the heck they were talking about, a blanket of pale gray mist shot from his hand and wrapped around her throat.

"I'm only here for the food," Kaja said, her voice lilting and musical. Definitely not sounding like normal Kaja.

"What the—?" My eyes widened, and I nodded at the bouncer. The next thing I knew, my voice was a bit lower, still female but more like the singer Adele.

Score!

"Have fun." He winked, and we stepped inside the giant entryway.

Holy mage babies.

Now *this* was a house. The large staircase led to an open loft area where half a dozen people lounged, chatting. A circular staircase led to the third floor, and I couldn't see any more of the upstairs beyond the halls leading to separate wings of the house. Past the giant staircase, a massive three-story great room flowed into a kitchen. I stared at the group of chefs, and one in a tall white hat barked orders at the others, making me avert my gaze. This party was catered?

Yum.

"Stop gawking," Nell said, grabbing my wrist and pulling me toward the wall of windows on the other side.

Music blared from outside, and it was only as we approached that I noticed the wall of windows was a set of sliding doors, all pushed to the side and opened fully. We stepped through the opening and onto the back patio.

"You know this place?" I asked, still freaked by the sound of my voice. If I knew no one would know, I'd be tempted to sing.

Hello, it's me...

She nodded. "The Midnight princes grew up here before they moved into the dorms. They hosted the party here last year too."

Of course they did. I rolled my eyes heavenward and then looked around with increased scrutiny. The virtues grew up here? Pretty posh. Not that I expected anything less of the alpha king's children. Or nephews. Or whatever. *Heirs*.

Nell led us outside and down a set of patio stairs, through a garden pathway lit by ground lanterns. When the walkway opened up into a large clearing, I gasped.

I don't know what I'd been expecting but ... not this. This was absolutely *magical*.

"I heard their mom, the headmistress, does all the decorating," Kaja whispered.

Mom ... headmistress? That's where I recognized her! The woman who gave the concluding speech had the same dark hair as her boys, and those green eyes were a dead ringer for Justice and Rage.

"The king's wife?" My brow furrowed in confusion. "Wouldn't that be their aunt?"

Nell shook her head. "Their father, the king's brother, died. So when the alpha king took over, he took her and the boys in. Married her and made them his heirs."

Whoa. That was actually kind of sweet for a total douchebag psycho who screamed abusively at them. King A-hole had to be sterile, or maybe their mom wouldn't sleep with him. Before I could ask any more questions, my gaze was pulled to the party.

The back yard, if you could call it that, was like a mini forest, at least an acre of manicured green land with thick canopy trees with *glowing* purple flowers.

I pointed to the flowering tree. "My dad told me about those." These were all over the island, not just the academy grounds, so my father was able to talk about them. Too bad everything else about this school was a mystery.

Kaja nodded. "Those flowers make a powerful sedative."

I knew that too. The extract was distilled and sold both in the mortal and magic world. The exclusive location of the flower accounted for a large portion of the werewolves' wealth. Well, most werewolves' wealth, the ones who weren't excommunicated.

My gaze ran over the white silk tents set up on the lawn and the swimming pool, glowing blue to green to purple. The most amazing part was the fireballs suspended in mid-air, illuminating the magical space.

"Like what you see, ladies?" a man asked, his deep voice unfamiliar.

I spun to see a large muscular guy in a black tuxedo and black mask grinning at us like a fool.

Hmm. Nolan? Rage? Justice? Could be anyone. All the males were huge and probably said douchy things like "Like what you see, ladies?"

"You live here?" I hedged to him.

The dude scoffed. "Breaking the rules. You must be a *newbie*."

I crossed my arms. "Second year actually."

Hey, if I was going to be someone else tonight, I might as well go all out and full-blown lie.

The guy looked from me to Kaja to Nell, who'd just joined us, and the music slowed to a soft and sexy beat.

"Dance with me?" He extended his arm to Nell, who grinned.

"I'd be delighted." She took it, and the two of them strolled over to where two other couples swayed to the beat.

Kaja eyed a food tent and yanked me toward it. "Let's grub. I heard they serve mage wine at this thing."

Mage wine. My dad let me have some once. A trader had brought it in with our usual haul. I'd laughed hysterically at everything Lona had said and then started crying and told my dad I wished I'd grown up with a mother. Suffice it to say, a full glass was not recommended for me. Train wreck city. I'd be staying far away from that stuff tonight.

"Ohh, chocolate fountain!" I squealed, spotting the liquid deliciousness, and ran over to the tent. I started plucking strawberries and marshmallows from beneath the flowing decadence and dropping them on a plate.

"I'll be right back. I'm going to track down the mage wine," Kaja told me and left.

I saturated a marshmallow in chocolate and then shoved the whole thing in my mouth.

Yummmm. Food was one hundred percent my love language.

"A woman who isn't afraid to eat. I dig it," a deep voice said from behind me.

I quickly swallowed the food, wiping my mouth with my hand. Turning around, I faced a giant of a man.

Midnight Kisses

At well over six feet tall, he towered over me. His black tuxedo strained against his muscles as if they were begging to be freed.

"I don't know what you're talking about. I was just looking for the salad bar," I joked.

The dude grinned, and my stomach flipped. Straight white teeth and a killer smile was my kryptonite. This dude had both.

"Wanna see something cool?" he asked, holding out his hand.

My heart pounded in my ears. What if this was freaking Nolan? Or Noble? The latter had already become like a brother to me. I remembered Nell's warning that I'd not just be here for the food…

I must have paused for too long because he dropped his hand. "It's cool. I get it."

He started to walk away.

Damn my curiosity! I did want to see something cool, especially if it was with that giant dude carved of stone with kissable lips and a nice smile.

I grabbed a strawberry and tore after him. "What cool thing?"

He looked back with a grin, and I nearly melted. Whoever this dude was … he was majorly yummy and, so far, super sweet. No way in hell could it be Rage or Nolan. They didn't have a sweet bone in their bodies.

He reached out again, and this time, I took his hand. I had no idea why because touchy-feely on the first date, or whatever this was, wasn't my thing. But I did. It felt … good. Warm and tingly. I stepped closer, my heart fluttering when he tucked my hand in the crook of his arm.

"I heard this place has a secret garden." He cut into the woods, and I froze.

"Umm." I pulled my hand back. *He could be a murderer.* "Out here?"

He looked back at me with a halfcocked grin. "I'm not going to hurt you. I promise. Besides, aren't you an alpha heir? I'll bet you could wipe the floor with me."

Hah!

He had a good sense of humor too. I laughed, genuinely. "I could probably make you wish you weren't born, yes."

Maybe, but not before he overpowered me with his 'roid monkey physique. Dude was jacked, and if he was at this party, he was an alpha heir too.

"Look, I get it." He retraced his steps, holding his hands up in a gesture of peace. "If you don't want to come, it's cool, but my friend said this place is magical, and … I like your blue hair."

His rambling softened my heart, but still, I hesitated.

He dropped his hands, and his voice softened. "I would never hurt anyone at this school. It's just … this is the one night a year we get to be … *free*."

Something crossed his face after he said the last word, and his lips turned down. He looked … sad. Like every other day of the year, he wasn't free.

"I really do like your blue hair." He reached out and touched the end of one curl before lowering his fingers.

Every other girl here had done normal colored hair, black, blonde, brown, red. I was the only one crazy enough to ask for blue...

He turned then and walked into the forest, leaving me by myself.

I like your blue hair. Gah! That was kinda sweet!

"Fine!" I shouted and traipsed after him. "You don't have to beg!"

I heard him chuckle as I caught up.

"I think it's right over here. If my buddy is telling the truth." He took a right.

Trying to maneuver over a log, I lifted the hem of my dress. My foot caught, and I sucked in a breath as I pitched forward.

But I never hit the ground. Somehow, the dude spun faster than lightning and caught me mid-fall. As he pulled me back upright, my body pressed into his chest, and all rational thought left my brain.

The music. The cool night air wafting his yummy scent to me. The glow of the moon through the trees. This was magical. A night to be free, like he said.

"Careful." He backed up a few inches and I found my last two brain cells. "That's why I was trying to hold your hand earlier. Those shoes are weapons."

I smiled. "They are. Thanks."

His hand slipped into mine again, and we continued

our walk until we happened upon a magnificent steel gate.

"Are those ... wings?" I gasped, dropping his hand to caress the metal in the shape of two giant angel wings. It was stunning.

He nodded. "I think so."

Reaching out, he plucked the gate open, and I was grateful it wasn't locked.

He bowed. "After you, Miss Blue."

A grin tugged at my lips. He was a charmer, and that was dangerous. I loved a guy who could give a good compliment. Hopefully, whomever my father picked to be my breeding partner and mate would be a charmer too. Pushing those thoughts from my mind, I stepped past the sweet talker.

"Thank you." I whisked forward, my huge dress skimming the sides of the gate as he stepped in behind me and closed it.

My breath hitched. "Whoa."

Every single flower in here was *glowing*—blues, pinks, purples, greens so vibrant it looked like paint. Even tiny white flowers crawled along the ground, covering the garden floor in a soft glowing blanket.

"It's the most amazing thing I've ever seen." I spun, and he watched me.

He kept his gaze on me. "It's a close second for me."

I rolled my eyes. "You're a charmer."

He shrugged. "I call them as I see them."

The music wafted through the trees, reaching us, soft and almost haunting in a way.

He held out a hand. "Dance with me, Miss Blue?"

Why resist? Tomorrow would start four years of hell. Four years of me proving to myself, Nolan, my clan, and everyone else that I was the best person to lead my pack when my father either died or retired. Why not let loose for one night?

He pulled me in a respectable distance to his body, but I pushed us closer. I don't know if it was the music, the magical garden, or the entire party atmosphere, but I felt like we were magnets unable to pull away from each other in this moment. His fingers trailed down my back, causing goosebumps to rise up my arms.

Without overthinking it, I reached up and traced his jawline. His eyes were the most captivating, searing green I'd ever seen. A slow buzzing sensation filled my body then, and my breath caught as he stiffened against me.

Something white and fluttering caught my eye, and I glanced up to see over a dozen white glowing butterflies descend upon us. His whole body tensed further as the butterflies landed on us, one by one.

Laugher pealed out of me as he held me tightly.

"Oh, my mage, this is crazy!" I said.

The buzzing grew stronger; the urge to draw closer to him seized me. I dropped my gaze, and my lips parted. His hands gripped my hips, his eyes widening, and his skin blanched as the butterflies settled onto my shoulders and his arms.

"It's you," he whispered, his voice filled with awe.

"What?" I didn't have time to process anything more because, in that moment, he leaned in and captured my mouth in a kiss. When our lips touched, warmth exploded within my chest and traveled downward, pooling low in my belly. The buzzing tingle saturated my entire body, and I reached up and threaded my fingers through his hair, pulling him closer. He nipped at my bottom lip, and I opened my mouth to him. He tasted of honey and promise. I kissed him harder; his fingers kneaded my back, reeling me into him until I was smooshed against his hard body. I'd never been kissed like this. Not James from the clan, not Kevin the farm boy who lived next door. Not ever. This kiss was earth-shattering. I was hungry for him in a way I'd never felt before. He deepened the kiss, and our tongues tangled, causing him to moan against my lips.

I swallowed his breath, wanting more of him. As I pushed my hands into his hair, the rest of the world faded until there was only him and me and this heat between us. I needed his kiss like I needed air. I needed *him*. I—

"Friend!" a voice that sounded a bit like Kaja shouted. "Blue-haired friend that I came with and now can't find…!"

I froze.

Crap, she couldn't say my name without giving me away.

Just like that, he pulled back, breaking the kiss, and the butterflies that had landed on us took flight and disappeared into the forest.

We stood there staring at each other, panting, lips swollen and red from our kiss.

"Who ... who are you?" Screw the rules. I needed more of that kissing, and I wasn't about to leave this party without this guy's name.

"No." He backed up, chest heaving, his gaze looking me up and down as if I were the plague. Okay ... maybe he did care about the rules.

"FRIEND! I'm calling werewolf 911, AKA the king, if you don't—"

"She's in here!" the dude called out and turned away from me, booking it for the gate.

"Wait!" I called after him. "Seriously?"

He reached the gate and looked back at me, his eyes, like glittering emeralds, brimmed with sadness.

"I can't. I ... won't." Then, he left.

What. The. Mage?

"There you are! You had me so worried." Kaja was nearly falling over, holding two glasses of mage wine and looking over her shoulder at the mystery kisser's retreating form.

"I'm ... fine." *Was I fine?*

No. I'd never be fine again.

Not after a kiss like that.

Chapter 7

I'D STARED at his retreating form until he disappeared, and even then, I just kept staring at the gate. Legit ... what ... the ... mage ... just happened?

"I can't ... I won't." What did that mean? I didn't initially take sexy-shmexy homeboy for an asshat, but what did I know? Maybe he really was one. I mean ... obviously, he was! Who kissed a woman like that and then *left*?

Green-eyed asshats.

"Who was that?" Kaja asked, toddling over to me with two half-filled glasses of mage wine. "And what did you do to freak him out?"

The sparkling liquid glowed golden in the crystal glasses, and the sinking feeling in my stomach needed to be quenched. I was not going to cry over someone I didn't even know—especially if he was douchy enough to run off after kissing me. Did it matter if that kiss

Midnight Kisses

was the best I'd ever had? Nope. I'd just have to find someone else to give me a better one.

"*That* was a douche-canoe," I said, plucking one of the crystal flutes from her hand. "And this"—I raised the glass—"is me taking charge of the rest of the night. We're going to eat enough delicious food to last a lifetime *and* find someone else to kiss who makes our toes curl."

Kaja nodded with a grin and solidified her role as my new BFF by raising her glass. "Challenge accepted."

We both drained our glasses, and the heady concoction tickled my insides as it slid through my chest and into my stomach. My anger over the asshat-wolf melted away, and I grinned at the prospect of kissing another stranger. "Did you see they have a chocolate fountain?"

Kaja licked her lips and then smacked them loudly. "You betcha. The only thing better than that is the mage wine. I could swim in it and not get enough, ya know?"

"Swim in it?" The idea had merit. "Let's go." I grabbed her wrist and tugged her along with me, determined to have fun. "One night to live it up, right?"

"Yass!" She giggled as she stumbled alongside me. "I knew there was secretly a fun chick hiding in there with all that sass. Let's go live it up, Blue!"

Blue. It reminded me of the best kisser in the world, AKA asshat-wolf calling me Miss Blue ... but we obviously needed code names. Staring at her black hair and silver dress, I dropped the first nickname that came to

105

mind. "You call me Blue, and I'm going to call you Ash. It's perf."

"I love that," Kaja said, her eyes wide as she clutched the empty flute to her chest. "I've never had a nickname before."

We exited the magical garden, and I resisted the urge to look back. Not going to happen. If a dude was going to kiss and bolt, he shouldn't be allowed to take up space in my thoughts. However, no matter how much I tried to steer my thoughts, they went back to that kiss, those green eyes and soft lips. Didn't Justice have eyes like that? Rage? And one dude from Daybreak I saw earlier. Maybe more … I hadn't exactly been an eye connoisseur. Until now.

The full lips reminded me of another guy I'd seen at the ceremony. I was desperate to know who I'd just made out with.

"I think the wine is affecting my thoughts," I announced with a giggle. We stepped back into the house, and I turned to look back the way we'd come. "Oh. My. Mage. Did we float here?"

Kaja blinked and then burst into peals of laughter—which only made me laugh harder.

"What's so funny?" a guy said, sidling up to us.

I glanced at him dressed in a black tux and wearing a black mask, and my snicker died off as a lump formed in my throat. Was this the same dude? His hair was black, but my interest waned as soon as I noted that his eyes were honey yellow. The guy was hot. They all were, but he wasn't my kiss stealer. It hit me then. They all...

I scanned the room, and my laughter returned. Oh mage ... no flippin' way. Every single dude in here was wearing a black tux—and a black mask, his hair dyed black. Asshat dude could be *any* of them. We only had about fifteen heirs here between the four clans, and those all ranged from first to fourth years. But there were at least thirty people at this party.

Palace guards. The king probably didn't let his four heirs party with the other clans without protection.

"Blue?" Kaja poked me.

Both she and the male wolf Clone #7 stared at me as if I were unhinged, but I was 70.3% sure there was no one else in the house dressed like me, so that was good.

"Mage wine is funny," I told the dude with a wink. My gaze shifted to the clone, and I raised my eyebrows. "You look like"—I waved my hand in the air, indicating the other occupants—"everyone else. "

The guy grinned, "All the males took a pact to magic ourselves with the same look."

Great. *Just freaking genius*. They all had the same onyx colored hair of the Midnight princes. But the dude I'd kissed wasn't one of them, because he'd referred to the secret garden as a place his friend told him about. Which meant my magical kisser was friends with the Midnight princes or worked for them.

Awkward.

Half of me wanted to go through the entire room and kiss every single guy just so I could find him and then kick him in the balls for leaving me like that. Why did that kiss have to be so amazing? I couldn't deal—I needed more wine and chocolate before I could enact operation *Kiss Every Dude Here*.

"Let's go, Ash." I tugged on Kaja's arm. "Nice to meet you!" I yelled to yellow eyes and walked away briskly with my new bestie.

Three mage wine drinks and a dozen dipped strawberries later, and still, all I could think about was a certain sexy-schmexy wolf dude. I needed to start kissing other guys pronto; someone was bound to make my toes curl … or make magical butterflies descend from the sky? Now, where was my wingwoman? I swayed on my feet, bumping into a tux-clad body as I spun away from the chocolate fountain. "Shh-orry."

Note to self: three drinks were *a lot* … way too much … for me to think … right. Although shifter metabolism was a thing of beauty, I had not burned off the effects of those drinks. The good news, no tears. I was doing better than I had a few years ago when my dad gave me that glass.

"You all right, princess?" the dude in the tux asked, his voice like liquid honey.

Grinning, I nodded. "Very much yes—I think."

Staring at his eyes, I noticed his were green—like spring grass. "Do people change their eye color tonight?"

Reaching out to touch his eyelids, I reconsidered and let my hand fall onto his chest. Hard as a rock. I patted it, wondering if chests could be magicked too.

Was this my kisser?

"Some do." He seemed amused by me, allowing me to pat his chest as he looked down at me with a half-cocked grin.

"Are yours really *that* color?" Because if they were, there was a fair chance this dude could be one of the asshole Midnight brothers, Rage or Justice. Too bad I didn't know if my magical garden asshat's eyes were really green or just magicked-green.

"No." His lips pulled up in the corner. "Why do you ask?"

No way was I going to tell, but there was something I wanted to say to this dude. Leaning forward, I dropped my voice and narrowed my eyes. "Are you trustworthy?"

He grinned, a feral, wild grin that made my heart leap. "Not at all."

"That's..." I held my fist up, index finger extended to make a point. "Huh ... that's very honest of you." Which required me to pat his chest again with approval. *Dayum*. "I like your chest."

Please don't be Nolan.

He chuckled. "Really? How interesting. I find yours quite to my liking as well."

Laughter burst from me as my belly warmed at his

words. Mage wine and chocolate were *life*. Where was Kaja? My bestie was missing out on all the fun.

"That's good." And totally factored into my kissing plan. Tilting my chin so I stared above his square jaw, I demanded, "Tell me what you think of my lips."

Leaning over me, he traced his finger across my collarbone, up the side of my neck, and then rubbed his thumb over my lips. His voice dropped, going husky with desire. "They're ripe for kissi—"

Dude disappeared. A blur, almost too fast for me to see, whizzed past, and when I looked up, he was gone.

Huh? How drunk was I?

I blinked, and there was a new man towering over me, definitely not the same guy who'd been there seconds ago.

"Hey, what the—?" In fact … those emerald eyes, those lips.

"You *asshole!*" I screamed at my garden kisser. How did I even recognize him? Who knew? Maybe it was the eyes or the way my body gravitated toward him like he was the frickin' sun.

Looking to the right, I saw the guy I'd been speaking with now lay among the forest bramble a dozen feet away. He'd literally flown out the open, white food tent and into the trees. He climbed to his feet, leaf-litter and twigs stuck to his coat and hair.

Shaking my head, I looked back at Asshat Extraordinaire. Un-freaking-believable. How dare he act possessive now? I splayed my palms out on his chest and tried to push past him—which was like trying to shove a tank, impossible—even for a werewolf.

Glaring up at him, I growled, "Move."

His jaw clenched. "You shouldn't be with that guy."

He grasped my hand softly and started to walk me out of the silk tent and back into the patio garden, leading me up to the house. I was too tipsy to put up much protest, and I needed to find Kaja anyway. We walked inside the packed living room, to the sound of bustling music, before he slipped me into a little alcove holding a potted plant. My pulse quickened as he leaned closer and sniffed the air in front of my face, and his lip curled. "You're drunk."

Hah! "That's rich! You don't get to do that. You scurried off like a rat, remember? So don't act like—"

"You're mine," he said, gripping my hips, eyes flaring emerald, and his possessive words melted into my body like warm butter. He pulled me closer, slamming my body to his; my pelvis pressed into his hips. The raw need in his voice made my knees tremble.

"*Only* mine," he added, and his chest heaved.

Whoa.

I swallowed hard. In the back of my mind, the little bit of rational-Nai screamed about healthy boundaries and psycho-controlling males. But the rest of me ... I grabbed the lapels of his tuxedo jacket and gave him a half-lidded gaze as the world fell away. Nothing else existed in this moment—just me and him.

"Prove it."

He growled, low and possessive, and then traced the tip of his nose up the side of my neck, scenting where my pulse pounded.

Scent. I'd forgotten to smell him before, but it was our greatest tracking device. In our human form, the aroma of an individual was best detected at the pulse points. In this crowded area of the house, even in our little alcove, the best place to scent him would be the neck, like he'd just done to me. If I got a good whiff now, I could figure out exactly who he was later...

My breath quickened. I gripped his arms. Desire blossomed low in my belly, and I inched closer.

"You smell like sunshine and home, Miss Blue," he whispered.

The warmth of his breath made my skin prickle, and I might've moaned—a little. "Like home?"

I inhaled, but my mind was fuzzy with mage wine. Cedarwood? Sandalwood? Sage? What was it? He traced the outside of my ear with his tongue before capturing the soft flesh between his teeth. Slowly, he worked his way across my jaw to my lips with his tongue, drawing out the tension until my desire for him was agony.

Holy mage!

"You're mine," he whispered, his lips brushing my skin. *"All mine."*

"Yes," I panted. I was his. I could feel that in my very core.

This time when he captured my lips, his kiss was

fierce and dominating. He nipped my bottom lip between his teeth, and I parted them. Our tongues tangled as he pressed me back against the wall, our bodies fitting together as if made for one another.

All alone in this magical little nook, the world around us fell away. Nothing else mattered.

His hand pressed between the laces of my dress on my back, nudging me closer. I couldn't get enough of him. I couldn't be close enough to him. His hips rotated, and I clung to him, throwing my head back to give him better access. He kissed my neck, sucking and biting as he pressed against me. I moaned, begging for more because this ... was ... *magic*.

"Mine," I growled, my wolf rising to the surface as instinct took over. I needed to stake my claim, to mark him as mine and make sure any female who got near him would know he was taken.

Searing heat flared beneath his palm, and I arched my back as the warmth became an inferno. Need, passion, and fire swirled around us, building and expanding, consuming us.

"What is happen—?" My question became a cry, and I clung to him to stay upright as the burning sensation tore through me, an explosion of pain and pleasure. His hand came up, fingers lacing through mine as all of that pain weaved through my body and wrapped around our encircled fingers. When I felt the final bolt of stinging flesh on my left ring finger, I gasped.

Looking at our clasped hands, I stared at fated mate

marks on our ring fingers, a glowing white swirl pattern in place of where a human couple might wear rings.

Holy mage.

I spun out of the alcove, switching places with him as I wrestled with my wine-soaked senses. His green eyes were wide with shock. His gaze bore into me. His chest heaved. But he didn't let me go, didn't give any indication he regretted this.

Green-eyed secret garden kisser was my freaking *mate*! I couldn't think, couldn't breathe— Fated mates? The phenomenon was rare, but not impossible. Except—

A hefty hand landed on my shoulder, and then I was ripped back, away from Green Eyes and our little alcove, and pressed into the chest of another man as his arm encircled my waist.

"Hey," a man snarled, his voice faintly familiar. "She was mine first."

The dude I'd been trying to kiss from before growled, and his grip tightened as he hauled me into the crowded living room where people danced around us.

Oh, Cursed High Mage Council.

The murderous look in Green Eyes' gaze told me shit was about to get real.

I felt, rather than saw, my mate's movement. My stomach lurched as I was ripped from Yellow Eyes' grasp and tucked back into my fated mate's embrace.

"You'll die for that," Green Eyes seethed. He released me, and the sound of bones cracking behind me alerted me to exactly how my mate intended to enforce his claim.

Oh frick.

His physical presence behind me dropped, and when my hands fell to my sides, my fingertips brushed against the soft fur of a ... wolf. *His* wolf.

Shock fried my brain; my saliva turned to cotton. I blinked and tucked my chin to stare down at ... a jet-black wolf. Baring his teeth, he snarled, a low rumbling that sent a thrill through me.

My mate is badass.

Yellow eyes grabbed my upper arm and squeezed. "Get back over here and dance with me."

Hard.

Oh, hell no.

The rest of the room swam in my periphery, and I swiveled my head to the left, looking up to meet the yellow-eyed gaze of the dude holding my arm.

"Let go." Fur rippled down my arms as my wolf sprang to the surface. She had an iffy record of coming out in times of need, but it looked like this time, she was ready to go.

Before he even had a chance to follow my command, the black wolf lunged, ripping into the guy's arm and tearing him away from me.

Holy mate-shifters!

"Don't kill him!" I yelped, afraid of what might

happen to my mate. With my luck, someone would tell the king, and my mate would get the boot from the island. I lunged after the black wolf, trying to get him to calm down. "I'm okay."

The music ground to a halt, and people spun to stare at the black wolf snapping at the yellow-eyed dude's throat.

"That's it," another guy shouted from behind me. "Party's over."

"Everyone out!" bellowed another dude, both in matching tuxes with black, gelled hair. "Now!"

People fled the garden, running past the pool and back inside where we were. Several women screeched, darting out of the rooms half-dressed and into the hallway. It didn't take a genius to know that the impromptu liaisons upstairs were coming to an untimely end. Yellow Eyes fled, and my black wolf looked back at me as if deciding whether to go after him or stick with me. I tried to inch away toward the door, and he moved with me, growling at anyone who approached within two feet of me.

My little, sexy kisser was being *possessive as hell*. Just like a newly-mated male would be, except…

This couldn't be happening. Fated mates were *always* from the same pack. *Always*.

Until now … because this obviously wasn't Nolan. Thank the Mother Mage for that blood spell.

I reached down and dug my fingers into his fur, my tension dissolving as I stroked my mate's neck and then behind his ears. As soon as my hand landed on his head, he tipped his muzzle up and rubbed it against my leg.

"So that was quite a display," I said in my most soothing voice as people ran around me to the exit. "But I'm not hurt."

I'd been in a pack for a long time and recognized all the signs of a protective mate. His wolf came out when that guy grabbed me. He was protecting me, not knowing if I could protect myself. It was sweet. My heart fluttered with the thought. I had a mate ... a *fated mate* ... who would apparently rip off the head of any male who touched me. There were only two fated mate pairs in Crescent Pack. They were rare. Less than one percent.

He licked my hand, tasting my fingers before growling at the others still in the living room.

Unfortunately, his wolf was out now, and anyone who came near me would be a threat.

"Hey, blue girl," one of the tux-clad-clones who'd kicked everyone out said, waving to me. "Tell the wolf you have to go," he said, eyeing the mate marks on my left hand with alarm. "If you do, he'll let you leave and be able to calm down enough to shift back to human."

I ran my fingers through his fur. "I don't want to leave him."

The mage wine was still hitting me, but the adrenaline rush had dissolved a good bit of it. Still, I wanted to stay here with my soft wolf-mate forever. I didn't want this night to end.

The guy cocked his head. "Do you want him to rip out the throat of every man in this room?"

I gulped. "You don't have to be so condescending—"

My wolf-mate bared his teeth at the guy, hackles raising. Then, he stalked toward the man.

Oh, wow.

My irritation evaporated. "Hey, Green Eyes," I called to my mate. "Come back over here, and don't hurt the dude."

Well, whaddya know ... the wolf listened, padding back over to me, sitting by my feet. Ha. I could get used to this.

Now bring me a cheese pizza.

Kidding.

"You need to leave. Now," the tux guy said. "It's just a matter of time before—"

Howling erupted upstairs, followed by snarls and snaps.

"Shit!" the dude muttered. "It's happening."

His eyes shifted from grass-green to yellow, and the last remnants of the mage wine burned out of my body in a flash. He was shifting ... they were all shifting.

All that sexy-shmexy mate-desire was basically coitus-incompletus, making me a lusty-beacon to every single male wolf on campus.

"Hey, wolfie," I muttered, kneeling to get on my

protector's level. "I gotta go. Uh ... will you walk me home?"

Before I even finished the sentence, I was moving toward the door. It was a race—get out of the house before the fighting reached here. Whenever wolves fought, it took a tremendous amount of willpower to keep yourself from shifting and asserting dominance. But a fight like this would be pointless. Better to protect my mate and get the hell out of here. A fight this big was bound to have repercussions. Alpha king repercussions.

Hard pass at that.

"Thank the mage," I said, relieved when my mate's wolf followed me out. As I passed the guy fighting against the call of his instinct, I felt my own skin tighten, and then fur rippled down my forearms in response. Why couldn't she do this during sparring matches at home? Right now, it felt like she had a mind of her own.

I raced out of the front door and padded along the trail, the sleek black wolf right beside me. My fingers were wound into his black fur, and my heart raced a mile a minute.

Mate.

Fated mates.

Holy frick.

He wasn't from Crescent Clan—which was a problem. Big problem. Mating outside of one's clan was forbidden; it diluted powers.

Besides, my father had a plan for me: I was supposed to go home to Montana, take up his position as alpha, and mate with a nice man from Crescent. My dad suggested Garret every chance he got, and the guy wasn't bad, so I'd never been opposed to the idea. But that was *before*.

Intentionally mating with another alpha heir from another clan would be treasonous. But could fate be wrong?

Lost in my thoughts, I didn't even realize when we'd reached the back door of my dorm. It was dark out, the moon high in the sky, only casting a small amount of light, and there wasn't a soul outside the building except me and my mate.

I knelt down and met the wolf's yellow eyes threaded through with blades of green. "You can shift now. I'm safe. You don't need to protect me anymore."

His eyes flared from yellow back to green, and as his form shifted, he stood tall and muscular, wearing the same tuxedo and black mask.

Damn.

Only really strong alpha heirs had enough magic to shift and hold on to their clothes while they did so. My mate was powerful.

He tucked me into his body, and I nestled closer. This was where I needed to be. It didn't matter which clan he was from or who he was beyond *mine*.

My mate.

Wanting him to know who I was, I tugged off my

mask and peered up at him. "I'm Nai, from Crescent Clan."

He nodded once then swallowed hard. He pursed his lips, and his jaw stiffened as if he were trying to control his expression, but a frown slipped over his mouth anyway.

I tilted my head and studied him, trying to make sense of his reaction as much as trying to connect the dots.

Wait ... *his* wolf had led *me* to my dorm.

"I know." His voice was rough and sounded slightly familiar. Was the spell wearing off?

I froze in shock.

Before I could draw any conclusions, he leaned in and kissed me, a quick brush of his lips against mine, before pulling back to smell my neck. My skin prickled with pleasure, and I tilted my head back to give him better access. Grinning, I faced my mate, ready for him to reveal himself.

Only ... his green eyes grew somber, and he made no effort to remove his mask.

No bueno. I needed to know who he was, so if he wouldn't take it off, I'd help him not be so shy.

I reached up, but before I could hook my fingers around the edges of his mask, he grabbed my wrists. Gently, he brought my hands away, holding them while we stared at each other, and as the seconds stretched, I realized he wasn't going to lower his mask. The rejection sucked the air from my lungs, and my lower lip quivered.

He brushed the curls away from my neck.

"Forgive me."

My brow furrowed as his words registered, but before I could say anything…

What the—?

He struck. The fleshy outside of his hand popped me in the neck. Before I could even gasp, blackness consumed me.

Chapter 8

A LOUD BANGING yanked me from sleep. My eyelids peeled open as the noise rattled my brain. Pain shot through my skull as the mother of all mage wine induced headaches arrived.

"No," I moaned as I sat up, hoping to stop the incessant knocking. Memories of last night flooded my brain, and I bolted out of the dusty bed—nearly tripping on the hem of the blue ball gown.

Staring down at my left hand, I saw that last night was not a dream. "Holy mage!"

Mate marks.

Real. It was all real.

The pounding at the front door grew louder, and I stumbled through my house and tugged the heavy door open.

Kaja stood there with two to-go coffee cups in her

hand. Her gaze dropped to my ring finger, which I was still inspecting, and her jaw went slack.

"It *is* you!" She pointed to my left hand, stumbling into the house. "You flipping found your fated mate at that party! Who is he?" she whisper-screamed before slamming the door behind her. She quickly followed me up to my bedroom where I shut and locked the door in case Nolan was nearby.

My thoughts went from the searing hot kisses to his lame-ass apology before he'd knocked me out with some karate mojo, and tears filled my eyes. "A huge asshole, that's who! He … he *left* me." I swallowed the lump at the back of my throat. "Knocked me out before I could lift his mask and dumped me in my bed without even giving me his name."

Kaja's face fell, and she held out the cup while shaking her head. "Whoa, that's heavy. Probably because … it's *forbidden*?"

She handed me the coffee, and I took a long swig, hoping the caffeine would prevent my head from exploding.

No more mage wine. Ever. Again.

"Yeah, I guess so. But … I wanted to know who he is." Was it so irrational to have wanted to throw caution to the wind and forget about the rules? I didn't care if it was forbidden. He was my fated mate! But *he* did care. Enough to leave me without a name, and that stung. His rejection of me over "rules" was a wound I'd never forget. Ever.

Midnight Kisses

"Okay, no biggie," Kaja said, holding out a muffin. Legit, this girl got me. Food and coffee were the things I needed first thing in the morning to function. "We can figure this out. Your mate will have mate marks, so we just look for a guy who has matching marks, and boom! Mate found."

I snickered before stating the sobering truth: "Yeah... well, I'm not sure I want to go out to my first day of class parading this around." I held up my hand. If the teachers saw it, or the king, I'd be kicked out so fast it'd make my head spin.

Kaja winced, tipping her coffee cup at me in acknowledgment. "Right." She walked over to my suitcase and flipped it open. "Where are your uniforms? I have an idea, but you need to get ready for class."

I shrugged. "Never got any. Hey, when I opened the door, you said, 'It's you.' Please don't tell me everyone is talking about the mate marks."

Bad enough being the new girl, a year early, banished clan...

Kaja winced, and I had my answer.

"EVERYONE is talking about it. Blue girl and her black wolf, fated mates. They had to break up the party... " Kaja pressed her lips together. "Didn't I tell you that everyone is talking about it already?"

Frick. This wasn't happening. "*I* don't want to talk about it anymore."

"Come on. I've got an idea—or two." Kaja pulled me out of my filthy dorm and across the courtyard into her

125

castle-like house. As we approached the west wing, I could hear her sisters bickering in the kitchen.

"Nell!" Kaja shouted.

Nell popped her head into the hallway and, upon seeing me, grinned. "Hey there, Cinderella, that was some heavy petting last night with your prince. Have fun?"

Kaja shoved my ring finger into her face. "The dude never revealed his identity. Total asswipe. He knocked her out and left. Can you hide this before first period?"

Nell's mouth popped open. "Holy crap. *Mate marks?* I thought that was a rumor. Figured Fiona was joking when she said she saw them last night on your hand. Well, not yours but Blue Girl."

"Can you hide them?" Kaja repeated while I sank into my own mortification.

Hide them? I rolled the idea around in my head, frowning. Yes … that would be ideal. Mate marks were usually worn with pride, but all that was assuming one knew who their freaking mate was *and* it wasn't forbidden! "Yes, please. Hide them."

The last thing I needed was more rumors. No, the last thing I needed was getting kicked out of school before I mastered my elements, but the rumors would seriously suck.

Nell's twin, Rue, peeked her head around the corner. She was the quiet one who didn't attend last night. Smart girl. "He's probably hiding his too. Scandalous."

"Rue!" Nell snapped as her sister shrugged and disappeared back into the kitchen where I heard Fiona and Mele, the eldest Harvest girls, all gossiping.

Great, now all the Harvest girls knew my secret.

"Yeah, I can hide them, but my magic is only strong enough to conceal them for a day. You'll need to come by every morning so I can repeat the spell."

Relief poured through me, and my shoulders dropped.

Yes. This was good.

Maybe I could just forget this mate thing ever happened. Clearly, he didn't want it—not to mention the fact that it was super freaking illegal and against pack law.

Nell held her hand over mine, and a cool blue light covered my ring finger. A moment later, all traces of the mark were gone.

That was easier than I expected and made me long to be as far along in my studies as Nell.

Kaja looked at Nell and then behind, through the doorway at Rue and the other sisters, "We don't know who Blue Girl was last night, got it? And we certainly haven't seen any mate marks. The mage wine was cray-cray."

All three redheaded girls poked their faces out through the kitchen doorway and nodded.

Fiona, the eldest, winked. "Hoes before bros. We got it."

They disappeared back into the kitchen, and I faced

Nell. Her Harvest moon mark on her forehead was three-quarters full, and for a small second, I wished I'd been in another clan. Not because I didn't like being Crescent, but I longed to have sisters—or any siblings for that matter.

She looked … sad for me.

"I'm … I'm sorry, Nai." Her voice cracked, which caused my throat to tighten. Meeting your mate and then having them taken from you was about the worst feeling in the world.

"Come on, you can have a couple of my uniforms. I've got a dozen." Kaja pulled me away, and I thanked the Mother Mage I'd met such a loyal friend.

∼

I HAD NO SCHOOL SCHEDULE, no uniform, no books, and no money. What the hell was my father thinking when he allowed me to come here?

Kaja had shown me where the headmistress's office was and then had to leave for her own studies.

After hounding the secretary for five minutes, which felt like an eternity of explaining how I didn't have a schedule or uniforms, she allowed me to speak to the headmistress.

"Come in," the woman's soft trill came from behind the large oak door.

I gulped. Pulling the doors wide, I stepped into a relatively small office: bookshelves stretched from ceiling to floor, filled with tomes and knickknacks—crystals and multiple different colored stones in green, blue, purple, and yellow—sculptures in dark wood; a golden candelabra; and a large white bowl. I could lose myself in here for days.

"Nai!" Headmistress Elaine, AKA Midnight Princes' mom, AKA the freaking king's wife, pushed away from the large mahogany desk. Her green eyes lit up when she smiled. This was the same woman who'd given birth to Rage and Justice? She seemed too cheery for that.

"I was just going to look for you." She had a piece of paper in her hand. She smiled, and I just stared at her awkwardly. "I was supposed to have dropped this off at your dorm early this morning, but I've never had a student with two affinities before, so it took some working out to get you a proper schedule."

Relief poured through me, and I returned her smile as I took the schedule.

I finally found my voice: "Thank you."

Her smile deepened. "I believe you met my sons yesterday."

That was the understatement of the century.

When she nodded, my thoughts bounced to Rage's foul temper, and I muttered, "Yeah, I did. They're ... nice ... boys."

Yep. I totally lied, and she laughed, deep and heartily.

"Rage and Justice will grow on you." She made the

statement as if she didn't believe my "nice boys" comment extended to them, and she followed it up with a wink. "Sorry about the summons mix up. The king is quite upset with whoever pulled that prank."

Hmm. Yesterday he'd called for the prankster's head. But maybe his perspective had changed. Relief washed through me. If she thought it was just a prank, then maybe nothing more sinister was going on like I'd originally thought.

"No worries…" I didn't expect her to be so cool and nice. She was probably a big part of how Noble and Honor got their personalities.

I glanced down at the paper, and the smile slid from my face.

NAIMA, Crescent Clan Heir:

7:00-8:00 A.M.: Work the coffee cart, east side of campus
    8:05-11:00 a.m.: Fire Element studies with Master Carn
    11:05-12:00 p.m.: Serve lunch in dining hall
    12:05-3:00 p.m.: Water Element Studies with Master Jin
    3:05-5:00 p.m.: Alpha Studies Main Gym
    5:05-6:00 p.m.: Serve Dinner in dining hall

"COFFEE CART?" I gulped and reached up to scratch my neck.

The headmistress winced, bringing her shoulders up, her discomfiture shrinking her posture nearly half a foot. Shaking her head, she said, "All of the clans pay an Alpha Island tax, which covers tuition for their heirs, along with books, maintenance of the dorms, and uniforms and such. Your father and Crescent Clan don't pay, so you'll have to earn your way here. I'm so sorry."

Why the hell would my clan pay an Alpha Island tax when we didn't even live on Alpha Island like the others? I wanted to scream with frustration.

I scrutinized the schedule more. "Serving lunch and dinner too? When exactly am I supposed to eat?"

I tried for a light tone, but it came out laced with sarcasm.

Her frown deepened. Nolan was right. We would be worked to the bone just to get by.

"I'm afraid the king made your work chart, I'm only in charge of the classes. I tried to persuade him to only give you one dining duty, but..."

"It's fine." I shoved the paper into my back pocket. "I'll be fine."

If King Douchebag wanted to try and break me at this school, he had another thing coming.

"Books for all your classes can be checked out from the library in your free time," she informed me.

Free time? Hah. I had none of that.

With a nod and a thank you, I left the room and

headed for Master Carn's room to start my first day of Fire Studies.

My thoughts drifted to my father. He'd be so proud to learn I was a fire elemental too. It would be nice to call him ... but obviously impossible between the magic lands and Earth. Maybe I could get a letter to him through a trader. How much could I reveal with the magic binding me?

My gaze fell to the paper in my hands. Based on this map, my class was clear across campus, and I was already late.

I broke into a jog, turning a corner quickly, and slammed right into someone's chest.

"Oof!" I clung to his shirt, and the heat from his skin radiated through the butter-soft material as he steadied me.

Pulling back, I looked up into the deep green eyes of Justice Midnight. I swallowed hard, and my gaze dipped to his lips. Green eyes, full lips ... I tried to imagine what he'd look like with a mask on...

"Sorry." He let me go with a small smile.

A smile?

"What?" Was he ... being nice to me? Suspicion rose in my gut. Justice was the number two asshole on the island—no, number three, just behind Rage and the king. My gaze fell to his left ring finger.

Nada.

No mate marks.

"Nai?" He waved his hand in front of my face. "You were running like a madwoman. Are you late?"

His gentle reminder was too nice. Then his words registered.

"Shit!" I side-stepped him with a wave and shouted thanks before taking off in a run, my mind racing just as fast.

Could Justice be my fated mate? He certainly had the eyes, and he was being way nicer today than yesterday…

After finally finding the room, I wrenched the door open, panting.

And … of course, Rage was here.

Mother Mage, have mercy.

Master Carn's head lifted, but my attention was captured by the Midnight Prince standing beside him.

My knees went weak as I zeroed in on his green eyes.

I was going to lose my mind, thinking that every guy I ran into with green eyes and full lips was my freaking fated mate.

"What is *she* doing here?" Rage snapped.

Well, maybe not *every* guy. Surely my mate wouldn't talk to me like *that*. Was it my imagination, or did his gaze flick to my fingers? Just as quickly as the thought came, his attention was back up to my face. His cold, hard, and unforgiving gaze.

I let my own eyes linger on his fingers, my heart sinking a little when I saw they were bare of marks.

What was wrong with me? Rage was the last man I should want to be mated to. I returned his glare, adding a middle-finger salute when Master Carn faced him.

"I'm sorry, Prince Courage, we weren't expecting an extra student this year. Especially not one with two affinities." He pivoted and looked down his nose at me.

Even for a mage, Master Carn was tall, at least six and a half feet, and he was thin. But I'd long since learned that bulk didn't necessarily equal strength. His eyes swirled like a high mage's, only the colors were limited to his affinity: red, orange, yellow. He was an elemental mage. There were different kinds of mages, as many as there were shifters: healer mage, potion mage, war mage, the list went on. He pursed his lips as he assessed me, and I tipped my head high, feigning strength I didn't feel inside.

"Does she have to be in my private session?" Rage asked the master, his voice low.

The teacher's mouth pulled into a frown. "The high mage was the one who ordered me to work with her, but you're right. I'm sure she can join someone else's private hour. I'll speak to the headmistress at once."

Rage waved off the professor quickly, his eyes narrowing at the mention of this being reported to his mother. "Nah, it's fine. Don't bother my mother with this. I'll need a moving target for practice, and this will be a trial by fire for her."

"Ha-ha." I crossed my arms, giving Rage a scowl.

Midnight Kisses

"You're sure?" Master Carn wrinkled his nose as if the idea of me studying with Rage was disgusting.

Rage nodded. "If she gets in the way of my progress, I'll speak to my mother myself."

Ouch.

Snitches get stitches, buddy.

"Very well," Master Carn said. Looking at me, he pointed at the door. "Go to the library and get the text *An Intro to Fire Elements* and return promptly."

"The library?" It could be on the other side of campus for all I knew. "Could you tell me where—?"

He sighed, pinching the bridge of his nose.

"Just sit down," he snapped and rolled his eyes. "In the interest of time, I'll get it. But you will get the remainder of your other books on your own time." He walked to the door with an air of superiority. "Be right back."

As soon as the door closed, I stepped closer to Rage, determined to go into full-on detective mode.

"So ... were you at the party last night?" If my mate was a friend of the Midnight brothers, then maybe I could get some names from him.

He crossed his arms, his expression giving away no emotion. "Obviously, it was at my house."

"Riiight." He wasn't giving me any help. "Were many of your friends there? Like friends who might know about a secret garden in your woods?"

He stiffened. "What?"

My heart pounded, climbing up into my throat. "I

135

mean, you know … what friends of yours were there?"

Rage furrowed his brow, looking at me like I was an alien. "All of them. Pretty sure the entire student population was there, all fifteen of us plus some guards I grew up with. Why?"

"Hmm." Really not helpful. "Can I get a list of your closest friends? Ones who—"

"Umm, no, psycho stalker," he said, shaking his head. "I'm not giving you a list of names."

"Why not?"

"Let me guess, you hooked up with someone, and you're trying to find out who it is now? They said they were my friend?"

I felt like I'd been punched in the gut. "Yeah… how did you…?"

Rage chuckled, but the sound held no mirth. "You and every girl in school. It's common after the masquerade party for people to try and find out who they got together with, but it's against the rules. It's why we have it masquerade-style. And it's why the Samhain party will stay fun too."

My throat went dry. "You do a party like that for Halloween?"

He nodded. "In the past, it's been a regular costume ball, but we're thinking about making our Samhain masquerade-style too."

That was months away, but it gave me something to hold on to, a date to put in my calendar when I could walk up to my fated mate and punch him in the face.

"You totally should!" I blurted out too eagerly.

"Yeah?" He drew back, his expression suddenly serious. "You really wanna see this guy that bad again?"

My body gravitated closer to him, and my gaze dropped to his lips. It wouldn't be Rage, right? He's not that good of a liar.

"Rage?" My voice was small.

He swallowed hard, and I fought the urge to reach up and trace his jawline. "Yeah?"

"Where were you last night when that fight broke out downstairs?"

Something flared in his eyes, a flash of yellow, then it was gone. He cleared his throat, heat pinking his cheeks. The silence stretched, growing awkward before he muttered, "Hooking up with a redheaded chick. But some hothead ruined that, and the party broke up."

My heart plummeted into my stomach, and I took a step back. I hated Rage, so why did I want it to be him?

"Right."

Before I could further my interrogation, Master Carn was back. He dropped a five-billion-page book onto the desk in the corner and glared at me. "Read the entire thing three times ... and then, *maybe* I'll let you try fire magic."

I eyed the four-inch-thick spine. "That'll take me weeks!"

"Then you'd better start reading."

He couldn't be serious, but by the way Rage was grinning, he totally was.

Master Carn turned back to Rage, and they resumed their lesson, talking about balancing heat and light.

Great!

I spent the next three hours reading an ancient *lame* history of fire wielders and all they could do. Occasionally, I stole glances at Rage making cool fireballs in his palms.

So cool. Ever since I was a little girl, I'd longed to do what my father could do. Boil water with a thought, toss a fireball into the lake on the Fourth of July, boil a rogue wolf's blood and kill him instantly. Fire magic was arguably the strongest element, and I was sitting here, reading a book. My father's magic had trickled to me as a member of his pack, but other than making my index finger a lighter, I couldn't do much. And apparently, Master Carn wanted it to stay that way.

When the bell rang for lunch, I was nearly catatonic from boredom.

"Don't you need to go, Nai?" Rage asked, tapping the schedule that I'd set at the edge of my desk, one he'd obviously been nosy enough to read.

I blinked and—*Crap!* I was serving lunch.

Without a word, I bolted toward the cafeteria that Kaja had pointed out on our way to campus. Darting through the courtyard to the right, I opened the large double-doors and was greeted with a legit movie-style high school cafeteria—Formica tables and everything.

"Umm, hello?" I called out, scanning the large and —thankfully—still-unoccupied room.

Crossing the space, I stepped behind the counter of the lunch line. Kids piled in behind me, but no one was here.

Please don't tell me I have to do this on my own!

"I'm guessing you're Nai," snapped a woman. Her tone held zero tolerance.

I froze, spinning on my heels, and faced a terrifying woman.

Holy frickin' mage!

Her black hair was neatly plaited all the way to her waist, and the symbol for dark magic hung from a necklace at her throat. Tattoos covered her skin, crawling and moving underneath as if vying for territory, with the exception of her face, which was unblemished. She looked maybe twenty-five, but she might be four times that.

Why would the school let a dark mage work here?

"Yes, ma'am," I muttered.

She noticed my gaze at her throat and rolled her eyes. "I owe a lifetime of servitude to the king for turning one of his wolves into a goat. Are we done with that?"

My eyes snapped back up to hers, and I nodded. "Yep. Totally. That's cool. We're cool."

She rolled her eyes. "I'm Kalama. Your cousin is in the back. You'll dish out front while I ring."

She tossed me an apron, hairnet, and plastic gloves.

Hairnet.

Hairnet.

Hairnet.

I couldn't look away from the small piece of social suicide I held in my hand.

"Put it on, princess. We've got hungry wolves to feed!"

Oh mage.

Why me? I quickly tied the apron and—*gulp*—slid the hairnet over my high ponytail. Then, I slipped on the plastic gloves.

"Come on, honey, we don't have all day," a catty female called out as I made my way behind the counter.

My gaze flicked up to the young wolf shifter. The bitchy blond chick glared down her nose at me. She was Daybreak Clan. *Shocker*. I recognized her from the ceremony last night. Mallory, the Barbie girl. Clearly an evil Barbie.

Daybreak thought they were superior to everyone, including Midnight. My father said they had a history of always talking about making a bid for the crown, but their alpha changed too often to make definitive plans. Superiority complexes seemed to run in their pack. According to my father, their heirs were cutthroat and constantly fighting for dominance.

I swallowed my pride and picked up a pair of tongs.

I looked down at the options. "Pizza or burger?"

"Burger, no bun, with avocado on the side." She tapped her foot, and I looked up to see over a dozen heirs behind her. Kaja waved to me. And just behind her were the Midnight brothers. *Great. Freaking hairnet.*

I yanked off the bun and threw a meat patty on the plate. "We're out of avocado," I told her, handing her the plate.

"You didn't even look!" she hissed.

"Come on, Mallory," a girl who looked a lot like a Barbie too, only older and with short-cropped bangs, called to her. Sisters or cousins?

Mallory, AKA Evil Barbie, flipped her ponytail at me and stormed off with her relative ... who was, apparently, not eating today.

I filled plate after plate, keeping my attention on the food to avoid having to see the stares of the other students, ignoring the whistles and pick-up lines.

Why did everyone have to...?

"That hairnet is super sexy," Noble said.

I looked up at his familiar voice and grinned.

"I'll be teased forever for this, won't I?" I grabbed some pizza and a burger and loaded up a plate for him.

He nodded, his lips squished together like a duck. "I need a picture"—he turned and held his phone out for a selfie—"Smile!"

I flipped him off but mimicked his duck face. After he took the pic, he looked at the image and laughed.

Noble was my homie, BFF spot #2.

"Hurry up! Hungry back here!" Rage called out from where he stood with Justice and Honor.

I ignored him but started fixing the three boys' plates while I continued my convo with Noble. "Hey, when you have time later, can we chat about the party last night? I want to ask you something about your friends."

His face fell, body going rigid as he turned somber. "Sure, but—"

Whatever he'd been about to say was drowned out by the sound of high-pitched screaming.

What the—?

Everyone in the entire cafeteria slapped their hands over their ears, myself included. The pressure in my head swelled like my eardrums were going to explode and bleed. Then, the screaming waned in volume, becoming a hissing sound like a teapot about to boil.

"Shit!" Rage burst out from the lunch line, diving under a nearby table. He reached underneath and pulled out a long, sleek *sword* as he shoved something into one ear. He switched the sword into the other hand and put his other hand up to his ear...

I was still processing *why* he was touching his ears when Rage said a word that made my blood run cold.

"Selkies!" he hissed. "Call the palace. We're under attack."

Selkies. Seal-shifters, who mortals mistakenly called mermaids or sirens, had once guarded this island. Why were they here, and why were we under attack from them?

Rage turned to Justice and cocked his head toward the kitchen. Justice nodded.

As the doors of the cafeteria blasted open, Justice leapt over the counter and reached for me.

"Nai, come on!"

I followed his lead, ducking to the ground, my heart pounding against my chest.

Why were the selkies attacking?

"Let's go. There's an exit behind the kitchens," Justice whispered, tugging me forward in an army crawl.

"Huh?" I scrunched my face and stared at him. Did he think I couldn't hold my own in a fight? "The school is under attack. Why would we run?"

More importantly, was this an alpha test I'd fail if I was a coward?

Justice gripped my underarm tightly. "You don't understand. The selkies' call—"

Just then, a beautiful melody picked up and carried throughout the air.

Chapter 9

THE COMPLEX MELODY dipped and then soared, the beautiful singing nearly spellbinding—

"Nai!" Justice bellowed, pulling on my arm.

I shook my head, wanting to hear the music, but my attention caught on the other shifters. Every single one of them stood rigidly, staring at the air in front of them. Nell, Honor, Kaja, evil Barbie, they all stood... frozen. Everyone except for Rage.

"What's wrong with them?"

Pivoting to face Justice, I frowned. He held a squished piece of foam between his thumb and forefinger, but he—like most of the other students—gaped slack-jawed at the doorway, from where the song flowed.

Frozen.

"Justice!" Rage sprinted forward as a stunning woman stepped into the room.

Her arms outstretched as she sang, water ran in rivulets down her legs, leaving small puddles where she walked. Clothed in a gauzy white dress that left little to the imagination as it clung to her soaking wet form, the woman wore her pale green hair down, hanging in loose clumps, resembling seaweed. Without breaking her song, she pounded a fist on the wall.

A dozen men entered dressed in slick black sealskin armor. With their swords drawn, they split into teams of two and advanced on the alpha heirs.

Selkies were a proud race of shifters. The females had spellbinding voices with the ability to sing in high frequencies—like mind-numbing, ear-bleeding noise. The males were fierce warriors. Why were they attacking *us*? We were just innocent kids at a school.

I grabbed the foam earplug from Justice's hand and stuck it in his ear as Rage skidded to a halt beside me.

"What are you still doing here?" he growled. I could see the yellow bit of a balled-up earplug sticking out of his ears. Then, he looked down at me, gaze zeroing in on my ears. "The song doesn't affect you?"

I had no idea how to answer that, but we didn't have time to discuss it now.

Two of the selkies charged us, and I scanned the area for something—anything—I could use as a weapon.

"Here," Rage snapped, shoving his sword at me, his only weapon.

I wanted to ask him if there were more deadly

weapons secretly scattered about, but there was no time. Hopefully, he had something else to use against our attackers.

Hefting the weapon, I shifted my stance and zeroed in on the two selkies.

A fireball soared through my peripheral vision, startling me. I glanced at Rage, who was conjuring another sphere of live flame.

"I hope you know how to use that." His gaze dropped to the sword, and he shook his head.

Like he didn't believe me capable and he was mad he had to babysit me.

"You worry about your fireballs," I snapped. If he thought I'd spent the last nineteen years in Montana picking apples, he had another thing coming.

The selkie warrior on the left dodged the fiery mass and lunged at me with his machete. I stepped forward and swung to meet his blade. The clash of metal rang through the cafeteria, interrupting the female's song. I slid in closer and followed up with an elbow to my opponent's nose, smiling at the satisfying crunch of bone and spurt of black blood.

He grunted and doubled over.

Rookie mistake.

Both hands on the hilt, I rotated and clobbered the man right in the temple with the pommel.

As he dropped, I spun to meet my next foe.

Only, no one was there. With a moment to breathe, I scanned the cafeteria, trying to absorb the scene. All of the students still stood rigidly, staring at the singing woman while Rage, Justice, Honor, and Noble, all with little foam earplugs, fought the selkies. Maybe Justice had been busy shoving earplugs in his brothers' ears. If the cafeteria was equipped with swords and earplugs hidden under tables, then maybe this was a regular occurrence.

Rage hurled another ball of flames, his lip curled in disgust. But magic could be just as hard to wield as a sword, and the flames crashed two feet from its intended target, extinguishing on the ground upon impact.

I pried a deadly machete from the unconscious male selkie's fingers and closed the distance between me and Rage. "Here," I said, returning Rage's blade now that I had my own. "I hope you know how to use it."

Take that, asshole.

He plucked it from my hand, giving me a small glare. "You worry about yourself. I've got this."

He rotated and swung the massive blade in one fluid movement. The two selkies advancing on us screeched and tried to get out of the way of its deadly arc.

One of the selkies darted to the side, but the other...

The metal slid through him from shoulder to hip like a hot knife cutting through butter. One second, he was standing; and the next, his knees buckled, and his torso toppled forward.

Rage obviously didn't need any help. Which meant I needed to protect the frozen students, specifically the five Harvest girls whom I'd grown to love. If Evil Barbie got whacked during this attack … oh well.

Miss Mariah Carey was keeping everyone entranced. Only those with earplugs seemed fine. I should probably have pressed my father further when he spoke of selkie powers.

Spinning around, I spotted a large kitchen knife on the counter and scooped it up.

Jackpot. Could never have too many weapons.

I glanced across the cafeteria and spotted Kaja, frozen but safe in the corner with Nell. Her other three sisters stood just behind them. No selkies were advancing on them. However… my gaze landed on Honor and Noble, who were cornered by *four* selkie warriors.

The pair were outnumbered; we all were.

We needed the ratios to change. I needed to stop this damn song.

Blood rushed in my ears as I sprinted forward, bumping the inert Evil Barbie—totally by accident—and I forced my attention to narrow until only my target existed. *Sorry, selkie, your show is getting canceled.*

"Nai!" Rage yelled, his voice buzzing in the distance, a mixture of panic or anger. "Stay put!"

No time for chitchat. I didn't care if he approved of my battle plans.

Tipping my wrist back, I flicked the kitchen blade

just as I had a billion times in the woods of Montana. The slender silver knife sang as it sliced through the air, and the female selkie's voice became a wet gurgle as a thin line of blood beaded on the right side of her neck. Her eyes widened, and she clutched her throat. The strike had hit true, just as deadly as Rage's.

Within seconds, the rest of the cafeteria roared to life, no longer frozen.

I pivoted to get to Honor and Noble, and pain exploded up my arm. My vision turned white, and I screamed. Agony pulsed up my arm; my fingers went limp as the machete tumbled from my grasp, clattering on the ground.

Blood ran from my elbow to fingers, and I clutched the injury and spun ... to see a Siren warrior bringing his blade up for a death strike. I flinched, preparing for the blow, but the pain never came.

There was a wet thwack followed by a thud at my feet. My eyes sprang open to see Kaja standing over the selkie. She pulled the blade from his body and held it out to me.

Total BFF.

"Thanks, girl." I snatched it from her and spun, bolting for Noble and Honor. Thank the mage that the selkie warrior only grazed my arm, or I might be missing it right now.

Darting through the melee, I pushed away those rousing from their cursed sleep until I reached my two favorite Midnight boys.

One selkie lay on the ground, blood pooling beneath him, but the other three were raining blows onto Honor and Noble. At any given second, it was two on one, and I tried to assess which brother was in more need of help.

Noble slid his weapon out from underneath the selkie's and went on the offense. The risk was big, given the numbers, but it seemed to be working.

Honor reached up to deflect another selkie's sword, leaving a gap from his armpit to his hip.

Time seemed to slow as the other warrior lunged for the kill.

"No!" I screamed, darting forward. I crashed into the selkie, using my momentum to drive the machete into his side, right between his ribs. He stumbled back; the knife dropped from his hand, and then he slumped to the ground, pulling me down with him. I released my hold on the machete and scrambled off the warrior. Climbing to my feet, I stared at the gore pooling beneath him.

Holy mage. I...

The selkie's eyes widened, and he grabbed for the blade, but his fingers slipped from the slick surface. Without considering my actions, I reached forward, and in one swift movement, I yanked the weapon out and ... dropped it.

Bile burned the back of my throat. My stomach churned. I spun away from the dude with his silvery and pink entrails spilling out of his abdomen.

I had to fight not to close my eyes. I'd been preparing for battle my whole life, only to discover I wasn't that prepared.

I'd never killed anyone before...

Noble shouted, and it snapped me from my stupor. There were still two selkies fighting to take the brothers down, but now they turned their focus on me. Stepping back, I reached over by the trashcan, picked up a metal food tray, and then whacked the selkie nearest me, right at the base of his head. The edge of the metal cut right into the side of his neck, and he went down screaming. Noble took care of the other one, cut him open like a fish.

Gross. Training with my father did nothing to prepare me for *this*. Seeing a man bleed out and—

My thoughts derailed as Rage suddenly swam into view.

"What the hell were you thinking!?" Rage grabbed the front of my shirt and yanked me forward until my body pressed up against his. "You could have been killed!"

The motion, combined with my nausea, wrenched my insides, and I pushed his hand away.

"You're welcome," I growled, stepping back and turning away from the blood and guts for fear of puking.

Around us, dozens of people were shouting, but the attack had died down. No more sounds of fighting. Mother Mage, I hoped the others were all okay. But...

The nausea churned my guts, and my breath grew shallow.

Just like that, in a split second, I took a life...

Saliva pooled in my mouth, and I sprinted for the nearest trashcan. Leaning over it, I grabbed the rim and vomited.

"It's one thing to train for killing and quite another to actually have to do it," Noble's sweet voice came from behind.

I thought it was him resting his hand on my shoulder until Honor spoke.

"Thank you, Nai." Honor's voice was barely a whisper, and he rubbed circles onto my back through my shirt. "You saved my life."

Why were these two so sweet and Rage so douchey?

I nodded and spit the last bit of bile from my mouth. "It's all good."

I'm fine. Everything is fine.

Does this school offer therapy?

I'd never seen someone's insides spill out like that. Even the occasional skirmishes with the rogues were nothing like that. Even hunting with my dad and taking down a deer, I'd never seen insides become outsides. He was young... at most in his twenties... with his whole life ahead of him...like me.

"Come on," Honor said, cupping my elbow. "Let's get you cleaned up."

"I'm in charge here, Nai." Rage invaded my space, pushing Honor back. "If I say *stay put,* you better *damn well* listen. You pull something like that again, next time, I'll throw you in the dungeon of my father's castle for a week."

Did he say *dungeon*?

His eyes glowed orange, and I knew his wolf was close to the surface, but legit… what … the … hell? Definitely not my mate.

"Everyone here—" I waved my arm in a wide circle "—might bow to your every whim, but *technically*, you aren't the alpha king yet, so you're not in charge of me." I was 67.3% sure of this.

Or was *he* in charge of me?

The fuzzy swirling in my head made it difficult to put a percent on that—maybe not 67.3%, more like 43.9%—but I hated bullies more than I was worried about being right.

Towering over me, Rage glowered, running his eyes over the length of my body, causing my cheeks to warm. "Actually, as first prince, I *am* in charge of you, along with every other student when it comes to safety."

Well, damn.

Fury burned away the nausea, and I straightened my spine to get every last inch of height as I glared at Rage. First prince? *Whatevs*. I offered him a one-finger "first prince" salute. "Don't tell me to stay put next time, and I won't have to ignore you."

I crossed my arms, and my wolf growled. Dude

better back down, or his pretty face was going to get up close and personal with my snarling teeth.

Rage stepped forward, and dark fur rippled on his arms. "It's *my* job to keep the students at our school safe when the king isn't around. He gave me that charge. Don't test me, Nai. Understood?"

Dammit. Maybe he did have some power around here. Where was my rulebook? Probably with my supply list and official uniforms.

I wanted to demand to see it in writing, but I knew better than to poke a wolf covered in blood and surrounded by the bodies of his enemies.

My nostrils flared, but I swallowed my pride and choked out, "Understood. Also, your school sucks."

Honor bumped Rage. "Don't be a douche. She saved me from getting skewered."

"Dude," Noble added, snickering as he stepped up to join us, "she got to the singer before any of us could. Well done, Nai."

Rage shook his head, glaring at his brother just as Evil Barbie stepped up next to him.

"Prince Courage!" she gushed. "That was *so* brave—oh, oh, what happened to your pants?"

I blinked, seeing the situation with new eyes. His crotch area was all wet with selkie blood, but his pants were really dark, so it looked like…

"I think he got a little nervous in the scuffle," I told her, holding back a grin.

Rage narrowed his eyes at me as he cocked his head to the side, but he didn't look pissed. He looked…

Holy mage. Was he about to smile?

A warm feeling spread throughout my chest when his lips curled into a smirk, and I rubbed the area because—no way was I getting warm fuzzies over this a-hole.

"You're a pain in my ass, Nai." That was all Rage said, still trying to fight the smile that *wanted* to grace his sexy face.

No. Not sexy. *Ugly*. Ugly troll man who must get off on misery.

Noble burst out laughing first. "Damn, girl," he said, patting my arm. "I think I love you."

"It's selkie blood, idiots!" Rage barked, but his grin ruined his attempt at acting pissed with his brothers.

My stomach flipped over that smile, and I knew in that moment that this man would be the death of me.

MY ADRENALINE WOULDN'T SHUT off after the selkie attack. School was canceled for the day, and the king was rumored to be beyond *pissed*. Rage and the other brothers had been called to the castle for a meeting while I sat in Harvest Dorm and recounted the entire story to Nell, Rue, and Kaja. We all sat around a pristine wood-polished coffee table while Mele and Fiona, the other Harvest girls, had their respective noses shoved in books whilst hiding in the corner. Clearly, they wanted nothing to do with today's drama.

"So, then, Barbie asked what was on his pants, and I was like, yeah, he got scared." I finished the story, my eyes flicking over to Fiona to see her wearing a grin. She was totally eavesdropping.

The girls erupted into laughter, but then Nell's expression furrowed with confusion.

"Wait, why didn't the selkie song affect you? Selkie magic freezes shifters."

I shrugged, popping a piece of popcorn into my mouth.

"No idea. I mean, it was captivating but didn't really bother me." I hadn't given it much thought until now. Maybe because I had two affinities?

Nell and Kaja shared a look. "Weird, because we were all like ... super helpless. I wonder if it has to do with your clan being—"

She stopped, seeming to realize what she was about to say could be hurtful.

"Cast out?" I finished for her. This used to be an issue for me. When wolves visited us from the magic lands and brought magical supplies and news of Alpha Island, I was so embarrassed. Back then, it made me angry that we weren't allowed back.

She winced. "Sorry, I just meant ... it's the only thing that's different."

"No, it's fine, and that's a good point." I shrugged. "Maybe that's why I have two affinities too. Although it was probably because I couldn't decide which one I wanted and wasn't focusing on the right color." I chuckled.

All three of their foreheads creased. Even Fiona and Mele set their books down from their reading chairs in the corner and stared over at me.

"What?" Mele asked from across the room.

"You know..." I considered how to explain the strange experience without sounding even more weird. "When the high mage dude whisked you away to your favorite landscape, made you pick your affinity, and then brought you back..."

The longer I spoke, the deeper the creases in their foreheads grew. Why were they looking at me like I was an alien?

"What are you talking about, Nai?" Kaja asked, her face furrowed like I was speaking a foreign language.

A chill ran the length of my spine, and gooseflesh prickled my skin.

"Didn't the high mage let everyone pick their element... at the beach?" I asked. "Maybe I misunderstood when he asked if it was my favorite place—"

"There was no beach..."

Nerves churned in my gut as I realized that maybe no one else had had the same experience as I did.

"Not a beach *for real*," I hurried to explain. "More like a mental landscape. I couldn't see you all for a few minutes, and we were on the beach—like a relaxation technique and then—" Their wild looks made me realize that my suspicions were correct. He'd only done that little number for me. But why would he do that? All the thoughts whirling through my head only scared me more. High mage equaled bad news, and I didn't want any favors from one of them.

"Never mind." I shook my head and waved away my previous words. "I'm a bit traumatized from today, and clearly not thinking ... clearly."

Was this something to do with that water symbol on my solar plexus? Now, there was no way I was going to ask them about it for fear they'd put me on the crazy train—one-way ticket and all that.

"You wanna lie down? I mean, you just got in a full-on battle." Kaja pointed to her room while the other sisters nodded and started to fawn over me.

I wanted to be alone and rock in a corner and cry—definitely not going to say that out loud though.

Instead, I just nodded. "You know what. A nap sounds great. I'm gonna head over to my place though and lie down."

All five of them winced.

"That condemned rathole?" Kaja grimaced, her expression an exclamation point.

I chuckled. "Yeah, but it's *my* condemned rat hole."

Nell pouted, her bottom lip stuck so far out it was almost comical. "If we were allowed to co-mix, I would totally give you a room here. We have more than enough."

Her sweet offer was so typical of Harvest generosity.

I gave her a sad smile and patted her hand. "Thank you. But rules are rules."

Grabbing my borrowed fire textbook, I forced a cheery smile. "I'll catch you at dinner. I'm serving!"

Because my life was awesome. If the blood and guts weren't cleaned up by then, I'd definitely be looking into therapy.

With that, I ran out of their house, afraid one of them would say something else about my weird beach encounter with the high mage. Hauling my butt across the courtyard, I glanced over my shoulder to make sure Kaja wasn't coming after me, and when I turned around, I skidded to avoid full-on crashing into—*ugh!*—Rage. I *barely* bumped into him, only a little. And then I stood in front of him, clutching my book with both hands and gasping for air.

We just stared at each other. I waited for him to yell at me, but he just kept *looking* at me, his gaze darting over every curve of my face. The silence stretched, weirding me out a little, or a lot, but legit, I could stare at his face all day and be okay with it.

Yummy ugly troll.

Finally, he sighed. "Thank you for your help today with the selkies."

My mouth popped open.

Did he just compliment me? I reached up and felt his forehead. No fever.

"You feeling okay?" I narrowed my eyes. "Are you really Rage? Or maybe Noble beefed up a little?"

I tapped his giant bicep as if I couldn't tell him and his brothers apart. A slow grin curled one side of his mouth into a lopsided, sexy smirk, making my insides melt.

Mother Mage, why did my internal compass point to the bad boy?

"You can't tell?" He stepped closer, and I could feel the heat rolling off his body. "You've never seemed to have a problem telling us apart before?"

His gaze dipped to my lips, and I sucked my bottom lip in—to make sure I wasn't drooling. Or slobbering. Or panting.

I wasn't sure what was happening here, but I didn't want to be done. I wanted nice Rage to stay and never leave.

"Where'd you learn to fight like that?" he asked, looking my body up and down like I was a prized specimen.

My cheeks warmed. "My father."

And just like that, his expression fell into a mask of indifference. "Right. Almost forgot there—*Crescent girl*."

He spun to leave, and I felt like I'd been slapped.

"Excuse me? How dare *you*!"

I glared after him, lifted my book high in the air, and threw it. Hard.

The solid thump against his head wasn't nearly as satisfying as watching him lurch forward, which made me grin. But the smile slid from my face as the book landed with a thud.

Oh, shifter babies. What had I done?

He was the first prince to the king, in line for the alpha throne.

He froze.

"I ... uh ... I'm sorry." I rushed forward and grabbed the book off the ground, holding it in front of me like a chest plate of armor.

Spinning slowly, he stepped closer to me.

"I like it better when you're nice," I said by way of explanation. "Grouchy Rage is an asshat. Why can't you just stay nice?"

He glared down at me with those big, beautiful, green eyes. "You don't know, do you?"

Pain flickered in his gaze, and the bravado he wore like a mask slipped. For the first time since I'd met him, he looked vulnerable.

"What?" I relaxed my death grip on the book and brought it to my hip. "What don't I know?"

"Your uncle killed my father, and I'll *never* forgive your clan for that."

His words cut into me like knives. My jaw hit the pavement. Before I managed to find my voice, he spun and stormed off again.

"That's not true!" I shouted at his retreating back. "Your dad and my uncle were best friends at school!" I marched toward where Rage now stood but stopped several feet away. Even so, I dropped my voice and whisper-shouted the truth. "The alpha king killed your father, not anyone from *my* pack!"

I believed the story my father told of what happened to his only brother that fateful night. My father had no reason to lie, but the alpha king? All the reason in the realm, no matter what Rage said.

Rage spun and laughed in my face. "You naive little pup! A Midnight alpha and a Crescent alpha *best friends*? My uncle killing his own brother? Listen to yourself! *You've* been lied to."

Tears sprang to my eyes. Did all of the Midnight princes think that? That my uncle killed their dad? The horror of it shook me even if it wasn't true. No wonder they hated me that first day. Could I blame them?

"Rage, listen…" I started to tell him the story I knew, but he cut me off.

"I can see you believe what you're saying, but you're wrong. Uncle Declan was commanded by the high mages to attack Crescent after my father's murder. It was my uncle's first assignment after he became alpha, to punish your pack because of a high crime. What about that? If your uncle didn't kill my father, what was the high crime?" His chest heaved, and tension rolled off him in waves.

"Well… I don't know," I admitted with a shrug. Shame burned my cheeks as all of the fight left me. "My father doesn't like to talk about it." Was an alpha killing another alpha a high crime? Did the mages get involved with that? I didn't know. I didn't know anything apparently.

Rage shook his head. "Sounds like a guy who is all about the truth."

When he turned to walk away this time, I let him go. I wondered then if everything my father told me had been a lie. Had my uncle killed Rage's dad and that's why we were cast out of Shifter Island? Was the alpha king only protecting his family when he'd taken over the throne and kicked Crescent out?

All the emotions I'd bottled up the last few days swelled beneath my chest until everything felt ready to explode. Turning on my heels, I raced into my dorm, slammed the door to my shitty room, and collapsed onto the bed just as the dam burst. Sobbing into my pillow, I cried for my father, my pack, and then finally for me. Had my father lied to me? Or possibly deceived me with a lie by omission? On the story of who killed who, I believed him. Even so, I wanted to know what high crime was committed that would have caused our entire clan to be cast out. Would I have to wait four years to find out?

Chapter 10

MASTER JIN TAUGHT my water elemental classes. Short and stocky with tattoos covering pretty much all of his visible skin, he looked like a Hell's Angel biker dude. Unlike the fire mage, Master Jin had my books waiting for me the second afternoon.

"Any chance you did the summer reading?" he asked as soon as he dropped the books on my desk.

I stared up at the ceiling and snorted. "There was summer reading?"

How was I ever going to catch up?

"Don't worry. Most of it is stuffy theory, mages pontificating just because they want to. I've highlighted the chapters you should read and X'd out the ones that are worthless."

Wow. "Um, thanks for that."

"Don't thank me yet. After today, I'll make you read on your own time. Here, in class, this is where we practice. You'll need to have the first four of those chapters read by tomorrow so we can start training."

A smile stretched across my face. What a contrast. "No problem."

When I opened the textbook, my jaw dropped as I stared at the same three wavy lines that were burned into my solar plexus. Without thinking, I raised my hand.

"Master Jin." I pointed at the lines when he returned to my desk. "Do we get marks related to our affinities? Like after we graduate…"

His eyes lit up, and he chuckled. "Sorry, no. Nothin' like that. You get magic. That's enough."

I frowned, debating whether I should ask him what it meant, when he continued.

"Though, if you really want something like that, I know a tattoo artist that can put one on ya."

Hmm. "That's okay. I was just curious."

Note to self: ask old high mage man. He was the only one who seemed to already know I wasn't normal.

I bent my head over the book and started to read.

THE FIRST WEEK of school passed in a blur. There were no more selkie attacks, thank the mage. And I'd gotten a bit of a reputation for being a badass. The other students gave me respectful nods and glances, a far cry from that first day. All except Rage. Needless to say, our fire element classes were beyond awkward. I read my book in the corner while he shot nasty glances my way and ignored me when I spoke. I worked the coffee cart in the morning and then the lunch and dinner periods as well. By the time I got home to study, I usually fell asleep with my face in a book. But today was Friday.

I bade "Madam Scary Dark Witch," aka Kalama, goodnight, and grabbed my box of cold pizza and cheese sticks before heading to the door. The cafeteria was mostly empty—all traces of the Selkie attack gone. A few groups of students still sat at the Formica tables even though dinner was over, all of them chatting about ... who knew? Probably weekend plans or sucky class assignments. I had far too much of the latter to worry about the former. Not to mention the sorry state of my dorm.

Ugh. The only food I had was the three meals served at the school or what I could snake from the coffee cart if it didn't sell and was near the expiration. We'd literally been given nothing. I was surprised we had running water.

"Hey, Nai," Noble shouted from across the room.

I spun, and my boxed dinner slid from the stack of books I carried. Reaching out, I managed to swing the stack and prevent the loss of dinner and then looked up.

He sat atop the table with Justice and Honor on either side, a cluster of girls spread on the benches at their feet. Evil Barbie was one of them. Anyone who needed a reminder of pack hierarchy needed only to see this. The princes appeared as if ministering to a harem of admirers. Funny, Rage wasn't here with them. Justice muttered something to Noble, who cut him off with a shake of his head.

"Are you coming tomorrow night?" Noble asked me, raising his chin, his smile promising mischief.

Sighing, I shook my head. "Nope. Not even sure what activity or thing you're referencing. I've got too much work tomorrow."

The corner of Honor's lips turned down. "You don't have work tomorrow. It's Saturday. No work. No school."

Must be nice.

I snorted. "I've got homework and housework, things I can't do when I'm working my three jobs. No. Still not going."

"But it's the bonfire," Noble explained. "You've got to come. We're going to eat s'mores—"

"And drink mage wine," Honor added. "Everyone gets happy drunk. You should totally come. You need happy—I can tell."

The girls at his feet shot me a glare, which I gladly returned. Okay, maybe I was in need of *happy*, but I had no time for it if I wanted to pass my classes.

Justice took a deep breath and met my gaze, his green eyes searing into me. "You do look like you could use a dose of happy."

I rolled my eyes.

"Everyone will be there," Noble added as if that would sway me.

I tore my gaze from Justice and forced a swallow. "No can do. Sorry, guys."

I was used to Noble and Honor being nice, but Justice? What was going on? Before they could intervene further, I bade them goodnight.

Their farewells followed me out of the cafeteria and into the evening. I crossed campus to Crescent House and entered through the side door. The kitchen lights worked as did the refrigerator now, a bonus of having Nolan and me working to pay our clan tax, so that was mage-freaking-tastic.

After devouring the pizza, I caught up on homework, reading ahead in the fire textbook until my eyes practically bled.

The biggest problem with sitting in class all day was the sensation of wanting to crawl out of my body. I was an active girl; I liked hiking in the woods behind our house in Montana or chasing my packmates down to the creek. Now that the school week was over, and I was at home, I had a solution.

Stepping outside into the cool night, I sucked in lungfuls of crisp clean air. After ducking behind a hedge, I stripped down naked, folding my clothes off to the side. Closing my eyes, I relaxed, letting my wolf surge forward and fill my being. I hadn't shifted since I'd gotten here. A week without shifting felt like an eternity to a wolf. Taking deep breaths, I let the change come over me, my bones cracking and rearranging, my pelt of fur rolling down my arms and across my back until I was on all fours. It didn't even hurt anymore; it just felt good to finally let my animal slide free of its human cage.

Run? her voice, my voice, *our voice*, asked.

Yes.

I darted into the woods, taking in the scents and sounds surrounding me with a sense of familiarity and wonder. Soft mulch, spongey beneath my paws, churned with the smell of decomposing leaf litter. Around me swirled the scents of verdant growth of the forest: pine, cedar, honeysuckle, lavender, sweet wild onions, and leaves—everywhere. Scat from rodents and deer, droppings of birds, and Nolan's markings were here too.

Huh ... I could fix that.

In wolf form, instinct usually ruled our being. Typically, only the very powerful or very practiced shifter could maintain full control of their human mind when in the being of their wolf. I was neither, and yet I'd always been able to access that rational portion of my mind that allowed me to reason, even as a wolf. Still, I was going to pee on Nolan's markings as a big eff-you to my cousin.

I raced through the woods, smelling hundreds of different wolves, some scents old and others very recent. Not surprising, considering the school was crawling with wolf shifters. Beneath the layer of wolf, there were other scents: fox, hawk, and, as I drew close to the shore: seal. All of the shifter races had once had a place of royalty among the elite of Shifter Island.

Rumors trickled out to us in Montana that the High Mage Council had supported the division of shifter races right after my uncle died. They said that the new alpha king, Declan of Midnight, was given permission to remove all shifter races from the island but for the wolves. Most of the hawks/falcons flew away; the selkies shifted and swam away. The kitsune, bears, panthers, and other land-based shifters were given boats, but one old woman, who visited years ago, said only a few boats escaped. I shivered to think what happened to the rest.

Suffice it to say, the new alpha king was not known for his mercy.

Slowing my pace, I caught the strong scent of a wolf, and I turned, facing the woods behind me with a snarl.

A low growl answered back as a black wolf stepped from the trees. He sniffed the air and then dipped his head low, rear up in the air and tail wagging with his ears erect like he was going to pounce on me. His sleek fur was as dark as the night sky above us. My heart flipped, and a deep yearning pulled at me when I recognized him.

Mate. My wolf's instincts identified the wolf just before my rational human side, but I strangled down the portion of me filled with excitement.

No freaking way. This was the same guy who knocked me out, dumped me on my bed, and left me not even a week ago. I wouldn't let him near me except to rip his eyes out!

My fur bristled, and my ears remained erect, tilted toward the offender. I curled my lips back as I crouched, ready to fight if necessary.

He might be an alpha heir, but he wasn't *my* alpha, and I had zero problem showing him that I was dominant too, something many males on this island seemed to forget about the females. My father had trained me in multiple fighting styles. I was not going to be dominated by Mr. Kiss and Leave.

'Mate?' The wolf's eyes narrowed as the low timbre of his wolf's voice coursed through me, filling me with want. *'Mine.'*

My heart stopped. *No way.* This wasn't happening. I knew mates could speak into each other's minds in wolf form, but having it actually happen was another story.

'Mate,' he said again as if wondering why I wasn't pouncing on him and humping his leg. He stepped forward, his posture relaxed; his tongue lolled out as he wagged his tail.

Bullshit.

His wolf might have been into me and protective, but his human surely wasn't. I slammed the door on desire and pulled my lips back so my incisors displayed as I snarled with menace: *'Don't you dare come near me.'*

I pushed the words into his mind, hoping he understood me.

He stopped, and his eyes narrowed in question. The way he cocked his head to the side reminded me of a scolded dog. *'Mate mad? Why?'*

Damn right mate mad. Mate gonna mess you up if you get close to me.

'You don't get to be with me,' I growled again, gnashing my teeth to reinforce my point. *'You betrayed me.'*

'No.' He stepped closer, but the only act of submission was the slight drop in his tail, which could mean nothing more than a drop in his happiness. *'Mate. Protect. Happy.'*

Was he kidding? I laughed, the sound of short barks hard and cutting. He stepped closer, closing the gap between us, and I lunged. With a sharp snap, I grazed his muzzle, and the coppery taste of his blood filled my mouth.

He yipped and jumped away from me, landing in a crouch of bunched muscle with his teeth bared. *'No.'*

His wolf looked like he was in shock. Clearly a far cry from his human side.

'Damn straight, no,' I snarled at him again. *'Don't follow me. I hate you.'*

I turned my back on him, keeping my tail up in a clear show of dominance, and walked away.

Mate ... my wolf practically whined to me in protest. The urge to go back to him, to lick his wound and nuzzle his neck, swelled as I ran. I couldn't sprint fast enough to escape the bombardment of my instinct. But I refused to give in. Refused to be with a wolf who would hurt me and abandon me like he did.

As soon as I arrived at the edge of the woods behind the hovel I called home, I shifted back into my human form. The need for my mate waned though not nearly enough, and I quickly dressed and ran inside, sighing with relief to see everything as I'd left it—gross and dirty with a stack of textbooks on the table.

∽

THE NEXT MORNING, I understood why Nolan had no energy for cleaning this place, but it needed to be done. I'd dust as much of this place as I could now and worry about the rest later. The blessed weekend had come, praise the mage.

It was just after 8 a.m., and Nolan was still sleeping because that's the kind of lazy bum he was. I, however, was up on my tiptoes with a wet washrag in hand, wiping down all the cupboards in the kitchen. The murky black water of the bucket was disgusting, but it felt good to get this place cleaned up.

"Knock knock!" Kaja yelled from the entryway.

"In here!" I shouted back.

Kaja and Nell had asked me to the same beach party that Noble and the boys had been asking me about last night. But I'd told them I'd had housework to do. They were probably here to beg, but I was going to put my foot down. I couldn't live in this dump any longer. It was depressing.

When they walked into the room and I looked up, emotion tightened my throat. Nell was carrying a mop and bucket while Kaja held a paint roller and a gallon of paint.

Kaja set the paint bucket down. "We thought you might need help."

"You guys … you don't have to." They were *heirs* for mage's sake. They'd been waited on hand and foot their whole lives. Living on Alpha Island as an heir meant you had a household staff and certain amenities. I'd bet my life Kaja had never painted a wall in her entire existence. And Nell wouldn't know the first thing about mopping. But having them show up was so sweet I rapidly blinked to keep from crying.

Nell held up the mop. "Oh, honestly, how hard can this be?"

I grinned. "You guys just want me to go to the beach party tonight, huh?"

They both nodded, and Kaja said, "Yep."

"The king sent word that the border around the island is secure again," Nell added. "So the party is on."

Laughter pealed out of me. "Well, whatever your motives, I'm grateful."

The next eight hours were brutal. We cleaned, mopped, and painted my bedroom and the kitchen, covering the old stained walls with a fresh lemon yellow. By the time we were done, the place looked decent. The kitchen was spotless, entryway clean, and living room livable, and my room was perfect. The rest of the house would have to wait for another weekend because I was dead. Nell and Kaja had just left to go back to their house and get ready for the night. I was supposed to meet them in an hour. They'd finally worn me down about going to the party. After hours of helping me clean, I owed them big-time.

Chapter 11

"I don't know why I agreed to this," I muttered, following behind Nell, Rue, and Kaja as we made our way down the sloped trail. All of us wore bikinis under our shorts and t-shirts. I tugged on my tank-top, self-conscious of the wave-like mark on my solar plexus. I wouldn't take my shirt off tonight, not after seeing the Harvest girls' unmarred skin. I wasn't about to reveal it to anyone else until I knew what it meant.

We stepped barefoot into the sand, me and the apparent supermodel Harvest girls. I would kill for those long lean legs. At least they'd pulled their red hair up into messy buns, mimicking mine. Loose strands fell around my face and neck, and for every single one I tucked up into the elastic, two more fell out.

Nell glanced over her shoulder at me and grinned. "Because you know we'll have fun."

The sun dipped below the horizon, twilight painting the sky in rich fuchsia and violet. Wolf-shifters occupied the beach, most of them crowding around the three fires, roasting marshmallows or drinking mage wine. One girl squealed as a guy hefted her over his shoulder and ran into the surf. Not all of them were students. I recognized a few king alpha guards who patrolled the palace and school grounds.

My gaze fell to Noble and Honor, both wearing huge grins as they waved me over.

Kaja told me to find her in a bit and left to follow her sisters, probably in search of food, leaving me with the two princes.

Noble settled back in his beach chair and pointed to the empty one next to him. "Come sit with me. Tell me how your week's been. You've got meal duty every day, right? That sucks."

I rolled my eyes, thinking of my sad little life here at school in comparison to the others, but accepted the chair. "You don't have to remind me how much my life sucks. I'm living it—one hundred percent of it—so I know."

Honor set down two more chairs on the other side of the coolers and winced when he came down on his right leg.

Noble froze. "Pain bad today?"

Honor nodded, but I didn't dare ask. Whatever made my friend permanently limp must have been a bad injury. Wolves healed from almost anything, and pointing out weaknesses could be considered a challenge.

Honor opened the lid of the cooler, and my mouth dropped open. Bottles and bottles of mage wine were interspersed with water in one and food in the other. Kaja went to the wrong place. I wanted to cry when I saw chips and…

"Is that pico?" I asked, reaching for the chips and chunky salsa. I hadn't seen anything resembling salsa in a week. Belatedly, I remembered my manners. Meaning my mouth was already full of chips and salsa when I mumbled, "May I have some?"

"Umm, are you getting enough food?" Noble poked me in the ribs when my shirt rode up as I reached for a bottle of water. "I don't remember you being this bony when we picked you up last week."

Last week? It seemed like an eternity ago. "How would you know if I lost weight?"

Hey, man, I only got a bagel from the coffee cart some mornings, two meals, and barely any snacks. For a shifter's diet, that was practically starvation, but Nolan and I were getting by. *Kinda*.

Noble shrugged. "I may or may not have noticed your body. I am a *guy*."

"You totally checked me out!" A grin pulled at my lips before I shoved another chip in my mouth.

"It doesn't take a genius to see it." He leaned forward, looking past me at his brother. "Don't you see it, Honor?"

I dipped another chip and shoved the entire thing loaded with tomatoes, onion, cilantro, and jalapeno into my mouth.

So good.

Before Honor could answer, I felt someone approach at my back.

"Answer his question, Nai," Rage growled. "Are you getting enough food?"

His voice washed over me, and heat radiated within the narrow space between us. The strength he exuded was like a magnet. I gritted my teeth, steeling myself before I turned to look at him.

Snapping my mouth shut, I nodded, nearly choking when I forced a swallow. Rage and Justice stood there; both their sets of emerald green eyes skimmed over my body like hungry wolves.

No pun intended.

The Midnight boys were paying attention to my weight? Noble was all goodness and kindness and light, so I could see him looking out for me. But Rage? He'd spewed his eternal hatred a week ago and ignored me ever since. Why the hell did he care now?

"I mean our fridge isn't exactly stocked, but I eat three times a day." My cheeks flamed red. I'd shifted for a run at night, and that burned at least a thousand calories, and I hadn't exactly been eating as much as I would've back home ... but I couldn't really afford to.

Rage's eyes flashed orange. "Are you ever hungry?"

"Doesn't the school deliver groceries?" Justice chimed in with a growl.

"Nai, are you seriously not getting enough food?" Noble asked as his voice crashed in with his brothers.

I dropped the chip in my hand and cringed. Too bad I couldn't shrink myself or turn invisible.

"Dudes, drop it," Honor snapped at his brothers. "You're embarrassing her. Can't you see that?"

Bless you, Honor.

Rage shook himself, eyes back to green, and the other brothers pulled their gazes away from me.

"Sorry, Nai. No offense intended." Noble cleared his throat and shared a look with Justice.

"It's ... uh ... fine. No worries. Seriously." I burbled the words, nearly incoherent as my mind spun. The boys were acting very, very weird. Like super protective.

If all of the Midnight princes knew and believed the same backstory of the Crescent Clan's banishment, that my uncle killed their dad, then why would any of them be nice to me? Either some of them questioned those events, or they knew I had nothing to do with it. I was a baby at the time. Their actions didn't seem fake or forced, but was I reading them right? My instinct said yes, and I was 87.2% sure they liked me.

Maybe even Rage—well, 'liked' might be a little much. Tolerated was better.

I studied Honor and Noble; they both had hazel eyes, not the same vibrant green like my mate's. I certainly didn't get mate-vibes from either of them, more like pack-support vibes. Which left only Rage and Justice as mate-possibilities if, in fact, the asshat who kissed me was one of the Midnight princes.

"Hey, guys. Hey, Nai." A blond dude who I'd seen around campus plopped in the sand at my feet, *mercifully* providing a distraction from the conversation about my eating habits.

The guy was stacked, his muscles jacked like a football player's—the big ones who always tackle the smaller guys—and his emerald green eyes were warm as he appraised me.

How did he know my name? He was a guard, and though I'd waved to him going from my late-night dinner shift, I'd never spoken to him.

"You in for beach volleyball?" he asked as my eyes flicked to the Midnight Pack moon mark embroidered on his t-shirt.

But he had those green eyes. I was a connoisseur of green eyes and full lips now. Was this my mate?

I raised my eyebrows. "You want to play volleyball … at night?"

It wasn't super dark yet, but volleyball wasn't my thing. I was more of a stroll along the sand kinda gal. If dark worked as an excuse, I'd use it.

"It's not like we can't see," he responded, his smile softening his reproach.

He was a looker—that's what Lona would've called

him—and while I leaned more toward tall, *dark*, and hot, this guy had me rethinking my preference.

"Touché." I scooped up another mouthful of salsa while I asked his name.

"I'm Beowulf," he said, grinning. "Like the poem."

I choked on my food—again—because I'd read that epically long poem from a billion years ago for English lit. After I finished my coughing fit, I asked, "You do know what happens to Beowulf at the end, right?"

"Yup." He winked. "But that's after a good *long* life."

This time when he grinned, his smile was feral, and his eyes sparked with fire. He radiated power so strong it was a palpable force, and it took conscious effort to raise my chin in defiance. While I could respect Beowulf as a dominant male, I refused to submit to his display of power.

He extended his hand. "Come play with me, Nai. I promise not to bite—unless you want me to."

Before I could respond, Justice growled, "Go hit on someone else Beo. Nai's with us."

Um, what? My eyes widened, and I glanced at Justice out of the corner of my eye. Did he really just say…

"That's how this is?" Beo glared at the princes before grumbling, "Fine."

He kicked the sand and then waltzed off.

That was … awkward. And weird. I sucked in a breath and turned to tell Justice I could handle myself when Noble stole my vehemence.

"He's a total player, Nai. You dodged a bullet," he said.

"Beo probably has herpes," Honor added.

I shook my head, trying to reboot my brain so I could make sense of this new version of reality, and my gaze collided with Justice's. His eyes narrowed in a look I could only call possessive, which made zero sense, unless...

My heart skipped a beat.

Glancing away, my attention landed on—*surprise!*—Rage. Vitriolic anger poured off him like it was intentionally his namesake. The tension simmered just under his skin, his muscles clenched so tight I thought he might explode.

What ... the ... hell? How dare they?

I stood, setting the chips and salsa down, and faced the four boys. "Listen, I'm not your little sister. Most of the time, I'm not even sure you all like me, okay? So whatever game this is, stop it. The last thing I need is for you all to scare off any guy interested in me or I'll die a virgin!"

The second it slipped out, I slapped my hand over my mouth.

Kill. Me. Now.

"I gotta go ... find Kaja." I spun on my heel and strode away, mortified, pausing to call over my shoulder, "Thanks for the food."

Why did I say that?

As female alpha heirs, we were expected to stay

virgins until we took a breeding mate. Most never followed the rules. I did. My dad said it was important to him and one day I'd understand. Pretty sure that was *never* going to happen though. I'd just freaking admitted my V-status to the four Midnight princes.

Kill me now.

I rolled my shoulders, trying to dislodge the discomfort settling there. Maybe it wasn't as big of a deal as I was making it. Maybe they didn't care as much as I thought.

Sucking in a deep breath, I decided to take a peek over my shoulder and see. If they were staring, I'd leave the planet and go live on Mars. If they weren't, they'd probably already forgotten about it.

Here we go.

Four sets of yellow eyes tracked me like prey, and my stomach flipped.

Mother Mage, have mercy.

Mars it is. Right after I find Kaja.

Pushing my virgin confession from my mind, I scanned the beach for my BFF. How long ago did Kaja leave to find her sisters? Ten minutes? Fifteen? Twenty?

I jogged away from the princes and sexy-but-possibly-herpesy Beo playing volleyball and looked over the crowd. Evil Barbie glared back at me, but other than that, I found no one I really knew, besides when I was serving food to them. Heading up the beach back toward the wooded path, I hollered, "Kaja? Nell? Rue?"

Nothing.

Maybe I'd missed them and they went the other way. I spotted a set of rocky cliffs melting into the sand. A great place for football or tag but too far away to see whether people were there. If nothing else, it was a good place to hide. The sun had fully set, and only the moon lit my path.

When I got away from the hubbub of my schoolmates on the beach, I picked up on the sound of someone sniffling up near the cliffs. The sound was high-pitched enough to identify the person as a female, and those broken sobs meant she was crying.

"Stupid Nai," she wailed.

I pulled to a stop in the sand as her words and voice registered. Was this Kaja? Was she upset that I'd lingered too long to hang with the boys?

"Kaja?" I called, picking up my pace and drawing closer. The overwhelming scent of seawater and sunbaked sand made it difficult to scent my friend by smell.

"Nai?" she called back, her voice breaking. "I'm over here."

Her voice came from behind a rock jutting up out of the sand, and I jogged toward my friend's voice. I turned the corner ... and *nothing* was there. "Kaj—?"

My breath caught in my throat as a massive wolf launched from a nearby sand-dune right at me. His mottled fur was impossible to distinguish in the darkness, only that he had a multitude of dark gold and brown shades.

The thought barely registered before the wolf crashed into me. We toppled, and he pinned me to the sand with a teeth-baring snarl.

Shock ripped through me, and I brought my forearm up, *just in time*, as he lunged for my neck. My vision turned white, and I screamed with agony as his jaws shattered the bone in my forearm.

Shit. He's trying to kill me.

The searing pain overwhelmed me, slowing my thoughts. Nausea roiled through my stomach, and I whimpered.

Pull it together, Nai! You know what to do in a fight.

Breathing through the pain, I grabbed the back of the wolf's head and then shoved my own forearm deeper into the wolf's mouth to gag him.

The wolf choked and instinctively loosened his jaw, but I wasn't done. I'd practiced this a million times with my dad—although not injured and bleeding like this. Adrenaline coursed through me, keeping most of the pain at bay.

I pushed back harder, still holding the animal's head and pressing my forearm into his mouth, climbing to my knees. The wolf fell backward, gagging, and yanked his head away from me, releasing my arm from his jaws. I'd been able to get to my feet, which increased my chances of survival, but it would take a few days for the damage on my arm to heal—even with our quick healing regeneration.

Time to go on the offense. I called up my wolf, there

just under the surface, but when I tried to shift. Nothing.

Dammit! Plan B.

Reaching out, I grasped the wolf by the back of the neck, bunching his fur into my fingers. It was risky, but there was no way I could run from this fight. He'd attack me from behind and then leave me to bleed out. Whoever this wolf was, he wanted me dead.

I drove my knee into the animal's neck, aiming for the larynx but hitting the wolf in its chest instead. It yipped and tried to back up, but luck was on my side. Still holding its neck skin in a firm grasp with my good hand, I drove my knee forward a second time just as the animal dipped toward me. The crunch of bone made me grin as my knee smashed into its throat. As the wolf tore loose from my hold, the glint of broken glass caught my eye. *Perfect.* Reaching over, I grabbed for the broken bottle while blood continued to pour down from the open gash in my arm, saturating the sand. After picking up my makeshift weapon, I then faced the wolf.

"Let's dance, asshole!" My vision tunneled, but if I showed weakness, I was dead. 91.5% of these fights were bluffing. I might still die, especially if I fainted from blood loss, but I needed to appear strong. "Come on!"

The animal lowered its head, wheezing and sputtering. Hopefully, I'd smashed his trachea. Go, me. Dad would be proud ... if I lived to tell him. I sucked in a deep breath through my nose to scent the wolf.

Male musk and heavy pinewood smoke, something wolves did to mask their scent. Of course it was a male. Females didn't initiate dominance fights nearly as often as males. I stared him in the eyes, begging my wolf to come to the surface.

Come on, baby. Shift and tear this guy in two.

The wolf stilled, cocking his head to the side.

My wolf hesitated, and shame burned my cheeks.

Not again.

"Nai?" Noble called.

His voice was far off, but it was enough to spook the wolf. He snarled at me before darting into the trees.

"Coward!" I screamed as my legs crumpled. I collapsed in the sand, dropping the glass shard and staring at the stars above me while they swirled.

Shit. My arm *hurt*. As the adrenaline from the fight wore off, pain throbbed through my arm from my wrist to my elbow. I panted, trying to maintain consciousness while blood seeped through my fingers and soaked into the sand.

Someone set me up. They set me up *good*.

This wasn't a dominance fight. That was done in front of peers and witnesses. This was a mother-freaking ambush.

Even though I didn't know *why*, I did have an inkling as to *who* could've set this up. No matter how many times my father and I did that damn drill, calling up my wolf when under duress had always been my biggest weakness. Only someone from *Crescent* could know that.

But was Nolan's wolf that psycho? He would benefit from my death, but to do it like this, in a dark patch of forest without anyone around, it was low, even for him. I wasn't aware of any other enemies though.

So before I died here, bleeding out on the sand, I wanted to know one thing:

Did my freaking cousin just try to kill me?

If I survived, I'd ask him with a sword in my hand for good measure. The coward.

"Help!" I managed to get out before weakness pummeled me. How was there so much blood? I leaned over and saw the stained red sand around my arm. It was clumpy; my gash was still free-flowing.

Did he *hit an artery?* More dizziness gripped me. Or was that fear?

Things started to spin when I heard Noble shout; his voice louder than before which, *hopefully*, meant he was closer.

"Over ... here," I gasped.

Seconds later, I felt his presence, and relief coursed through me. As the darkness rushed up to meet me, I was scooped up by a pair of giant muscular arms, and the owner's smell hit my nose like a truck.

Rage.

"Get a healer!" he shouted, and I looked up at his

face. Those eyes … were they the eyes of my masked mate?

His fingers went to my pulse. "Who did this?"

I knew then, without a doubt, that if I said Nolan's name, my cousin wouldn't survive until morning, and I was only 48.3% sure it was him.

"Your eyes … so green…" I mumbled, trailing my fingers along his cheek before finally losing consciousness.

Chapter 12

I came to with a pounding headache. Muffled voices filled my ears and clanged through my head. As I pried my eyes open, images solidified with a snap.

Kaja and Nell stood on either side of the bed, both leaning directly in front of my face.

"Thank the mage!" Kaja gasped, her hands fluttering over me.

"You scared the magic out of us! Don't ever do that again," Nell warned.

Kaja nodded, her expression pinched.

Behind them, Noble stood at the foot of the bed, his nostrils flaring; his eyes practically shot fire. Honor leaned against the window, arms crossed as he stared. When our gazes collided, his eyes narrowed.

I sat up, and Nell grabbed pillows from the bed next to me to stuff behind my back for support.

Two rows of beds ran parallel the length of the brick

walls, all the beds made up with white sheets and all unoccupied except mine.

I was in a hospital. One hundred percent certain of that. The castle? Maybe 50/50 sure. The alpha king probably wouldn't invite me into his personal space. The memory of the attack roared through my mind then, and I stared at my forearm, tracing the puckered scar.

Yikes. The skin was pale—even for me—but the jagged wound was healing.

"You lost a lot of blood," Honor said, pushing away from the window. He winced as he came down on his right leg.

I wondered again how he'd gotten the permanent injury and why it didn't heal. Also ... why didn't anyone talk about it? There was a story there, but could I ask him? Not today. Today, I was the patient.

Frowning, he stepped forward and then halted as Noble approached my bedside, cutting Honor off.

My gentle friend growled, and Nell scurried back, allowing Noble ample space.

"Who did this?" he demanded, his voice sharp and full of anger.

I blinked, thinking it was Rage or Justice, but no. Gone was my sweet friend; he was all fierce and full of hatred.

A vise closed around my chest.

Shit.

My suspicion that Nolan was at the bottom of it was

just that—suspicion. What with the shock and all, I wasn't even 50.7% sure.

Noble was scary though, and I rethought my earlier assessment of him. That was a creepy-ass-scary-as-hell-Mr. Hyde-switch he had going on. I was 99.99% sure if I told him I suspected Nolan, my cousin would be dead.

"I'm not sure," I croaked, the statement sounding more like a question. After sipping at the lukewarm water Kaja held out for me, I tried to deflect. "What time is it?"

"Bullshit," Honor said from the growing shadows filtering in by the window.

Fear trickled in, and I let it fuel anger as I glared at the silent brother. "Excuse me?"

He approached my bedside again, limping softly as he did.

"I read people," he said, nostrils flaring. *"Very* well."

My palms broke out in a sweat. What was with my two sweet boys going all ragey-alpha on me?

Noble nodded to his brother before facing me. His fierce expression softened, barely. "This is an official investigation, Nai, so tell the truth. Do you have *any* idea who did this?"

Official investigation.

My heart pounded, climbing up into my throat. I really didn't know. Not a hundred percent. I couldn't implicate someone and ruin their life over a hunch. Even if it was my asshat cousin Nolan. I sighed and then said, "No. I tried to scent him, but he covered it with pine smoke."

"Why didn't you shift?" Honor asked. "Your wolf is better suited for a fight like that."

I frowned, hesitant to share my secret, and Noble patted my good arm.

"Whatever it is, you can tell us. We want to help."

After sucking in a deep breath, I blurted, "Stress makes it hard to shift. Always has. I ... can't control my wolf."

Every wolf I'd ever known had no problem shifting when in danger. In fact, it was easier when in mortal peril. *Not me.*

"What?" Noble stared at me like I'd just grown another head. "That makes no sense."

Honor snarled at Noble, more animal than human, maybe because he didn't like his brother pointing out my weakness when he had one of his own. But when he spoke, Honor's words were clear and full of pity. "How? The wolf instinct makes it impossible *not* to shift."

I rolled my eyes to the ceiling, "Well, somehow my wolf never got the memo on rules of instinct."

I had no idea why she hesitated. After years of trying to force her, my father decided extra lessons in hand-to-hand combat were the best backup plan for my wolf, who locked up in life or death situations.

"Does your entire pack know your weakness?"

Honor asked, his hand going to massage that spot on his right leg that must be causing him pain.

Calling it a weakness hurt, but he was right.

I knew where this conversation was headed. "Yes, but I doubt the wolf who attacked me was Nolan." Moving my position slightly, I winced when the movement sent a sharp zing deep into my bone. I knew Nolan's wolf's markings and smell, but there was magic to cover that up, so I wasn't sure.

"Damn," Honor said as if he wanted it to be Nolan.

Noble shared a look with Honor, and the latter nodded.

"You need lessons," Honor said, fur rippling down his arms. "That's a weakness no shifter can afford."

"Sure," I said. "Where do you propose I squeeze that in? Saturdays might work, assuming I'm not cramming for fire or water classes. Or the alpha studies in the gym. Not to mention serving meals in the dining hall." I shook my head at the absurdity of their proposal. "I don't have time for one more thing."

Noble sucked in a breath. "Nai—"

"You can't afford to *not* take time for this," Honor snapped. "How can you expect your pack to follow you if you can't shift when there's danger?"

I glared at him, forcing myself to keep my eyes off his injured leg; it was rich coming from him. "It hasn't affected me ... so far."

Honor crouched and stared at me eye-to-eye. "It just did, Nai. That's why you're in here." He gestured to the healing ward I lay in and straightened. "Lessons start Saturday night, 8 p.m. sharp."

Then he turned and stormed out of the room, slamming the door behind him.

"What the mage is his problem?" I grumbled, picking at the edge of my blanket. Lessons? Honor was going to teach my wolf to shift in danger? Hah. Good luck. My father had been trying for years.

Noble shook his head, making it clear he wasn't pleased either.

"You almost died, Nai. Everyone is really wound up about this attack." Noble pursed his lips. "No one knows if you were the specific target or just the best opportunity to strike at the heirs. Think of what it could mean if our own kind was uniting with the selkies and betraying us. It could put others at risk, not just you, and there's the tension with the other shifters too…"

Wolf shifters uniting with the other shifter races to pick off heirs? I shivered at the thought. I'd never asked anymore about the selkie incident, and the boys didn't offer anything up.

"But the attack on me was an isolated incident, right?" I argued, my voice still sounding raspy. "Or have there been others?"

"As much as I hate to say it, you're the only one. Hardly reassuring at this point." He gave my good hand a squeeze. "Feel better. I've got to report back to the king."

Then he, too, left the room.

My attention bounced from the door and back to my friends, who swarmed back to the bed again.

"Whoa," Nell said.

"Super whoa," Kaja agreed, her brown eyes as big as saucers. "What's up with you and the Midnight princes?"

Speaking of… "Where's Rage?" I asked. "He's the one who saved me."

I needed to thank him. Big-time. The memory of his green eyes flashing fire when he scooped me up set my heart fluttering.

Both girls shared a look, a look that one hundred percent promised I wasn't going to like whatever they said.

"He's briefing the king on the attack. Justice too." Nell forced a smile, the flat-lipped kind that wasn't really a smile at all. "You *legit* almost died. It's Sunday afternoon."

Sunday! I'd slept almost twenty-four hours? That was scary, but I was going to focus on the fact I was… not dead. "Why are they only briefing the king now? What happened? Why didn't they brief him last night, right after the attack?"

Kaja scooted onto the bed, and Nell sat at my feet, but Kaja's bouncing indicated she was nearly bursting with something.

"Spill," I told her more urgently.

She grinned. Leaning forward, she dropped her

voice to a whisper. "Rage lost it. He was white as a sheet when we arrived on scene, yelling orders at everyone. You looked like a ragdoll in his arms."

On scene. Yelling orders. In his arms. My stomach dropped. I wanted to hear more, but I also needed to tell someone my suspicion.

"I think Rage or Justice might be my fated mate," I blurted and then chewed my lip, waiting for their reactions.

Nell's mouth popped open into an "O" shape, and her eyes widened.

Maybe I should've kept that to myself.

I glanced at Kaja, who grinned hugely.

"That makes sense," my BFF said, nodding. "But which one?"

I sighed. "I don't know. They both have the same green eyes, but I'm leaning toward Justice … he's nicer to me."

Beowulf also had green eyes, but my gut was telling me my mate was a Midnight brother.

Saying Justice's name out loud caused a twinge of tightness just under my breastbone. Wait, did I want it to be Rage or Justice? Ugh.

This was going to kill me.

"If a Midnight prince is your fated mate, that's going to be some dra-ma," Nell concluded.

A sigh escaped me. "I know. Okay, tell me what happened at the beach. I don't want to think about who my mate is anymore."

Kaja nodded, picking up where she left off, "It was the strangest thing. After I found some mage wine, I was on my way back to the beach to look for you when a messenger told me I was needed urgently at our dorm. He delivered a note saying Rue had been badly injured, so I raced to the house to see—"

"The whole thing was a setup," Nell added, her voice low. "I told Rage—"

"I even gave him the letter," Kaja piped in.

What the heck? Whoever attacked me knew I was close friends with Kaja and that she'd be looking for me on the beach, so they lured her away? That meant this was a two-person job. One to attack and one to distract. Maybe more. "I was looking for you."

After I explained how the attacker drew me away by mimicking her voice, Kaja cursed.

"Maybe it wasn't a random attack." But was Nolan smart enough to coordinate something like that? Not at all. Leaning forward, I asked, "What about the messenger?"

"Gone," Nell said. "The guy wasn't any of the messengers from around campus or the castle, and Rage made them all do a lineup in case Kaja could identify him."

Dread slithered down my throat, through my chest, and settled at the bottom of my stomach—the cold weight making me nauseated. I sank into my pillows and closed my eyes, waiting for my stomach to settle.

"Anyway, Prince Courage brought you here, but the

healer mage couldn't wake you up. Justice was so upset he went *rogue*—totally disobeyed the king—and went to Dark Row." Nell swallowed hard.

I sat up so fast my head spun, "Wait, what?"

Kaja nodded, picking up the story. "He forced a witch there to make a healing potion to awaken you. He just left." She pointed to the door. "Otherwise, you might still be asleep."

I sat up straighter, my fear overcome by shock. Okay, that settled it. Justice was my mate…

"He went to Dark Row?" I cleared my throat and pressed on. "As in the deadly black market?" Even watching Kaja's head bob up and down, it didn't register. "As in the 'don't ever go there' market where people are murdered over magical things?"

I ended my question with a flourish meant to encompass all the artifacts and potions one could get— usually for a very steep price. It was legendary, and not the good kind. Definitely not a place for a prince. My father told me all about it.

They both nodded. "Rumor is, he had to give his blood to pay the price to save you."

Holy shit. Justice was my mate. That was proof. Right there. No one else would do such a thing.

"Oh, girl, you should've seen Prince Courage," Nell said as if to prove my conclusion wrong.

Kaja nodded. "Rage never left your side from the time he picked you up until Justice returned. We could hear him all the way from the hallway, *screaming* death threats at the healers."

"From the hallway?" I repeated, trying to process.

Nell patted my leg as she said, "They wouldn't let us in until you were stable."

Kaja snickered. "More likely they didn't want us in while Rage was thrashing that one guy."

I frowned. *Maybe Rage is my mate.* Oh mage, I was so confused.

I rubbed my temples, wishing I could go to sleep for another day or ten...

"Nai..." Kaja placed a hand on my shoulder. "You do have a hunch who did this, right?"

I sighed. "Maybe..." But would he go to that much effort? "Nolan was my first guess, but I'm not sure."

Kaja nodded as if this made perfect sense. "He definitely wants to be alpha of your clan, and he hasn't exactly been welcoming."

Nell scrunched her face in obvious disagreement. "But that's so *obvious*. Not to mention unethical."

Pretty sure ethics weren't at the top of Nolan's priority list.

"This would take some thought," Nell continued, oblivious to my judgy thoughts. "Who else hates you?"

I was barely out of ICU, and they wanted me to weigh-in on my nemesis' identity and evil plan?

"No idea. I'm so nice and lovable," I joked.

Kaja agreed, but Nell snorted. "I was thinking Mallory could have done it. You know, she and Rage dated last year for a hot minute, and she's been glaring daggers at you since you arrived."

"Mallory?" I asked.

"Evil Barbie," Kaja translated.

Oh yeah, blood loss had done a number on my brain.

Barbie would kill me over Rage? She had to know life didn't work that way, right?

"No," I huffed. "It was a male wolf. I could smell him."

Nell waved me off. "Well, *obviously* she wouldn't do it herself. I'll bet she hired someone."

Kaja shook her head. "Murder, Nell? Really? No, it's definitely Nolan. You should tell the princes so they can confront him about this."

Pretty sure I knew that wasn't the best plan—even without a gallon of blood.

"I'm a little overwhelmed, to be honest." Dizziness rocked through me, and I closed my eyes until the sensation of spinning passed. "Can we change the subject for now?"

"Definitely." Nell got up and walked over to the far corner of the room and pulled a wheelchair from an alcove. Bringing the contraption back to the bed, she patted the seat. "The healer said you need lots of rare steak and rest, so let's bust this sterile hellhole. Kaja and I will take turns playing nurse."

I looked at my two new friends and smiled. "Thanks for being here. You don't have to do all this."

Nell waved her hand, "We begged you to come to the beach party, so I'm only doing it out of guilt. And you went looking for Kaja, so it's practically her fault."

We all laughed. I knew she was lying, but the generosity made my heart swell. These girls were gold, and I was lucky to have them.

Chapter 13

KAJA STIRRED the pot of cream of wheat, and I frowned, eyes still blurry from sleep. We were at my place, having spent yesterday evening holed up at hers while her sweet sisters waited on me hand and foot. Today was Monday, which meant class. Ugh. My blood loss earned me a pass for serving meals. However, without the work, I couldn't eat at the cafeteria or snake breakfast at the coffee cart like I normally did. Kalama had just left my dorm after relaying the king's message, only to have a package delivered within minutes of her leaving my doorstep.

"You said this stuff has fifty percent of my daily iron requirements?" I grimaced as she let a spoonful plop into the pot of hot cereal and then shook my head. "I'm not eating any of it, just so you know. I'm..." My gaze flitted over the groceries laid out on the counter. "Having pancakes..."

She chuckled. "You can have both."

My stomach echoed her sentiments with a loud growl.

I ate the hot mushy cereal while Kaja cooked pancakes, my gaze drifting back to the *mysterious* box of fresh groceries. They'd arrived by official Midnight Pack messenger not even an hour ago. Pancake mix, eggs, steak, spinach, ice cream, the works. There was even a card, one I couldn't stop staring at.

I picked up the heavy cardstock and flipped it over for the tenth time. ***"Get well soon –Mate."***

Mate.

The rumor of my injury had reached my mate, and now he was sending food boxes. All while he chose to keep his identity a secret and ignore me. I wasn't sure if I wanted to kiss him or kill him.

Both.

Before I could think more on the box of food, Nolan sauntered into the kitchen. I snatched the card up and stuck it in my pocket.

My cousin was dressed in head-to-toe black, emo all the way down to his charcoal turtleneck. His hair still rumpled with sleep, he surveyed the room with the hungry look of a hyena.

Both Kaja and I froze.

Was he behind my attack? Maybe his fur had darkened, or been magically camouflaged, and I was wrong about his wolf. Because who in their right mind wore a turtleneck when it was eighty-five degrees out? It was way too hot, not to mention social suicide. Unless they were hiding something...

"Food," he mumbled, reaching for the pancake stack.

Still holding the spatula, Kaja whacked his hand, making him yelp. "I don't think so, assface."

He glared at her and growled, letting his yellow wolf eyes come to the surface.

I gulped, glad that it looked like Kaja wasn't letting him off the hook. I guess now was as good a time as any to do this.

"Why the turtleneck?" I asked my cousin. "It's not winter."

"Not even close," Kaja growled. "*And* it looks horrible on you."

Burn.

He glared from Kaja to me. "Why don't you both mind your own damn business?"

Kaja growled, low and deep, and I could see her losing control over her wolf. "Did you hear about Nai's attack?" Her words were barely coherent. "Aren't you going to ask how your cousin is doing?"

Nolan crossed his arms. "Yeah, I heard she pissed off a wolf at the beach party and they got into it." Waving at me, he said, "Obviously, she's fine."

Kaja took one step closer to him, holding up the completely useless plastic spatula as if it were a lightsaber. "Where were you during the party, Nolan?"

My muscles tightened, and I sighed, pushing myself

out of my seat. Might as well get it all out there. I rounded to his other side just in case he bolted, trapping him in.

Nolan laughed, legit barked out in full-on laughter. "You think *I* attacked her?" When neither of us disputed it, his face went deadly serious. "There's a time for contesting her future place as alpha. It's *not* now."

Okay. His not so thinly veiled threat made it sound like we were being absurd.

"You'll never take the pack from me, Nolan." My wolf surged to the surface with my declaration, fur rippling down my arms, and I had to force her back down.

Now she wanted to come out and play? What about when I was dying?

More important than the pissing match, he'd not given a direct answer or told me why he was wearing that stupid sweater. It was perfect for hiding a still-healing wound, and I'd damaged that wolf's throat. Sneaky as a rat.

"Answer the damn question or I'll report my suspicions to the Midnight brothers. Then, where will you be?" At least he had the decency to pale when I spoke of them. "Where were you when I was attacked, Nolan?"

Nolan drew himself up to his full height, and his nostrils flared. "Screw you, Nai!"

He turned to leave, and I realized he wasn't going to

answer. But... that turtleneck! I had to know why he was covering his throat. Kaja must've been on the same wavelength because, when I lunged for him, she did the same. We both grabbed at his shirt, high on the collar, and tugged. The seam ripped, and Nolan spun.

The force of his movement threw me off balance, and I crashed into Kaja, both of us tumbling back into the row of cabinets.

"What the hell, *psychos*!" He waved his arms as he bellowed. "What is wrong with you?"

Oh. My. Mage.

I stared, unable to take my gaze from his neck, now fully exposed. I shook my head and glanced toward Kaja, who likewise stared, jaw gaping, at the bright, red ... *hickey*.

Dammit.

"Oops," I said lamely, wincing as I climbed to my feet.

"So... sorry. We, uh... slipped." Kaja smiled and raced to the stack of golden pancakes. Holding a short stack of three on the spatula, she extended the peace offering. "Want one ... or some? I heard it takes a lot of sucking to do that well—"

I snickered as he ripped the stack of pancakes from her and stormed out of the room.

"Well, there goes that theory," I told Kaja.

She eyed the doorway Nolan had fled through. "I dunno," she said, shaking her head. "His voice was raspy, and that hickey could be a magicked mark. I still don't trust him."

Yeah. Definitely not. He was sketchy as hell, but was he a killer?

Kaja checked her watch. "We have class in thirty minutes. Time to go." She pointed to my left hand and said, "Better get Nell to cover that."

Crap! My mark was slowly coming back. Hopefully, Nolan hadn't seen it.

I nodded, grabbing two pancakes to munch on the way. "Thanks for all your help, girl."

She put down the spatula and gave me a hug. "Just watch your back. I hope this was an isolated incident, but…"

Yeah. "You and me both."

A half-hour later, I stepped into Fire Studies to find Rage already there, talking it up with the professor. The two of them stared at the giant, *perfect* fireball resting in Rage's palm.

I hadn't seen Rage since my near-death experience, or Justice for that matter, and I took a moment and stared at the beautiful boy who'd carried me from the beach to the hospital wing. My gaze flitted to the orange and red sphere and stayed.

Yep, I was one hundred percent done with this book-reading business.

I marched up to the desk nearest where they stood and slammed the giant textbook down with a loud thwack. They both jumped, Rage far less than the professor, and then turned to me.

"I've read it," I announced, grinning like a loon. "Front to back, three whole times. Now, teach me some magic."

Rage's eyes warmed as his gaze roamed over my face. Then, his attention slowly drifted down my body, and his eyes hardened into ice when he glanced at the fine scar on my arm.

Master Carn cleared his throat and looked to Rage, and I almost lost it when he—Prince Rage—nodded. Even the teachers took orders from him? The fireball in his hand dissipated, and then he said to the professor: "I'll go practice in the back."

Wasn't he going to say a word to me?

We'd had that big fight where he admitted to hating me and all my pack for one wolf's betrayal—which wasn't even true—then I almost died, and he saved me, carrying me all the way to the castle. After all that history, all I got was a look? That man was *infuriating*. If I knew how to make fireballs, he'd be dodging them right now.

"I'll be right back," Master Carn said. "We need water."

In case I set the building on fire?

Yikes.

With the professor gone, I refused to play Rage's game. I crossed the room, but my steps slowed when he kept his back to me. I owed him a debt of gratitude even if he was a bastard. Reaching out, I grabbed his shoulder and tried to turn him toward me ... to no avail.

Seriously?

"Hey ... Rage!" I called, waving my hand in front of him. "I want to talk to you."

He sighed, and I almost stomped off. But when he turned and faced me, my rehearsed speech evaporated, and my mouth dropped open, stunned by the emotion in his eyes. They were glittering with ... *rage*.

"Yes?" he growled.

Why was he mad? At me? And now that I looked closer, he looked exhausted.

"Thanks..." I shook my head, trying to clear the shock, and then mumbled, "You know, for saving me."

He nodded stiffly. "I take my charge over the safety of the alpha heirs seriously. It's a job bestowed on me and one I need to prove worthy of if I want to rule someday."

Oh. *So that's why he saved me.*

"Okay..." I wasn't sure where this was going anymore. "Well, why are you acting so pissed at me? Other than your usual hatred...?"

He clenched his jaw and forced a swallow before answering, his voice tight with fury. "I don't hate you, Nai. I do wish you'd tell me if you have any inkling as to who attacked you. I want to make sure this island remains a safe haven." The fire was back in his eyes. "For you—and all of the heirs."

I wanted to tell him Nolan, but I was even less sure now after we'd talked this morning. And I was still 64.5% certain Rage would kill him. His coiled body seemed ready to attack.

"I wish I knew," I said, lamely. "But I really don't."

Rage sighed, his eyes again falling to my injured arm. "Well, I'm... glad you're not dead."

His halting words registered, and I grimaced. *Wow*. "That's so sweet. They should hire you to write Valentine's Day cards."

I'd totally buy that. *Not*.

He rolled his eyes but said nothing.

"Okay, well, this was constructive," I muttered, turning to flee this bizarre convo. I could take a hint.

Rage cleared his throat, making me pause before rubbing the sides of his temples.

"You'll need to push the professors to train you. You're here a year early, and they're setting you up for failure by making you read books. If you don't pass the practical mid-year exam, then you can't come back to finish the rest of the year. You've got two and a half months to prep, so step it up."

My eyes bugged, and I stepped toward him, seething. "What! They can do that?"

I'd assumed each year had some kind of practical elemental exam, but I didn't know they could kick me out halfway through the year.

He nodded, stepping closer and bringing the scent of sandalwood with him. My heart flipped and then thumped against my ribs as if it could lurch me forward and close the gap.

"Time to be an alpha, Nai." He growled: "Demand what you want. You need practical lessons every day or you'll never be ready for the test."

I swallowed hard and nodded, again noticing how tired he looked. "You okay? You look exhausted."

He was silent a moment before his gaze dipped to my lips, "I was up late."

And then he left the room.

Just like that.

I wiped my mouth just to make sure I didn't have pancake crumbs leftover from breakfast, or maybe drool. Nope. All good on that. I shook my head, certain I'd never figure that man out, but not gonna lie, watching his cute butt leave a room wasn't half bad. I only hoped 'up late' wasn't code for hooking up with a girl because, as much as I didn't want to admit it, I'd care if he did.

At least the eye candy *partially* made up for his winning personality.

THE COOL NIGHT air was perfect for exploring the forest. I stared up into the sky, smiling when the clouds scuttled away from the white sliver of the crescent moon hanging in the darkness. Another week down, and Saturday had arrived. Specifically, Saturday at 8 p.m. All the conditions were perfect, and still, my wolf refused to rise to the surface. She perceived Honor as a threat. Not that he would ever hurt me, but his presence with the intention to provoke my wolf made her uneasy, and she stayed put—the opposite of what she should do.

"Can you feel her here?" Honor asked, tapping his chest.

We stood behind my dorm, at the edge of the woods, for our first class of "Help Nai Shift 101." So far, we'd had zero success, which was to say I was still human even after he'd waved a knife in my face.

At least, Honor wasn't rubbing my failure in my face by shifting back and forth. Pushing away the painful memory of my one lesson with Nolan from years ago, I sucked in a deep, cleansing breath.

Pine and mulch. Loamy earth and verdant growth. Sandalwood and sage.

'Mate.'

My eyes popped open, and I scanned the tree line. My skin prickled with anticipation, and my wolf surged forward. I took another breath, but then his scent was gone.

Just like that, my wolf retreated. She'd been like this ever since the attack. Hesitant.

"She's there," I said, patting my chest. "But also here," and I patted my temple. "She doesn't want to come out for you."

Running through the woods? Sure, no problem. But

my wolf was not a beck and call kinda girl. Not for me, my father, and apparently, not for Honor. The urge to ask if he knew who my mate was burned at the tip of my tongue, but if I disclosed I was half of the fated-mate pair, would I reveal a secret my mate kept from his brothers? Of all the green-eyed boys at this school … I was sure in my bones it was one of the Midnight brothers, most likely Justice or Rage.

Honor cocked his head. "What do you mean, 'she?'"

His question pulled me back to the lesson, and I held my hand out to stop what would surely follow. "I know, I know. 'She' is *me*."

My father said the same thing. In fact, every wolf-shifter I knew felt the same. The wolf was merely the embodiment of the animalistic instinct of their 'human.'

But that's not how I felt.

Honor limped closer. "Then why did you say *she*?"

How could I explain without sounding insane?

"I know we're one and the same as far as beings, and most of the time, it feels that way." Not completely true, but the best I could come up with. "However, whenever I'm in peril or under pressure—" I pursed my lips and shrugged "—she steps back, freezes up as if she thinks my human form is more powerful."

"That's not good," Honor stated just like every other wolf shifter who'd discovered my secret. "Are you sure she freezes up?"

"I don't know how else to explain it." I crossed my arms over my chest, frowning.

He chuckled. "There are shifters who fight their instincts as they get older, and some even say they can control whether or not they shift. But what you're saying..." He shook his head. "Our wolf is physically stronger than our human body, so when it comes to physical danger, the instinct to shift is almost impossible to stop."

Almost impossible wasn't the same as impossible. And it didn't matter what everyone else did or didn't do. I could only speak for myself. "You're not telling me anything I haven't heard before."

"All right," Honor said. "Then tell me what it's like for you. When that wolf attacked you, you didn't have any...drive or push to shift?"

"I wanted to, but I couldn't."

He shook his head, and I reached back to a conversation I'd had with my father, years ago, to try and explain.

"You know that feeling of presence as you shift, and I mean just before your instinct takes over and your rational mind goes away, that few seconds when both the human rational side and wolf instinct coexist in the same space at the same time?"

Honor stared at me, his gaze piercing. "That's like a millisecond."

I snorted. "Not for me."

Midnight Kisses

"You mean you can still think and rationalize even when you're in your wolf form?"

"Yep."

He shook his head. *Again*. But it wasn't in a disrespectful way. He looked ... amazed. "I've never heard of anything like that."

His words prickled my skin. *Dammit*. I'd said too much. Revealed too much. What if he told the alpha king? I grabbed his arm.

"Please don't tell *anyone*. The last thing I need is more scrutiny for being different. Everyone already treats me like a freak for having two affinities." I straightened, dropping his arm, and gave him an apologetic smile. "Maybe that's why. Maybe my two affinities are stronger than my wolf."

I was grasping for straws, but the pity in his expression twisted my insides. There had to be a reasonable explanation for this.

He pulled me in for a hug, surprising me. "Maybe. But I need you to be able to shift and defend yourself. We just want you to be safe, and I would never tell anyone your secret."

Without him saying it, I knew the "we" he referred to was him and Noble. Sweet and caring, both of them. Or could that "we" also include the other two Midnight brothers? Probably, at least one of them—*if* one of them was my mate.

Gah! Why did there have to be so many green-eyed boys at this school?

Emotion clogged my throat, and I sank into Honor's hug. "Thanks for trying."

Honor kissed my temple and then pulled away. "We're not done," he said, crouching to look me in the eye. "I'll meet you here same time next week."

I watched him leave, guilt pressed against my breastbone. As soon as he disappeared around the corner, my wolf nudged me.

'Run?'

Blessed Mother Mage. Really? Now that Honor was gone, she was willing to come out? No one told her what to do.

Granted, I'd been keeping my shifts to once a week so that I didn't run into my mate again. Staring out into the darkness, I found the normal skittering and hoots served to reassure me that, hopefully, I wouldn't see him. So long had passed that the odds had to be in my favor. Surely he wouldn't be out in the woods this late. Right? The stress was going to kill me. Or drive me mad—except I might already be there.

Ugh. I needed to connect to the earth. To feel the air in my fur.

Before I could formulate any further arguments, I marched into the woods, stripping out of my clothes as soon as I'd cleared the tree line.

With a deep breath, I relaxed, letting my wolf surge forward. The fur prickled as it spread down my skin, and I grinned as my bones twisted and morphed.

Seconds later, I let my tongue loll out of my mouth in the wolf-equivalent of a grin. I so *needed* this.

Racing into the forest, I left the tension of the last few weeks behind and thought of nothing but the night and the beauty of the woods. The scent of wolf was everywhere, but this deep into the forest, the *other* smells ruled. Early autumn's foliage, decomposing mulch, the scat of small rodents and birds.

And then I sensed him.

'Mate.'

I couldn't say if it was by smell or just the feeling, but I had time to flee. Only I didn't really want to. The large black wolf stepped from behind a tree, slowly approaching.

'Mate.'

Closing my eyes, I let him approach.

'*Missed you.*' He nuzzled my neck. '*Smell good.*'

But the intimacy of the gesture—of his touch—upset me, and I stepped back. '*No. You left me. You hurt me.*'

I used small short sentences his wolf could understand.

'Yes.' He nodded. '*Leaving you bad. Mate never leave. My human stupid.*'

True that. The "human stupid" comment won him a wolfish grin.

'*Human very stupid,*' I agreed.

'*Mate. Home. Safe. No Leave.*' His voice brushed over me as he nuzzled my neck, and the sincerity in his voice melted me. I could *feel* his feelings just the way my father described as pack alpha. Did all mates have this? I could feel my pack back home. I let him continue to nuzzle my neck before nipping playfully at his fur.

'I'm sorry I bit you last time.'

He cocked his head and then licked me from chin to ear. *'Sorry I hurt you.'*

My heart squeezed at his words, and I nuzzled him back. Why couldn't his human be as nice?

Chapter 14

TWO WEEKS LATER, and I still couldn't shift for Honor, not even when he threatened me with a knife. Not even when Noble jumped out in all his wolfish glory—a big *black* wolf, incidentally—and shocked me. Nope. For one irrational second, I thought the wolf was my mate's, but my wolf ... *she knew* and didn't even budge for Noble.

On a more positive note, I had made progress in my water elemental class, and fire was *finally* starting to click.

I watched the water stir in the glass I held, staring at the steady liquid as I pushed heat into the glass through my palm. The water stirred and started to boil, causing me to grin. When there was a good roiling boil, and I was confident that I held my magic energy tight within my being, I held the glass out to Master Carn. "There you are."

The tall mage wore a furrowed expression, his lips flattened until they nearly disappeared, but he said nothing. After accepting the glass, he stuck a thermometer into the contents as if confirming I'd done just as he'd asked.

Like we both couldn't see the water boiling.

"Now will you teach me fireballs?" I asked. Not that boiling water didn't have its usefulness and all. "We still have an hour of class left—"

He shook his head. "Not today, I'm afraid."

Then he turned, set the glass on his desk, and headed to the door—all without even looking at me. I stood slack-jawed, watching him practically flee after my success.

"Where are you going?" I asked. "I thought this was class time?"

"I've got a staff meeting," he said over his shoulder by way of explanation, pulling the door open. "Can't be late."

His deep voice bounced back into the room, and I frowned. Master Carn was acting whack.

Rage was missing today too, so it wasn't like I could ask him to help me. Not that he would. After our warm-fuzzy convo two weeks ago, he'd returned to pretending I didn't exist. Who knew how that boy's mind worked? Not me. One hundred percent not me.

Well ... if Master Carn wasn't going to teach me how to wield fire, I'd find a book in the library and teach myself.

Midnight Kisses

I left the room, hefting the stupid beginner's fire book, and practically skipped down the hall. If I never had to work with Master Carn again, it would be fine by me. He might be brilliant with his element, but the guy was stuffy and cold. *Zero* personality and unhelpful. Why become a teacher if he didn't want to teach?

Master Jin, my water teacher, was happy to have an eager student, and with his help, I was quickly catching up. Master Carn, on the other hand, treated me like a pariah, probably taking hints from Rage or even the alpha king. The fire mage left the room more than any other teacher I'd ever had, which shortened my lessons … like he wanted me to fail. Too bad. I refused to fail at anything.

I pulled open the door to the library, and the smells of parchment and leather assailed me.

"Can I help—oh … Nai." Mrs. Edi blinked at me through her Coke-bottle glasses as I pushed the beginner fire textbook to her. The advanced spell mage glanced down at the heavy tome. "All done with this one?"

"Yep." I grinned at the librarian. Her thick lenses made her eyes look bigger than they were. "I need *advanced* books on fire wielding, please."

She frowned, scooting off her chair, and disappeared behind the desk. "Is there a specific question you have? I'm sure Master Carn would be the best resource for you—"

"No, he won't," I grunted, and she stepped out from around the corner, her brow furrowed with worry.

After a long exhale, I met her eye-to-eye. "Master Carn is useless. He's always leaving me alone during class time. I'd like some additional reading. I need to learn enough to pass my test at the end of the term."

"Oh, dear. That won't do." Her eyes widened, magnified by the thick lenses. She patted my shoulder and offered a smile filled with sympathy. "Let me show you where the advanced texts are."

I followed the stout woman through the rows of shelves until we neared the back of the library.

Mrs. Edi pointed to a row of four bookcases filled with thick tomes and rolled parchments. "All the advanced practical information is here. It's organized by affinity, so everything with the symbol of fire on it should be in the second case."

She pointed to the second bookcase, and at the top of it, a dancing flame emblem stood etched into the wood.

My gaze flicked over the other bookcases, stopping at water, the three squiggly lines that matched the mark on my abdomen. "Thanks, Mrs. Edi."

She patted my hand. "Always happy to help a student wanting to learn."

Which is what all teachers should believe—like a motto or sworn oath.

She turned to go, and my gaze flicked past the shelves, landing on a black onyx stone door. Inlaid in gold was a symbol I didn't recognize: a large triangle with three overlapping circles inside, all spread apart like petals of a flower.

"What's in there?" I asked, pointing at the strange door. There wasn't even a handle for it.

Mrs. Edi's eyes widened, and she swallowed hard before following my gaze.

"That's ... not for students." With a curt nod, she spun and practically raced down the aisle. "Good day, Nai."

Huh. *Okaaay*.

I turned my attention back to finding a solution for my sucky teacher. Each of the bookcases was close to six feet in length. Stopping in front of the second one, I stared at the fire symbol. With nearly an hour before I needed to be in the cafeteria, I stepped back to the first bookcase ... and stared at the three wavy lines—exactly like the ones on my abdomen.

Maybe instead of looking into advanced fire magic, I should look into why the water symbol was seared on my body. I didn't even think about it anymore unless I was showering. I still hadn't asked anyone else about the mark. Not even Kaja.

I glanced over the books, their thick, embossed spines so similar to the basic text Master Carn had given me. At the end of the bottom shelf, a thin journal-looking tome sat tucked between two larger books. I plucked it from the shelf. After wiping the dust from the top of it, I turned it over. The leather-bound book held only the wavy line-symbol embossed on it. No title or author on the cover. The blue leather was worn, and as I traced the lines one by one, a deep feeling of resonance hit me. My heart fluttered with excitement, and I opened the text. This book was old; the paper was stitched together—

A single sheet slid from the book. I snatched it from the air before tucking it into the back of the book.

Notes on Water was hand-written on the first page, followed by a bunch of chemistry-like equations.

Cool.

I kept the book, deciding to read it later, and moved to the fire shelf, scanning it for a similar tome to the one I held. My attention snagged on a title, and I nearly laughed out loud. *Wielding Fire—An Advanced Guide for Self-Instruction.*

Take that, Master Carn! I don't need you.

I pulled the book from the shelf and sat on the floor, letting it fall open on my lap. There it was, in black and white on the table of contents page:

Creating and Transferring Heat I: Boiling Water

Creating Light I: From Lighting Candles to Live Flames in Your Palm

Creating and Transferring Light and Heat II: Fireballs

Grinning, I snapped the book shut.

Heading toward the door, I passed a shelf of books that all had the same width, height, and pretty gold lettering on the spine.

Squirrel.

Midnight Kisses

I stopped and my smile turned into full-blown curiosity. These were yearbooks! The gold lettering on the spines were years from the 1900s up until now.

I traced my finger over the years, counting down to when my father would've been here.

But the yearbooks for the years he would have been here ... were missing.

Gone was the year he graduated, along with the six before.

What the mage?

I climbed to my feet, intending to ask Mrs. Edi about the missing yearbooks, when I heard the large library doors squeak open, and the trickle of voices wound through the shelves.

"Edi, go to lunch early," a man's gravelly voice said. "And don't come back for at least an hour."

"But—" she interjected, possibly to tell them a student was still in here.

"Now!"

"Yes, sir," she squeaked.

What an asshat!

I glared at the air, offended for the librarian, and her shuffling footsteps disappeared, followed by the door clicking shut. Oh crap! What was I supposed to do now? I stepped toward the aisle to let whoever was here know of my presence when someone else spoke.

"It stinks like wet dog in here," another man said. His voice had the musical quality of a high mage, specifically the one in the royal blue robes who seemingly had it out for me.

Nervous anxiety crawled down my spine.

Hiding might be better.

"Are you certain there are no other wolves in here?"

Peeking through the shelves, I saw the high mage from the council standing near the door, and beside him was none other than the king himself. Not that I'd ever met the jerk, but his pictures were plastered *everywhere*. He had the same dark hair as his nephews as well as the jacked body, but his chin jutted with belligerence, and his muddy-brown eyes glinted with malice. Rage and Justice clearly took their mean-lessons from this douchebag.

The king locked the library doors with a click and then turned to the high mage.

Raising his eyebrows, the king said, "I'm sure you're not implying that I stink, Kian."

"How's our project going?" the high mage asked, ignoring the king's statement. "Any idea how Crescent trash was summoned early? I was hoping things would be further along than they are, Declan."

"The investigation is still ongoing. We've had some *odd* interferences." The king groaned. "Also, we've had our first fated mate-pair of opposite clans, but no one knows who they are. Another project I've been pursuing."

My throat went bone dry. The fact that they were working together was scary as hell, especially because both "projects" centered around me. I strained to hear more regarding the fated mates.

"A mated pair, from opposite clans?" Kian asked. "That's impossible."

"Indeed."

"That's... a high crime."

I swallowed hard, and then my heart stopped when the high mage said, "Find out who they are, and have them report to the High Mage Council."

Frick. I knew fated mates from opposing clans was bad, but a high crime?

Kian continued to talk, but I wasn't paying attention anymore. I needed to find a place to hide ... because they were coming this way.

I raced to the other end of the row, at the very back of the library, and my heart dropped when I realized the only way out of here was that black onyx door. The one *not* for students.

"I've put a lot of faith in you," Kian said, his voice louder as they drew near.

If they got any closer, one of them would smell or hear me. I reached out and splayed my palm on the cool black stone, hoping it was unlocked, and pushed.

Best luck ever.

The door opened without a sound, and I slid inside, closing it gently.

A light turned on automatically. I ducked down on my hands and knees, wishing for invisibility.

Please don't walk through the door.

Then, the strangest thing happened. Even though the door was closed, I could hear them while they continued their conversation—as if they were standing in the same room.

Okay. Maybe I shouldn't have opened the magic black door.

"...and the selkies killed four of our guards—"

"How did the selkies get past the barrier?" Kian, aka Shady High Mage, asked. "Something is amiss here, and I'm going to look into it. I suggest you do the same, Declan. We need to know who is sabotaging us and put a stop to it."

"Of course I'm looking into it, but only high mage magic could allow them to cross the barrier—and I don't have *that* magic."

The accusation was clear. Silence descended on their conversation.

There was no answer, and after counting to ten, I stood, intending to crack the door and peek out when a cold hand clamped over my mouth.

My shriek died in my throat.

"Shhh," a woman whispered from behind me. "If they catch you in here, you're dead."

My heart hammered in my chest, and I nodded to let her know I understood.

Slowly, she pulled her fingers back one by one.

My blood pumped through my veins, my heart slamming against my ribs so hard my head spun. I pivoted and came face to face with the most beautiful woman I'd ever seen.

"Holy mage." My eyes widened as I took her in. Silvery blue hair fell to her waist in a cascade of soft curls. I knew from the way she carried herself and her golden cloak that she was a mage. A high-level one.

The room I'd ducked into wasn't a room at all but a grand hallway leading to what looked like an even bigger library—of sorts. Bookshelves lined the walls with domed twenty-foot ceilings and stained-glass inlay. It was *beautiful*.

And I wasn't supposed to be here. "I … well … you see—"

She waved her hand at me as if she didn't want me to speak and reached for my hand. Pulling it up to her face, she traced the lines in my palm.

"You opened the door?" she asked.

Her expression showed no fury or menacing power, more just a quizzical nature, so I relaxed a little.

"Yes … ma'am. It was unlocked."

She winced. "Do I look old enough to be called ma'am?"

I grinned and shook my head. "Sorry. Miss?"

She nodded, dropping my hand. "That's better. Now, who are you?"

I swallowed hard. "Nai, of Crescent Clan."

Her gaze narrowed and seemed to run the length of my hair. "Crescent Clan?" A strange look of *shock? Surprise?*—something I couldn't quite place—flickered across her face, and then it was gone. "You really shouldn't be in here—"

Someone cleared their throat, farther down the hall, and a book snapped shut.

I frowned. "What is this place?"

She chewed her lip as if mentally wrestling with something.

With a snap of her fingers, a little table appeared with a chair on either side. The quality of the stained wood was excellent, the surface completely unmarred of graffiti or even nicks or pen marks.

Several books sat on the top, and my eyes widened when I realized they were a stack of yearbooks, the six missing ones from the shelf.

But how did they get in here? And why? Did she know I'd been looking for these only minutes ago?

She looked down at the book and then toward the door. "You must go now."

Okay ... was that code for "Take the books with you?"

"So ... can I borrow these?"

Another sound like the flapping of wings came from deeper down the hall, and her gaze sharpened. "Go!"

I grabbed the six books, spun, and pulled open the door, praying to every deity in all of history that the king and high mage would be gone.

Stepping into the Alpha Academy library, I sagged in relief to find I was completely alone.

Thank the mage.

Midnight Kisses

My mind reeled with the conversation Kian and the king had had but mostly with the secret library and the silver-haired mage I'd met. This school held more secrets than a beach had sand.

Pushing all of that from my mind, I sank to the ground between the aisles with an overwhelming need to see pictures of my father. I missed him so much it hurt.

Thumbing through the top book, I found that it was my uncle's graduation year. My father was two years younger and would have been a second year.

I flipped through it until I spotted my uncle smiling in his cap and gown, and a lump of emotion filled my throat. My father stood right next to him, holding bunny ears over his cap. He had his other arm around my Uncle Mackay. Mackay had the same lithe build and the same wide-set, pale blue eyes that both Dad and I had. What would he say if he were here now?

Tears pricked the corners of my eyes as I stared, and my throat tightened.

"Miss you, Dad," I whispered, running my fingers over the page. My uncle and father were the best of friends. They did everything together growing up and never had the typical alpha sibling rivalry. I flipped through the pages, stopping when a group photo caught my eye.

My stomach dropped.

I knew it! I knew my father would *never* lie to me.

There was Dad, in a suit, at some party, grinning ear

to ear. But my uncle was grinning like a lunatic, his golden-blond hair tousled and messy. Uncle Mackay leaned to the side, off-balance, pulled by another young man on his left. I stared, jaw gaping, at the young man ... the spitting image of *Rage*, except this version of him was laughing, arm around my uncle like they were the best of friends. Dark black hair, green eyes, and swoon-worthy smile. It wasn't Rage though; it was his dad.

I flipped through the other yearbooks, looking for pictures of my uncle Mackay. In every single group picture I found Mackay, Rage's dad was there too—playing volleyball on the beach, studying in this very same library, both of them with arms around girls, one of whom looked a lot like Rage's mom. Picture after picture told a story.

A bell sounded, jarring me from my trance, and I swore. Late for lunch service meant I got to march through a line of shame.

I shoved the six yearbooks into my bag and zipped it up. I mean, it wasn't stealing, right? The mage lady gave them to me, and they were technically staying on school property. Totally legit. Now I had the proof of what I'd told Rage. I might be wrong about a lot of things, but *this* wasn't one of them.

My uncle and Rage's dad were friends. Best friends from the looks of it.

Somehow, holding the proof in my hand wasn't nearly as gratifying as I'd hoped. In fact, the idea of going to Rage to shove this in his face made my stomach turn.

I ducked out of the aisle and then the library, racing through the building toward my lunchroom servitude, mulling over why I didn't want to march over to Rage and show him the pictures in my bag.

It was like the ultimate *I-told-you-so*, and while there would be some sense of vindication for me ... I spent most of my time on rocky ground with Rage, and this might push us past our breaking point.

I needed to wait for the right time, and even though I wanted it to be today... it wasn't.

Chapter 15

THE NEXT MONTH passed by in a blur of activity. The leaves on the trees started to turn golden yellow and burnt orange with the promise of fall and sweet pumpkin coffee. I went through the motions with Master Carn, letting him spoon-feed me while I studied by myself in the evenings. After weeks hunched over the advanced fire textbook, one night, at 1 a.m., I finally made a fireball!

The next day, I grinned like a lunatic when Rage made one and I stepped up next to him with one in my own palm. Master Carn nearly passed out and then fled the room—off to report to the king most likely.

I stood in Fire Studies with Rage watching me with his inscrutable gaze.

"How are your lessons with Honor?" His gaze traveled the length of my body as if he could see evidence of my progress on my exposed skin. Of course, he knew

I couldn't shift. They all probably talked about it at dinner. How embarrassing.

The fireball I'd been building fizzled out in my palm, but I puffed my chest out and muttered, "Fine."

"So you can shift on demand if danger appears?" Rage asked, stepping in front of me.

I took a step back and bumped into a table.

Rage inched forward. The weight of his attention made me aware of our proximity, and a thrill of excitement shot through me.

Gah! Why did I care about him or his attention? Worse, why did my body react every single time he drew near? Like my brain short-circuited.

Because he was a freaking hottie, that's why. All the Midnight boys were.

Keep it together, Nai!

"Why does it matter to you?" I raised my gaze to meet his, but all my irritation fled at the heat I saw in his eyes.

His lips parted as his breath grew shallow. He placed his hands on either side of the table, boxing me in. His gaze dipped to my mouth, and for one irrational moment, I thought he might kiss me.

I licked my lips, feeling heat pooling low in my belly. Without thinking through my next words, I spoke in a low breathy whisper: "It's not like you care."

Oh, but I wanted him to. I wanted to close the distance and see if he tasted like my mate. I wanted to kiss him—feel him. This energy between us ... could he feel it too?

Rage clenched his teeth and stepped back, shuttering his gaze. He swallowed hard, and when he spoke, his voice was rough. "It's my responsibility to see that each student is safe."

Meaning: he didn't care. Not beyond his "responsibility" and possibly a physical attraction he was more than willing to fight. If he were my mate, would he be able to fight it?

The spell broke, and I cursed my body for wanting him. At least, Justice was polite—even nice usually. Rage? Except for the occasional possessiveness or concern he exhibited on behalf of his position, he didn't care.

"Fine," I snapped, spinning away from him. "Then why don't you check in with my instructor, Honor? I'm sure he'll give you a report on my progress or lack thereof." I jerked my head toward the door. "Just like Master Carn is giving a report to your uncle."

Rage frowned. "That's not true." He looked at the door with worry as if he'd only now noticed that Master Carn had left me high and dry in the middle of my studies.

I grabbed my books and headed for the exit. "Sure it isn't. Just keep telling yourself that, *Prince Rage*."

As the door clicked shut behind me, I tried to shove away the sense of gloom our interaction caused. I shouldn't care what he thought of me or my clan.

Stupid alpha male.

~

AFTER SERVING DINNER THAT NIGHT, I headed out of the cafeteria, startled to see Justice waiting at the door.

"May I walk you home?" he asked.

Uh... "Okay."

He smiled, and my stomach flipped.

My thoughts went back to when I'd gone to thank him for going to Dark Row to get the spell to wake me, and he'd just nodded, letting me speak with zero interruptions. Then, when I finished, he'd said, "I'd do anything for you."

Total one-eighty from when they'd come to pick me up in Montana.

I felt like all the signs were there, declaring him as my mate, but ... every time I was firmly in Team Justice's camp, something happened to throw me off. Every time ... except now.

We crossed through the courtyard, and I felt like everyone was staring. One glance confirmed everyone *was* staring, which only made me feel weirder.

I stole a side glance at Justice and pulled to a stop at his intense gaze.

"What's wrong?" he asked, facing me.

Was he joking?

"I know it's one of you. It has to be." It slipped out of my mouth before I could stop it. I took a deep breath, but when I spoke, my voice still shook. "Just tell me."

His eyes widened for a second before softening, and he shrugged noncommittally. "I don't know what you're talking about."

Mother Mage of all things holy, I was going to kill him!

It was torture not knowing who my mate was. I stroked the covered marks on my ring finger, and his gaze lingered there. "Why even walk me home, Justice? Why be so nice to me *all of a sudden*?" I shook my head and waved him away. "I know how to get home, okay. I don't *need* company."

Unless you're my mate. Just tell me already! Then I can slap you for ignoring me all this time, and we can make out.

"No, wait." His expression cleared, and he offered a soft smile of apology. "I thought we were friends."

At least I thought it was a smile of apology. "Then what's up? What do you need?"

After a deep breath, he said in a rush, "Are you going to the Samhain party? Not that you have to, but it's kinda tradition for everyone to go. I mean—like with Kaja and them, are you going?"

He stepped in front of me to block my escape. The heat of his body radiated warmth, but ... it hit me in that moment: I didn't want it to be Justice. For whatever cruel reason, I wanted my mate to be his slightly larger, definitely meaner brother. The universe obviously hated me because it was so clearly Justice. He was nicer, *consistently nicer*, and he'd basically just asked me to the Samhain dance.

"Not sure," I said honestly. "The beach party turned out to be a shitshow, and the one before that..." I had no words for the yo-yo of emotions that had plagued me since the masquerade, so I shrugged. "Anyway, I'm not sure I want to go to another one."

Justice nodded, his green eyes flaring. "I get that."

"Really?" I asked, picking up my pace again. "Did you not have fun at the masquerade? Or did you and your hook-up get interrupted like Rage?"

Okay, I was prying, so he could sue me. Screw the stupid rules!

Furrowing his brow, he asked, "Is that what he said happened?"

I laughed. "What do you mean?"

Did Rage lie?

"Nai..." Justice said, leading me up to the door of my house. "No one talks about what happens at the masquerade."

"Yeah, yeah," I waved him off, annoyed. "I gotta run. Thanks for walking me and all that." I moved to go inside, and his arm snaked out, his hand grasping me by the bicep.

I spun to face him, and he pinned me with his vibrant gaze, causing me to swallow hard.

"So," he said, his voice low and husky, "about the Samhain party ... will you please consider going?"

Was he asking me? Like on a date? Could you even

have a date when everyone wore a mask and had voice modifications?

I shrugged again. "I dunno. The last party I went to, I almost died."

The occasional nightmare about the beach party still woke me up.

He frowned, his gaze going to the puckered scar on my arm, and his eyes flashed yellow. "That won't happen again. *Ever.*"

I didn't mean to trigger his instinct to protect, but clearly, I had.

I studied his face, and even though his features were nearly identical to Rage's, there was no way to confuse the two brothers. So why did my thoughts keep drifting back to the eldest brother? Probably because we had so much unresolved conflict.

But Justice was ... nice. He was being nice. And he'd been consistently nice ... for weeks.

After opening the door, I glanced over my shoulder.

Justice still stood there, watching me, his eyes wolf-yellow.

"I'll think about it." The words tumbled out of my mouth before I could think them through, and he rewarded me with a heart-stopping grin.

"Good." He winked at me. "See you there, Nai."

"Hey, I said I'd think about it!" I called after him, but apparently, we both knew I was going.

Dammit.

THE ENTIRE NEXT DAY, my mind was unsettled. I couldn't wait until that night so that I could go for a run. When darkness fell over the island and the moon rose high in the sky, I quickly changed and shifted into my wolf, hoping to see my mate. We'd been meeting up now for the past several weeks, running and playing in wolf form. It was carefree and beautiful without any of the human drama.

The second my nose hit the damp earth, I smelled him.

His wolf came out of the tree line and nuzzled me. *'Missed you.'*

I nipped his tail. *'You're it!'*

I took off into the trees, jumping over fallen logs, hearing him racing right behind me. His wolf was faster than mine, but he let me win. A lot. We raced into the forest, only stopping when we were both out of breath and panting.

He led me to a creek where we both lapped at the water.

Why couldn't it be like this when he was human? I didn't need him to parade around and tell everyone we were mated, but...

'Mate sad,' his wolf said.

I faced him, studied his features, and wished for the ten-millionth time that I knew who he was.

'Yes, I'm sad. I wish you trusted me—that your human trusted me.'

Before he could answer, a twig snapped, and we both scented the air.

'Male wolf.' I curled my lip in disgust. This wolf smelled of whiskey and smoke and foreign wolf.

My mate crouched low, growling.

Shit. The male was closing in.

'Rogue. Get down!' my mate snarled to me.

Something in the tone of his voice told me this wasn't a matter of dominance, and I ducked as he launched himself forward—into the air and over me, crashing into another wolf with dark, honey-colored fur.

Feral snapping bounced between the two males, their fur a moving blur as they snapped so fast I could barely tell who was who. My heart raced as I watched the fight, but for me to jump into the fray could make things worse, not better. A blur of fangs precipitated a flash of crimson…

Oh Mage! The moonlight came through the trees just in time to light up the two wolves fighting. The honey-colored wolf bit down on my mate's shoulder, and his low growl became a high-pitched whine.

'No!' I lunged forward, snarling, intent to intervene when the crunch of bone punched me in the gut.

Instinct took over.

Charging forward, I snapped at the attacker's tail, biting clean through the end.

The golden-colored animal yipped in pain, releasing my mate, and I darted away, spitting out the chunk of bone and fur. My mate pushed off the ground where he'd been on his back and lurched forward, reaching out with his uninjured paw to swipe at the rogue wolf's face. The hit was so hard it knocked the wolf off balance, and that's when my mate attacked.

The second the honey-colored wolf fell backward, my mate launched on him with the grace and speed of a seasoned hunter. The two wolves slammed into the dirt, and my mate dove forward with a vicious snap of his muzzle.

The golden wolf's howl of pain cut off with a wet gurgle.

The human part of me winced, but my wolf felt nothing but pride.

Much like watching my father fight, I was pleased my mate was fast and precise.

With one jerk of his head, my mate threw the hunk of honey-colored fur right at my feet like a prize. He'd just torn out the other wolf's throat.

He faced me then, his muzzle covered in blood.

I blinked,stunned with the emotion welling within.

'Go,' he said, drawing near me. *'Go home.'* He limped forward, nudging me with his bloody snout. *'Must keep mate safe.'* He nuzzled my neck.

'No, you're hurt.' My wolf sniffed his shoulder injury, and a high whine emanated from my throat. It was bad, the meat and bone exposed.

'I'm fine. Go home.' He nudged me with his head.

When I didn't move because both my wolf and I didn't want to leave him, he dipped his head low, in submission. *'Please? Guards coming. Go.'*

He'd *asked*, not as an alpha. As an equal. As if he knew this would be the best way to get me to agree. Fierce pride and ... *love?* Or ... maybe just pride flashed through me, and I nuzzled him back. If guards were coming, this would turn into a shitshow, and he was trying to protect me. My clan already had enough infractions on it—maybe this would get me kicked out? But not him...

'Go. Mate be safe. Please.' He pushed my chest with his head, and my wolf skidded backward a little.

'Okay.' I finally agreed. *'But send word tomorrow that you're okay. A letter. Something,'* I begged him.

I couldn't leave him like this. It was torture. A howl rose up in the night, and I knew the guards were coming. Had they scented all that blood? Maybe there were other rogues on campus.

With one last look at my injured mate standing over his kill like a hunter claiming its prize, I ran.

My heart hammered the whole way home. This strange feeling crawling through me tethered me to my mate—*willingly*—for the first time. Was this sensation love? Loyalty? I had no idea what to call it, but it was binding and freeing all at once.

The wolf of my mate fought *for me*—which meant the wolf part accepted our bond—accepted *me*—even *loved* me. But had the human side of him changed his feelings? Was he in agreement with his wolf? Or would he treat me as he had after the party—as something to hide, to be ashamed of?

If only I knew who, I could ask him.

After making it back to my dorm, I lay awake for hours, tossing and turning. How bad was my mate injured? Would he need more skill than a normal healer could give?

Why did I leave? I should've stayed and helped him or called a healer. The temptation to sneak over to the healing unit in the castle was nearly overwhelming. The only thing holding me back was the risk. If I got caught by one of the guards, what would I say?

The king and douchebag Kian were already "looking into" the fated mates. How could I explain a late-night gallivant that ended with an injured wolf and a dead rogue?

So I just lay there, replaying the scene over and over in my head. But the things that stuck out the most were... *'Mate. Home. Safe. Please.'*

Something warm and comforting unfolded inside my chest, the sensation blossoming as I thought of the black wolf. All the feelings of a tender ... mate.

Only ... we couldn't ever be together. Not really. We were from different clans.

At most, we'd have midnight runs over the next four years, fading kisses at masquerade balls before we'd both have to return to our respective packs. And take a breeding mate.

Tears pricked my eyes. I let them slide down my cheeks unchecked.

Either the Fates were wrong, or the rules were. Why did it matter if we were from different clans? How could being together with my mate be a crime? So many questions and zero answers.

Eventually, I fell asleep, my pillow damp with tears.

Chapter 16

THE NEXT MORNING, Nell burst through the door, her eyes wide. "Oh, thank the mages," she declared, her shoulders slumping. "I'm so glad you're okay."

I wiped the crusty remnants of tears from my eyes as I sat up, frowning.

"There was an attack last night, in the woods," Rue said, appearing over Nell's shoulder.

Kaja pushed aside her sisters, forcing her way into my room and shutting the door behind her. She held two paper cups in her hands, both full of French toast sticks. Crossing the room to my bed, she shoved one at me as she sat on the edge. "*Everyone* is talking about it."

She took a large bite, and her eyes rolled back in her head as she moaned. "You should eat those before I decide to take them back."

Nell grabbed my left hand to hide my mate marks while the last remnants of a bad night's sleep left me.

Rue chewed on her lip. "Attacks on students don't happen on Alpha Island. Like ... ever."

Here we go. I sucked in a deep breath and then blurted, "I know, I was there."

All three of them gasped, and Nell's grip on my hand went slack as it fell to my lap. Still, I trusted them. More importantly, I needed someone to talk to since the school failed to offer therapy. A big oversight, in my opinion, especially with their sucky security.

Rue's eyebrows hit her hairline, and Kaja gaped.

"You were ... there?" Nell asked.

I nodded. "Yeah. With my mate, who... got injured."

"Holy shit!" Kaja stammered, leaping to her feet, her breakfast now forgotten. "Mother of mages!" She paced the room, shaking her head. "I can't even..."

Weird reaction.

Not that I was exactly Zen about the whole thing, but ... picking up one of the sticks, I nibbled on the flaky sweetness. Oh, yummy. Around a mouthful, I asked, "What? What's wrong?"

A sly grin pulled at Nell's lips. "The student who was injured, the one sent away for a special *royal* healer off-island, was one of the Midnight princes."

The room swam, and the color must have drained from my face because Nell reached out and grasped my shoulders. "You okay?"

Midnight Kisses

I gulped, nodding. This was it, the proof I'd been waiting for. I told myself my mate could be a close friend of the Midnight brothers. Hadn't he said as much in the garden when we first kissed? That his friend told him of the place. But this ... this was proof. "So, my mate is..."

Kaja shook a French toast stick at me, flinging syrup onto the floor. "Obviously Rage or Justice! Oh, my stars, what I wouldn't give to mate with either of them."

Something about her statement made me laugh, but the sound was hollow. Having it confirmed that either Rage or Justice was my mate ... hurt. Why wouldn't he tell me? I could think of only two reasons:

1. embarrassment
2. cowardice

Well, plus, there was that whole thing about who's family member killed who. I'd call that resentment. So maybe three reasons. But the first two were stupid, and the third one was wrong.

My thoughts drifted to the two Midnight princes. Despite Rage's hot/cold and sometimes ugly personality, he lit a fire inside of me. Then, there was Justice. Equally icy at times, but lately ... he was definitely thawing.

All of Nell's excitement fell from her expression, and then she shrugged. "No details were given, so no idea which one it was. I heard the alpha king freaked out. *Livid.* But their mom sent them to a special healer off-island for a rapid recovery."

Huh…

An epiphany hit me like a truck then, and I grinned. This would be easy. If Rage was missing from class today … he was my mate. And if he was there, my mate was Justice. I'd find out once and for all who *he* was and then confront him.

Everyone grew quiet. I got dressed and forced myself to finish eating. As the morning progressed, a weight settled beneath my breastbone, echoing my fears from last night. My movements felt like walking through quicksand, and icy depression settled over me like a heavy blanket. Not knowing who my mate was but knowing he was a Midnight prince should've made me happy, but the confirmation only unsettled me, making me feel melancholy.

I didn't need a Ph.D. in psych to know that beneath my anger was fear. Fear that either Rage or Justice was ashamed to be mated to *me*, and that stung hard. I understood the rules, that we couldn't be public about it, but for him to not even tell me? His distrust stung the most.

When I opened the door to my Fire Studies class, Master Carn looked up from his desk, but the rest of the room was empty. The lack of Rage's presence sent my heart into my throat.

"Where's Rage?" I blurted, louder and far more demanding than respectful.

Master Carn furrowed his brow and straightened in his chair. "Off-island with his brothers."

Brothers? "They're *all* gone?"

He rolled his eyes. "Didn't you hear one of them was injured in the attack last night?"

My whole body tensed as I nodded. "Yes, but which one?"

"That is something you can gossip about with your friends on your own time."

Frak frick fook!

"But *all* of them went off-island?"

Of course they did. I would too if I had a sibling injured.

"Maybe you should stop worrying about boys and start focusing on your studies for the midyear test. It's only a month or so away."

I nodded. Time to eat humble pie. "Yes, Master Carn."

He gave me a curt nod. "Good. Then when you're done with your studies and dinner service for the day, meet me here."

"Why?" I studied him, looking for a hint of something.

"It's a surprise."

I hated surprises, *especially* here, because none of them were ever good.

I nodded and then settled into my coursework,

feeling the absence of the giant douchebag I'd come to miss. I hoped was okay.

The day dragged on with a special torture. Justice, Honor, Noble and Rage were all gone from lunch and dinner. Now, I had to meet Mr. Carn for my "surprise" when really, I just wanted to inspect the Midnight princes for shoulder wounds.

I headed down the hallway just as Master Carn stepped out the door.

"Ready?" he asked.

Before I could respond, he walked off, taking massively long strides further into the building.

Okay.

Please don't lead me to the king's dungeon and kill me.

We traversed the hall, and every snatch of conversation I overheard was regarding the attack or how one of the Midnight princes was injured. The one bit of news—or rumor—that caught my ear was that the attacker was a rogue wolf from the mainland.

Shady.

My thoughts were so deeply consumed that I bumped into Master Carn when he came to an abrupt stop.

"Sorry," I muttered, backing away.

Master Carn huffed but said nothing else as he drew a key from his pocket, which he used to unlock a stone door.

I glanced down the long concrete hallway, first to the right and then the left. "Where are we?"

Midnight Kisses

He grunted, pulling open the door.

My fears of dungeons evaporated with the sight of Kaja, Nell, Evil Barbie, and one of her sisters all seated on a gray mat. I passed my instructor and crossed the threshold into a gymnasium of sorts, but it was fully made of concrete, from the floors to the ceiling. On the far wall was a cache of glittering weapons.

Cool.

"Young ladies," Master Carn greeted the others.

Nell and Kaja waved excitedly at me while Mallory and her clone sister Heather just crossed their arms and glared.

Backatcha.

"The midyear practical is slowly creeping up, and with the recent attacks, the king has asked that all alpha heirs start practicing within a group. This will help strengthen your abilities, both individually as well as collectively."

Ugh. Why was Evil Barbie in our group?

"Nell will brief you on a few details of the exam and give you some strategies to help you do well. The other professors are doing the same with their students. Good luck."

With that, he left, locking the door behind him…

"Did he just lock us in?" Kaja said, her eyes widening.

Exactly my thought!

Nell chuckled. "It's for our safety as well as theirs. Imagine poking your head into the room and getting hit in the face with a fireball. This is a practical skills gym. No one in or out without a key. Don't worry. We can leave."

She held a key up as if for further reassurance.

"All right," I grinned. "So, give us the deets."

Nell cleared her throat. "So, here's what you need to know—"

"My sister already told me." Mallory pointed to her sister Heather and rolled her eyes until they stuck to the ceiling. "We play *magical* 'capture the flag.' A demonstration of our skills for the High Mage Council and king."

After Mallory finished with a huff, Nell snapped her mouth shut with a click of teeth.

"Yeah, well, it's a bit more complicated than that." Nell's gaze bounced to each of us, and she continued: "A student died two years ago. If you don't practice enough, not only could you fail to return for studies the second half of the year, you could fail to draw another breath. Did your sister tell you that?"

Nell glared at the mute blonde next to Mallory.

Mallory blanched and then glared at her sister. "No."

"All right! Well, now you all know." Nell clapped her hands together. "The trickiest part about the midyear practical is you'll need to show your skills to get high marks, all while protecting your flag. They change things around every year. Last year, we were teamed with heirs from other clans."

Midnight Kisses

My stomach dropped. What if they put me on a team with Justice or Rage?

I leaned forward, trying to absorb all the info I could. Should I be taking notes?

"But this year could be different. Don't count on anything. It's deep in the woods. Two to four teams, depending on the size of the class year. Capture the flag ... by any means necessary."

"I'm sorry ... what?" I asked. "Like anything goes?"

Nell nodded. "*Anything* goes. You can throw a fireball at Mallory's head and won't get in trouble. The king wants all graduates to be warriors. Only the best to lead our packs."

I grinned, imagining throwing fireballs at Evil Barbie. "That sounds badass."

"Oh, piss off, all of you," Mallory snapped.

"Get your weapons," Nell said.

We raced toward the far wall, which held an assortment of blades, and excitement replaced my previous gloom. I needed this. A solid workout, without almost dying.

As I was reaching for my weapon, booming thunder rocked the room, and the concrete floor swayed.

What the...?

My ears rang as I stumbled backward in shock.

"Get down!" Nell shouted, dropping to the ground and putting her arms over her head.

I dropped, following her example just as another blast rocked us.

My ears buzzed. Pieces of concrete rained down as smoke rolled into the room. Glancing to the side, I saw Nell pop up, waving her arms through the silty air. Following her example, I climbed to my feet, and Kaja bumped me.

"What the fu—" Nell's eyes widened as a half dozen figures strode into the room.

It took a nanosecond for me to process the situation and draw conclusions.

1. The people walking through the smoking doorway weren't *people*.
2. The assortment of shifters—including bear, panther, fox, selkie, and hawk—weren't here for a tea party.
3. We were under attack. *Again*.

"Weapons!" Nell shouted.

Practical practice just got *real*.

I grabbed a set of blades and tossed them to Mallory, who caught them smoothly and then spun with a ferocious look on her face. Barbie's clone grabbed another set while I handed a pair to Kaja.

I went to hand a long broadsword to Nell when she shook her head at me. "I'm shifting."

Before I could finish nodding, pelts of cinnamon fur rippled down her arms and across her chest, and she dropped to all fours as her clothes ripped from her body—her wolf body. I grabbed two blades and spun to face the attacking pack.

A selkie warrior, dressed in black leather armor, pointed his sword right at me. "You killed my mate."

Mariah Carey? The psycho who sang every student into a stupor while they tried to kill us?

Was I supposed to apologize?

"Then take her and go!" Mallory shouted, dropping into a defensive stance with her blades out.

Bitch. Note to self: never trust Mallory. One hundred percent treacherous.

The selkie warrior shook his head. "The alpha king stole this island from us, and we want it back for our kinds. Every single alpha heir will be slain in retribution."

Probably not the best time to chat about negotiation, but … really?

The bear shifter reared up on his hind legs and roared, a fierce and terrifying battle cry.

Wolf-Nell tipped her head back and howled, a deep and chilling answer of "Hell no!"

There was no getting out of it now. Where were the palace guards? This place sucked on security.

A blur of feathers drew my eye upward just as a hawk dove at my face, talons extended. Bird shifters loved to go for the eyes. Taking out the throat was then a lot easier.

Evil bastards.

Pivoting into my fighting stance, I raised my left

arm, blade in hand, blocking the hawk's path to my eyes. The bird tore into my arm with its talons and lunged with its beak. I crouched low as fiery pain scorched my skin. With a scream of defiance, I rotated and swung. In one fluid movement, I sliced through the hawk's neck, severing its head clean off.

The two pieces fell to the ground with a muted thud and then started to shift back to their human form—a fair-haired girl close to my age now lay beheaded at my feet. A sick feeling tightened my throat.

I'd killed *again*.

"Nai, Look out!" Kaja screamed, breaking through my stupor.

Spinning on my heel, I pulled my swords up just as the warrior selkie swung his blade. I parried.

Clack. Clack. Clack.

When his pace slowed, I glanced toward my friends to check on them, and my stomach turned with dread. The bear had cornered Kaja, and Nell's wolf was on his back—but he was big.

Too big for one or two wolves.

Barbie and her clone were locked in a fight with the fox and panther shifters, and props to Mallory #1 and #2, they looked to be holding their own.

The ringing in my ears from the explosion had faded, and the screams filtering in from outside told me that we weren't the only ones fighting. If the selkie spoke the truth, the entire campus was likely at war.

Focusing on the selkie warrior before me, I considered my options. This was kill or be killed, and I needed to hurry to help Nell and Kaja take down the bear.

Pulling from deep within my core, I let the power of fire fill me. As it coursed down my arms, I dropped one of my swords and slid in close to the warrior, grabbing him by the throat.

His eyes widened. "What...?"

I sent the flames out through my fingers; the fire licked up the side of his face, catching on his hair. The scent of charring flesh turned my stomach, but I wouldn't quit.

This was war.

A blood-curdling bellow ripped from his throat. Flailing, he dropped his sword, and his arm connected with my chest, the force throwing me backward, away from him.

I landed on my butt with a jarring reverberation. Climbing to my feet, I glared at the vindictive warrior, now set aflame. I'd worked with my water power enough that I could pull the water from the air to quench the fire ... but I didn't.

As he writhed on the floor, I scooped up my other blade and ran to help Kaja and Nell. When I neared, time slowed. The bear swiped at Kaja, his claws raking across her abdomen. As she pitched forward, he rotated... coming back along the same trajectory.

"No!" I screamed.

He hit her with the back of his paw, and my best

friend looked like a garish ragdoll as she sailed through the air. Her body hit the wall with a sickening thud, and she crumpled to the ground, blood dripping from the gashes on her stomach, seeping through her clothes.

Rage and heat exploded in my chest; fire blazed from my hands like flamethrowers. Nell's wolf glanced over her shoulder. Her eyes went wide before she rolled off the bear's back and scooted away several paces.

The searing pain in my chest expanded, and I let it fill me—welcomed it because this power would *destroy* that beast.

"Come on!" I screamed at the bear. "Face me!"

The black furry monster turned, and I raised my hands, now covered in live flame all the way up to my shoulders.

He roared, and I flung my hands forward, thrusting my fire magic at him. The fur on his chest ignited, and the flames spread, turning his body into a ball of flames in an instant.

Mallory's slight frame was a blur to my left, but I kept the majority of my attention on the burning bear.

Reaching back, she chucked her sword. It flew across the room, sliding into the bear's chest like a knife through butter.

The huge animal keeled over, landing with a thump.

I released the hold on my magic, but the searing pain in my chest continued to swell. Glancing down, I gasped as I saw the skin on my chest was glowing.

Tugging at the neckline, I watched as the mark of the flame element burned into my skin, right between my breasts.

What the mage?

"Kaja!"

Nell's scream ripped me from my thoughts, and I jerked my head up to see Nell holding her sister, my BFF, limp and bleeding out, in her arms.

Chapter 17

THE ENTIRE CAMPUS was littered with bodies. All around us, people lay dead or dying, but I kept my focus on Kaja. Nell and I carried her to the castle, desperate for the best healer, only to discover every healer in the castle ward had been killed in the battle.

Before I could ask Nell what to do, a male voice boomed through the air like a magical PA system. "Anyone with healing abilities, report to the castle. All other students, please lock yourself in your dorm until a teacher comes to check on you."

Nell magically staunched Kaja's bleeding abdomen with her water power and then went to work on the small gash on the side of her head. Then, we took her to Harvest Dorm, settling inside and locking the door.

"Stay here with her while I go get help?" Nell asked. "I'll see if any other healers survived."

Like there was anywhere else I'd go.

I settled in at Kaja's feet to monitor her, and both Nell and Rue dashed off to try to find another healer. Mother Mage, let the guard at the castle be wrong, that at least one healer survived. Kaja's other sisters, Mele and Fiona, hadn't been by either, and I hoped they were okay.

An agonizing half-hour later, the twins returned to the Harvest dorm, both wearing matching wary expressions.

"It's a madhouse out there. How's she doing?" Nell studied her sister, who lay in bed, still unconscious. I'd been staring at the rise and fall of her chest, but the rate of her breaths was increasing.

"Not bleeding anymore, but she hasn't woken," I told them. "Is it normal to breathe that fast?"

Nell frowned.

I'd cut away Kaja's uniform and wiped all the blood from her skin to better assess her stomach wound. No more bleeding, thanks to Nell's water magic, but what if Kaja had internal bleeding? She hadn't stirred once, and my anxiety continued to coil tighter and tighter until I felt I might burst.

"Did you find another healer?" I looked past them at the entryway, expecting one to walk through any moment. "A strong one?"

Nell's voice was hollow. "*All* the castle healers are dead."

Panic flooded me so fast my hands shook. I mean... the guard said as much to us when we took Kaja there, but I thought for sure she would have found at least one...

How could that be?

The twins stepped closer, and Rue pulled out a stethoscope and blood pressure cuff, which they must've gotten from the castle. After turning on every light in the room, the muted tones of twilight outside fled in the artificial brightness. Kaja's room was decorated in the vibrant greens of life, and with the lights on, the contrasts became even more noticeable. My bestie's skin was whiter than a ghost.

Thick scabs covered the once open gashes on her face and another on her stomach, but Kaja looked *bad*.

I hovered as Rue did her assessment, and ten minutes later, she shook her head.

"What does that mean?" I asked.

"Her vital signs are getting worse, not better," Rue stated, her voice shaking with emotion. "I'm not sure..."

She didn't finish her sentence, but I didn't need her to.

"How much blood did she lose?" I asked. "How much can we lose before we won't heal ourselves?" A wolf's regenerative capability was in the blood. Without most of it ... my gaze bounced from Rue to Nell because one of them should know this. Right?

Nell shrugged, and her gaze dropped. In the last half hour, she'd worked herself to exhaustion, leaving the skin beneath her eyes now dark and sallow. "I don't know."

Rue paced the room. "Not a healing mage left on the island. This was a heavily coordinated attack."

"So ... what are our options?" Doing nothing wasn't an option; I wasn't going to lose my bestie.

Nell sank onto the edge of the bed with a sigh, and Rue shook her head, her gaze downcast.

"Mele and Fiona must be in hiding or hurt. I don't know what to do!" Nell got up and paced the room too. "Our clan's land is a two-hour run from here, all the way at the south end of the island. But I'm not sure our father can do much better than me."

"What does that mean?" I waited, and when neither said anything, I screamed, "What does that mean?"

Rue swallowed. "Maybe if she's in a restorative sleep, she'll eventually wake up on her own..."

I strode closer to the bed and leaned toward Nell, narrowing my eyes.

"But..." I swallowed. "You don't think that's what this is."

Nell shook her head, but this time, Rue answered.

"Kaja's vital signs aren't strong enough for this to be a restorative sleep."

Which meant she was dying.

No way in hell would I let that happen.

I paced the room, frantic to think of something…anything…to save my friend. The colors of the sky deepened to black as I stared out the window, and then the answer hit. With a triumphant grin, I spun toward Kaja's sisters. "Didn't Justice go to Dark Row and get a potion to heal me?"

Nell's eyes widened, and Rue paled.

"We need to go there. Surely we can find a potion maker there who can heal her."

Nell glanced at Rue, and my gaze followed, but Rue dropped her chin to her chest.

"Well?" I asked Nell. "Can we do it?"

After a hard swallow, Nell said, "I don't know how to get there."

Crap. That was the reason I needed them; I had no idea either.

"Rue?" Nell prodded, her voice filled with sympathy. "Please? It's for Kaja."

When Rue lifted her chin, her eyes swam with tears. She nodded, but her expression was lined with terror. "We're going to need a boat."

There was a story there, one I wanted to hear later. Right now, I didn't care how Rue knew how to get to Dark Row; I just needed to get there.

As for a boat … pretty sure the selkies were royally pissed with us right now, but if I had to swim with the murderous warriors to save my friend, so be it.

"I know where we can find one," Nell said. "Let's get Kaja and head out."

Midnight Kisses

The night was pitch dark. The campus lights remained off, but we weren't the only ones carrying a makeshift stretcher with a body on it. I saw at least a dozen bodies still on the ground on our way to the boat docks, most of them royal guards.

We left the campus proper and wound down a set of steep wooden stairs to a dock. Several boats were moored there, at least a dozen, and I nearly bumped into Nell when she drew to a stop.

"Are you sure it's safe for me to return?" a man growled, his voice familiar. "Protect the ruler above all. Remember?"

Oh. My. Frickin'. Mother. Mage.

I knew that voice.

Nell pushed us off the path and into the shrubbery surrounding the dock.

"Yes, sir," another man said. "The attack is over."

I watched, feeling equal parts fascination and disgust, as King Declan snapped his fingers toward a boat, and two guards disembarked, joining the three other shifters on the dock.

"Malik, I want every student and teacher with an eyewitness account of the attack to be in my office in the morning. I will find which clan is involved in getting these usurpers on my island and obliterate them!"

"Of course, sir."

The guards scrambled to unload what looked like

the king's duffle bag, complete with embroidered AI insignia.

That bastard packed a bag before he fled to let us fight on our own?

"And what would you like to do about your wife? She was held captive and is badly wounded."

"Hasn't she been healed yet?!" Declan asked—or rather demanded. "How could you—?"

The group strode past us, and we shrank back into the shrubs.

"All of the healers from the castle were killed in the raid, sir," one of the guards said.

The alpha king snarled, and I shrank farther back at the raw power and menace in his voice.

"Well, get back on that boat, and go find me another one from the mainland, you jackass!" the king snapped, the threat clear as if he'd spoken it. "And you'd *better* hope she survives. My heirs adore their mother."

My heirs adore her, not him. Suddenly, I felt very stabby, and I forced myself to take several deep breaths to calm down.

We waited until their voices faded and the one guard had taken the small speedboat and was riding it full-steam ahead back to the mainland. Then, we inched our way out of the undergrowth. Both Nell and Rue's eyes were wide, reflecting the same shock I felt.

The alpha king fled while we were under attack. Even worse, he'd left his injured wife.

We boarded an Alpha Academy crested speedboat

and carefully loaded Kaja's limp form, trying to do all we could to not injure her further. Rue and Nell worked in tandem to unmoor the small craft. As we glided over the water, I leaned over Kaja and whispered, "Hang on, girl. We're gonna fix you, good as new."

Chapter 18

Rue pulled up to a long dock bustling with activity despite the darkness. Or maybe the traffic was because of the cover of night. Either way, dozens of people milled about, their hushed voices creating a low, indistinguishable buzz. Their transactions occurred with a rapidity that made my head hurt, a sleight of hand and exchange of goods. As soon as we tied the boat off, silence descended over the crowd.

Nell jumped onto the dock, and the crowd dispersed, casting wary glances our way. Probably because we were all covered in blood and holding an unconscious girl, driving a boat from Alpha Academy.

"That's quite a welcome," I muttered, sensing the first inkling of unease trickling through my insides. "So, how do we do this?" I glanced down at Kaja and then to her sisters. "Should two of us go and one of us stay here with Kaja? Or should we bring her with?"

Midnight Kisses

I didn't know how this worked. I just wanted to make sure we got a good potion, and Rue and Nell were both a little too quick to say their sister was dying. My attention drifted to the fleeing crowd, still confused that they would all bolt.

Every single one of them ran … except one.

Nell said, "I'm not sure—"

"What are you doing here, *wolves*?" the lone man asked, his deep voice coming from within the folds of his cloak.

Chills ran the length of my arms, and dread sank deep into my gut.

"We are here to do business." I gulped. "Same as any." My voice was firm, a relief because on the inside, I was a mess.

Still several steps away from us, he raised his head and took a deep inhale. "Are you here buying?"

He stepped closer, and my wolf squirmed. Yeah, I had a bad feeling too.

"Or selling?" he asked.

Selling? Selling what?

Before I could protest the absurdity of his question, Rue—*quiet, studious Rue*—replied, "A bit of both."

"I'll give you five gold coins for her liver." The man pulled his hood back and licked his lips, looking at Kaja's limp form. His face was covered with thin white scars draped over a network of black veins.

Eww! Also, hell to the NO!

Nell pulled her sword. "We're not here to sell *her*, you foul creature!"

The man lunged for the boat then and, in the next moment, *froze* midair.

What the...?

My jaw dropped, and Nell jabbed her elbow into my side.

"Oww," I muttered. Glancing up, I locked gazes with the swirly eyes of a high mage, his irises practically glowing from within his hood. He stepped up to the man frozen in midair and flicked his wrist, sending the now petrified body flying. Like a boulder, it crashed into an open tent stall fifty feet away.

Whoa.

He pushed his cloak back, and my jaw dropped with recognition. This was the high mage who'd asked me to choose my elements, the nice gray-haired one with the silver robes.

Crap. We were busted.

My mouth dried, and I waited for him to ream us for being here, only it never came. Still, my heart pounded against my ribs in a desperate attempt to flee. Maybe it wasn't us who'd caused the bedlam. Maybe it was the creepy, swirly-eyed mage.

He looked down his nose at us. "Welcome to Dark Row, ladies. I trust you have good reason to be here?"

I gulped. "Our friend is dying. We need help saving her." After swallowing again, I added, "Also, thanks for saving us."

Probably should've started with that.

He nodded, which I chose to take as approval. As soon as I disembarked the boat and stood on the dock, he spoke again.

"Let me offer you one bit of warning."

Legit, I'd take all the help I could get. Shifting uneasily from foot to foot, I asked, "Yes? What is it?"

I had no idea what he was doing here, and I probably didn't want to know. The high mages were the rulers of our society, and Dark Row was where all of the illegal activities of the magic world took place. Why would he be here? Unless he was here procuring something illegal as well...

He took a deep breath then cocked his head and continued. "Take your injured wolf with you if you mean to keep her intact."

Oh, Mother Mage. I shook my head. *He did not just say that.*

"Thank you," Rue said, inclining her head. "And what do we owe you for this?"

Wait ... why would we owe him?

The sinking sensation of *what-the-hell-is-going-on* settled over me, and I realized just how out of my element I was.

"You never saw me here," he replied and turned to leave.

Pausing, he looked back over his shoulder at us and said, "If you want your friend to be healed, there is only one mage strong enough to do this: Madam Surlama."

He spun around, and we all muttered our thanks to the dude.

I looked down at Kaja. My chest tightened as I thought of us carrying her on a stretcher through a market.

"What I wouldn't give for a wheelbarrow," I muttered.

Nell gasped, drawing my attention, but when I looked at her, she pointed toward shore.

The cloaked high mage was gone, but at the end of the dock sat a wheelbarrow.

Shaking my head, I blew out a long breath. "I have a feeling I'm going to owe him someday."

We set Kaja into the wheelbarrow, and Nell pushed while Rue and I flanked on either side. Rue said nothing as she directed us toward Dark Row and the glowing lights of the black market.

As we approached, my heart raced, and I reached down to give Kaja's hand a squeeze.

This had better work.

Dark Row resembled flea markets I'd seen on TV. Stalls stretched further than I could see, their walls a variety of colors and materials: painted wood and stained canvas. A myriad of scents perfumed the air: the yeasty scent of bread, roasted meat, and bitter herbs. Beneath the recognizable lay other smells, some acrid and others sweet.

We passed a stall filled with vibrant blue flowers, and the wafting scent made me yearn for something I couldn't even name. I reached out to touch one of the petals, and a woman smacked my hand away.

"Don't touch unless you're going to buy, missy!"

Ouch.

I nodded and murmured an apology.

"I smell wolf blood," a man said. Stumbling out from the shadows, he sniffed the air as we passed. Reaching out, he tried to lift the blanket covering Kaja, and I drew one of my blades, pointing it at his neck.

"Touch it, and lose your hand," I warned, pushing the long dagger into the sensitive flesh of his neck.

His gaze dipped to my chest, and he swallowed hard. "Yes, ma'am."

Okay ... that was a first.

Oh, cursed mages.

I'd forgotten. One glance downward confirmed my theory. The tip of my new fire mark poked out from the neckline of my tank-top. I pulled it up and narrowed my eyes at the creeper.

"If you want to sell her for parts, it would be far more merciful to slit her throat now—before you go into the market," he said, eyeing Kaja's body with longing.

I tightened my grip on the sword and growled. "She's going to be healed."

Luckily, he got the message and offered a wide-eyed nod before melting into the crowd.

Holy-frickin'-mage. This place was a nightmare.

"Why do they call it the black market if it's out in the

open like this?" I turned to Nell. Clearly, the high mage knew what was going on here and didn't seem to care.

Nell shrugged. "It's a necessary evil. Even the high council uses it at times."

Hypocrites. How did allowing an illegal market to exist keep the peace or encourage playing by the rules?

Kaja coughed, a wet gurgling sound, and fear gripped my heart in its icy grasp.

"We need to hurry."

I kept my attention fixed on Rue's shoulder as we made our way into the bowels of Dark Row.

"This is Madam Surlama's," Rue said as we approached a tall, black, silk tent. "You two can go in. I'll stand guard outside."

The black tent appeared uninhabited, no soft light beckoning us to come in and no one standing outside either.

"Are you sure?" I asked.

Rue nodded, and her breath quickened. "Just be careful, Nai. She's a dark mage."

"Rue! How do you know that?" Nell gasped.

Dark mages were bad, but the high mage had said Madam Evil-Magic was the only one who could heal Kaja.

"Do we have another option?" I asked Nell.

She blanched and shook her head. "But the cost will be high."

As if cost mattered. This was Kaja.

After a deep breath, I clapped my hands and yelled into the tent. "Madam...?"

Nothing.

Rue closed her eyes and clapped loudly. "Madam Surlama, we are seeking a healer."

The curtain parted, and I gasped.

I'd expected a gangly old hag of a woman, not this ... *goddess* who stood before me, dressed in boho chic. Her long inky black hair fell to her waist in waves, and her alabaster skin was so pale the blue-tinged veins traced her skin like a network of tattoos. Pursing her glossy red lips, she studied us with her vibrant blue eyes. Then, she beckoned us forward with a wave of her hand.

We wheeled Kaja closer, and the mage peeled back the sheet, exposing my friend's entire body.

The dark mage clicked her tongue against her teeth. "On death's door."

"What?" Nell cried.

"Come on, then. Better hurry if you want me to save her." She disappeared behind the black curtain, and Nell and I shared a look.

But we both knew there was no other option.

Stepping forward, we started to push the wheelbarrow into the split in the curtain when Rue's arm came out and clamped over mine like a vise. "If she asks for blood payment, don't let Nell do it."

Blood payment? Was that a thing?

"Promise me," she growled, pain flittering across her face.

"I ... promise."

Rue had clearly come here before, and whatever happened must've been awful. Somehow, none of that surprised me.

"I'll look after them both," I promised the shy twin.

Please don't let me regret that.

She nodded, and then I was pulled into the darkness. Nell and I traversed a dark hallway, following the sound of clinking jars and bottles.

"Where did she go?" I asked.

Nell shrugged, her eyes as wide as my own.

"Umm, miss mage?" Nell called.

"In here, dears."

Dears?

Her voice came from the left, so Nell directed the wheelbarrow that way.

Dark mages were notoriously selfish, so why was this one being so friendly? I didn't like it.

Light filtered into the hallway from a room ahead. A few steps later, we entered a wide-open room with a courtyard visible beyond.

The scent of smoked meat and wet feathers wafted in the air, and I shared an alarmed look with Nell. If it was anyone else besides Kaja needing a healer, I'd be out.

The woman beckoned us again with another wave. "Put her on the table."

She pointed to a gray marble slab that had intricate carvings around its perimeter.

"So you can heal her?" I pressed. "For sure?" I wanted absolute certainty.

She grinned, a full pearly white smile that didn't reach her eyes. "Honey, I know the keeper of souls. There's not much I can't do."

The keeper of souls was like the god of the dead. I gulped. Not exactly the reassurance I'd wanted.

"Come on," Nell nudged me as she hefted Kaja under her armpits with a grunt. I grabbed Kaja's ankles, and together, we hoisted her onto the cold, stone slab.

The mage walked around the marble slab, poking and prodding Kaja's body, finally leaning in at her neck where she took a deep inhale. She straightened and faced us, eyes narrowed.

"She's an alpha heir," she stated. "To heal her will cost you double."

Double ... what? I crossed my arms, but before I could speak, Nell nodded.

"Name your payment."

The dark mage flicked her gaze my way, letting her attention linger on my chest before running the length of my body. Magic washed over me, the same way as when creepy Kian, the high mage, inspected me.

"One thimble of blood." She nodded as if confirming the price to herself.

My stomach dropped. Blood? The one thing I promised Rue I wouldn't let Nell do.

"A thimbleful of blood every full moon, for a year," she added quickly.

"A year?" WTH? Shaking my head, I protested, "What about when school is out?"

That was only about seven months away. Maybe I could barter.

"I'll do it," Nell blurted out.

She thrust her wrist at the mage, and I stepped forward to cut her off.

"Not from you…" The mage waved Nell off and then pointed at me. "From her."

Relief and trepidation washed through me with equal measure. *Why me?* No sooner had the thought crossed my mind than I shook my head. Who cares? I'd help my friend and, for some creepy reason, also get to keep my promise to Rue.

Nell glared at the mage. "What? Why? She's *my* sister."

The stunning dark mage raised one eyebrow. "Because she's more powerful than you."

My cheeks flamed with mortification as if the statement were an insult to Nell.

However, Nell merely nodded before facing me with a pleading look in her eyes. "I can't expect you to do this—"

"Oh, I'm doing it." I extended my arm. "She may be your sister, but she's my bestie. I've got this."

Sort of. I hoped. Once a month, I'd take a boat trip over here, no big deal. *Right?*

Remembering my other friends, I faced the mage. "I'll do it *if* you give me enough potion to save two people."

The dark mage's brow furrowed, and she chewed on her lower lip. Finally, she shook her head. "I don't negotiate."

I frowned as if considering whether or not I was willing to drop my price. But I wasn't. The Midnight prince's mom had shown me kindness even if her husband was a total asshole. He'd left the island during the attack, and she'd nearly died trying to protect her students. I'd save her too. That was non-negotiable. One of them, either Rage or Justice, was my mate, and they hadn't been on campus to protect their mom, so this was the least I could do. This was how a mate should act. Maybe my mate didn't know how to be a good companion and partner, what with the way King A-hole treated his mother.

And Kaja…

I'd been clueless when I started school here, and it would've been an absolute lonely hell if it weren't for her barging into my dorm and befriending me.

I let the silence stretch, my heart thundering against my ribs as my panic swelled. *Come on, greedy witch…*

"Fine," she snapped. "Healing potions for two lives in exchange for a thimble of your blood."

Nell lowered her voice, stepping closer to me, and said, "I don't think you understand. A blood sacrifice is *dangerous*."

"I don't care," I told her, waving away her concern.

Holy-frickin'-mage, this had better work.

The dark mage grinned wide, and her elation made my skin prickle. Holding her hands into the air, she clapped twice, fast and sharp.

A stout hairy man with a hunchback shuffled into the room from the courtyard. "My lady?"

"Fetch two life potions from the dungeon."

Dungeon? I scanned the silk tent, realizing how much bigger it was inside than it had appeared outside.

Magic.

The dark mage crouched and pulled boxes out from under the stone table, muttering to herself.

Nell sidled up next to me, her eyes brimming with tears. "Thank you."

There was no way to tell her all I felt, so I just nodded and squeezed her hand.

"Come ... sit here, child." The mage motioned to a dusty couch at the back of the room that I was 99.5% certain hadn't been there when we first walked in. With one last squeeze, I dropped Nell's hand and walked over to the dubious piece of furniture. When my gaze landed on a jagged knife lying on the armrest next to a giant jar labeled "thimble," I got woozy.

"What's that?" Nell growled, pointing to the jar.

The mage turned, sneering. "This is my thimble."

Nell frowned, and my stomach churned.

Not gonna lie; when the dark mage started cackling, doubt hit me like a pickup truck.

"It's huge! That's not fair," Nell snapped.

The mage shrugged. "If you wanted something smaller, you should have stated so before the contract."

Contract? What the what? When did I sign a contract? Were verbal contracts binding ... *oops*.

Leaning in, she smelled the skin of my palm and then groaned, a guttural sound deep in her throat. "A virgin? I would have given you twenty vials of life potion had I known."

Frick. How did she know I was a virgin? Seriously, mortifying and creepy! Also, I might not be so good at this whole dark mage negotiation thing.

I glanced nervously at Kaja. "Just hurry."

The mage nodded and picked up the knife before she drew it across my wrist with one clean slice.

I hissed as the fresh wound seared across my skin. Holding the "thimble" under my wrist, the mage collected the dark crimson blood oozing in thin rivulets from my arm.

Mother Mage, protect me. The burning began to work its way up my arm, skittering over my shoulder and across the top of my back. Sweat broke out on my brow.

"Ahhh," I hissed, and my cry became a roar as fire exploded from the base of my skull all the way down my neck. Damn. That was another mark! I knew that feeling by now.

Why did this keep happening, and what did these marks mean?

"Are you okay?" Nell's voice warbled above me, and I blinked, trying to focus my now-blurry gaze. I glanced at the giant jar. Wait ... it was halfway full a moment ago, but now it looked empty again.

What the hell?

Wooziness overwhelmed me, and I scanned the area for Nell. As soon as I spotted her, she morphed into Rage.

"It's me. I'm your mate," Nell-Rage said.

"I knew it." My words slurred together, and I started to giggle.

The mage then turned into Justice. "No, Nai, it's me. I'm in love with you."

My eyes widened. *"You* are?"

I had no idea if the mage was professing her love or Justice. Something wasn't right here.

Nell's shrill scream burst through the hallucination, jarring me back to the present. "You're killing her!"

I stared at three blurry-Nells, and they all lunged at me then, yanking my arm out from under the mage's blade. The mage dropped the knife and pulled the jar to her chest with both hands as Nell swiped the blade from the ground and waved it at the witch.

"That's not fair. You tricked her!" Nell bellowed. "That jar is spelled. It never fills."

"If either of you had wanted something specific, you should've demanded it before we sealed the contract." The woman grinned. "Life's not fair; neither is death. Remember that."

She walked away as if Nell threatening her life didn't bother her one bit.

Maybe it didn't.

"Nai, are you okay?"

Nell's concerned face swam into view just before I shook my head to clear my thoughts of Rage and Justice.

Oww. Bad idea. The headache was akin to that cursed blade stabbing my brain. I held my hand out to examine the cut, which was now healing, and croaked, "Fine."

Two of the hunchback dudes shuffled into the room then coalesced into one, carrying two potions in his hand. The purple iridescent fluid danced in the small glass bottle.

Nell gasped. "That's the same stuff Justice got when he saved your life."

Shock ripped through me. Would Justice have seen the same mage? Would he have given a blood sacrifice to save me?

No way…

"Wake Kaja," I said, shoving one of the vials toward Nell. I took the other bottle, the one intended for the Headmistress Elaine, and uncorked it. I wasn't sure I was going to be able to walk out of here in my current state, so I'd have to follow my instinct. Tipping back the vial, I took a tiny swig of the syrupy liquid into my mouth and swallowed. Immediately, my entire body heaved at the revolting taste, and I would've spat the liquid out if I hadn't already swallowed. Even so, I gagged and spit, wishing for a mint...or even a drink of water. Peering back at the vial, I prayed that three-quarters full was enough to save the Midnight princes' mom.

"What is in that?" I rasped.

The dark mage ignored me, whistling happily in the corner as she poured my blood into a huge wine barrel labeled "Virgin Blood."

Before I could repeat my question, Kaja gasped and then started coughing.

Legit, almost dying sucked.

Stumbling toward my BFF, I swayed as the tent spun around me.

Nell tucked the now-empty vial into her pocket, tears streaming down her face. She turned and stepped away from Kaja, catching me by the upper arm just in time for me to avoid a faceplant. "Maybe you should take the other one."

I held my hand out to stop her coaxing. "I took a sip. I'll be okay."

That second vial was for my mate's mother.

We helped Kaja sit up, and Nell dipped her head to look her sister in the eye. "Hey, girl. How you feeling?"

My bestie's hair was matted with blood, and her eyes held dark circles. "Near death ... and jittery."

My head started to buzz, and my body twitched with a sudden need to move.

Nell chuckled. "Well, that's accurate."

Kaja opened her arms, and we all crowded in for a group hug. "I love you guys."

The dark mage stared us down from the corner of the room. "All right, wolves," she growled. "I've got another client, so it's time to skedaddle."

Would she have bled me dry had Nell not intervened? I pushed the thought from my mind. All I could do was bring someone with me next month who'd have my back.

Kaja was still weak, so we lowered her cross-legged into the wheelbarrow. Once she was settled, Nell pushed her toward the entrance of the tent with me trailing behind.

"See you next full moon, virgin!"

I faced the dark mage and gave her a brittle smile.

Next month, I'd tell her to keep the v-word on the down-low.

Geeze.

Maybe I wouldn't even show...

"Just in case you're wondering ... if you don't come, a curse will fall upon you and all of your future children."

Great. I should've known. "What kind of curse?"

She grinned but didn't answer. Of course not.

"See you next month," I growled, and followed Nell out of the dark mage's tent and back into the market.

"Kaja!" Rue screamed, throwing her arms around her sister. When she looked up at me, her gaze fell to the healing gash on my arm. "You did it?"

Nell's eyes widened as she stared at Rue. "Is this where you snuck off to every full moon last year? You were paying a debt?"

Rue swallowed hard. "I don't want to talk about it. Can we just ... go home ... please?"

I patted my pocket. "We need to get this healing life potion to the headmistress."

"Life potion you say?" a man asked, his voice low and growly as he grabbed my arm. "I'll take that off your hands."

I jumped, and a group of five thugs converged from between the tents, knives at the ready.

I was way too depleted of energy to make a fireball; my arms felt like they were filled with lead. We were grossly outnumbered here, so my adrenaline needed to kick in—pronto.

Nell growled beside me as fur sprouted down her arms while Rue stepped in front of Kaja's wheelbarrow.

Before either of them could shift, a dude jumped between us and the goons, bringing with him the scent of sandalwood.

I blinked, and all four Midnight princes appeared before us and then proceeded to kick the shit out of the thugs.

"Rage," I screamed, my heart thundering to life at the sight of my sometimes frenemy.

He pounded the guy in the ribcage, pummeling with his fists until the dude dropped the knife. As the thugs ran off, Rage spun, and—chest heaving—he ran his gaze from my head to my toes.

"Why are you bleeding?" he demanded.

"What are you doing here?" Justice asked.

Noble stepped forward. "Are you hurt?"

They crowded around me, and Rage grabbed my arm and ran his fingers over the still-healing gash. His gaze flicked from me to Madam Surlama's tent and back. "You didn't..."

"What's going on?" Justice growled, bringing the heat of his body closer to me.

I tried to see which of the two boys had been hurt, but it was impossible to tell. For all I knew, that's why they were here, but neither wore a bandage now.

"While you were gone, the school was attacked," Nell said.

Immediately after Nell, Rue said, "Dozens are dead, including all the palace healers."

All of the princes' eyes widened; they had no idea. They must've been here all day... while whichever one was injured healed.

"Kaja almost died," I said, by way of explanation. "And your mom was hurt too." Reaching into my pocket, I handed Justice the serum. "Now we're even."

His jaw dropped, and he blinked at me for several awkward seconds before he managed to swallow. "You ... did this for our mom?"

Rage stepped between us.

"Who attacked you?" he growled in a voice that was

barely human. Black fur ran the length of his arms, and his eyes gleamed yellow.

"Shifters. All kinds." I glanced back at Nell, Rue, and Kaja, and all three sisters nodded.

Nell stepped forward and added, "Bears, foxes, selkies. They've all banded together."

Honor swore. "Come on. We need to get back to the island and help."

I didn't have the heart to say they were too late. They'd find out soon enough.

Chapter 19

SUNLIGHT STREAMED in through my window, and I warily watched the warmth and cheeriness creep across my dorm room. As soon as the light hit my bed, I threw back the covers and rolled out with a groan.

My body was good as new, thanks to that tiny sip of healing potion, but I couldn't say the same for my mind. Legit, someone should have a chat with the alpha king regarding therapy for the students at the academy. Maybe he didn't offer it because any decent counselor would start by telling King Declan that he was a douche-canoe. Not that anyone needed a Ph.D. in psych to figure that one out.

I still couldn't fathom how an alpha could flee a fight; my father never would.

That night, as soon as our boat had hit the shore, Justice shifted into an all-black wolf and ran for the castle at full speed, the healing serum between his teeth.

I hoped it saved his mom.

The next day, classes were canceled for a day of mourning our dead. I laid around all day, resting and going from my dorm to Harvest's to check on Kaja.

Today, things were back to somewhat normal. After a restless night of PTSD, I showered off the crust of cold sweat from my skin and the sleeplessness from my eyes then dried off. Looking semi-zombie-ish, I pulled on my borrowed uniform and piled my silver locks up into a messy bun, only to yank it down again with a snarl as my new mark reflected in the mirror behind me. The three clustered swirls, the symbol for air, branded the back of my neck. I didn't even have power over air…

What were these marks? I'd never seen them on any creature. Only the moon symbol on our foreheads to mark us as alpha heirs.

One more reason I needed therapy.

As I shuffled down the stairs, I heard Nolan in the kitchen, probably rifling through the latest box of groceries from my mate. The Midnight boys had obsessed over my eating after that party on the beach, and then the boxes rolled in. It all made sense now. The temptation to scream obscenities at my cousin simmered just below my throat, but I ground my teeth and beelined toward the door. I needed to get my mate-marks covered before class.

Twenty-two Academy guards, one teacher, all the healers, and one student, Mallory's oldest sister, had died in the coordinated attack the day before yesterday. Not to mention the other shifters, which no one bothered to count, and where was my cousin? The whole frickin' time, he'd been cozy as a cockroach, hiding in our dorm.

Some alpha he'd make.

When I got to fire class, Rage wasn't there. Hopefully, he was with his mother, and she was healed, happy, and whole. If anyone in this hellhole deserved happiness, it was her. How had she put up with King Alpha-Ass for nearly twenty years?

Even though today was midweek, Honor slipped me a note at lunch, saying we had a training session tonight. Dude had no mercy. Granted, my wolf wasn't exactly cooperating, but couldn't I have one night off? Apparently not.

After dinner, I watched a movie at Kaja's and then dragged myself home. Opening the back door to meet Honor, I sighed with relief at his absence from the glen. Maybe he'd forgotten and I could go catch up on some much-needed sleep. Stepping down onto the crumbling patio, I felt the chill of the concrete soak into my bare feet as I stared out at the forest. I'd give him a courtesy five-minute grace period. Because it was Honor.

The weeks of failure, on top of the "you're not like normal wolves" vibe from my first lesson, were all adding up to a big fat no bueno for these private lessons, at least as far as I was concerned.

I glanced at my watch and smiled. At least, tonight was a wash.

'Mate.'

The low rumble of my mate's voice caused a shiver of pleasure to stroke through me, and I grinned with anticipation.

He was one thing both me and my wolf one hundred percent agreed upon.

While the human version of my mate might or might not be a total douche, most of which hinged on whether he was Rage or Justice, he was responsible for the weekly grocery box of fresh fruits, veggies, bread, pasta, and raw meats. It was SO male wolf to make sure a female was fed, but the timing and consistency of his gifts made it seem less a play for power and more a play for my heart. Either way, I couldn't totally hate him.

'Mate. Come.'

Desire to be with my mate brought my wolf to the surface. I stepped off the patio and pulled my shirt off, scanning the darkness. The cooler night temperatures made my skin prickle, but I didn't want to ruin my favorite t-shirt. I unbuttoned my jeans, the eagerness of my wolf driving me to hurry.

'Run? Mate?'

A low growl of a foreign wolf was followed by a yip, and I froze.

Midnight Kisses

No way those two sounds came from the same animal.

'*Mate?*' I sent the question out into the night and waited.

And waited.

Unease unfurled in my chest, and both my wolf and I hesitated as I stood there in my bra and underwear in human form.

Another low growl sounded, and then two black wolves stepped out from between the trees.

The pitch-black animals looked exactly like my mate, but the panicked fluttering of my heart told me that neither of the animals stalking forward was him.

I'd learned that all four Midnight brothers had jet black wolves, nearly identical.

"Honor. Noble. We tried this already, and it didn't work." I stepped back, and my heels bumped against the concrete step of the patio. They were constantly trying to scare my wolf out, to simulate an attack. I was in my bra and underwear, for mage's sake! Quickly crossing my arms over my marks, I glared at them.

"Knock it off!" I yelled at the black wolves.

'*Mate,*' he called for me from the woods, behind Honor and Noble or whoever the other wolf was. '*Come.*'

That voice was definitely my mate. My gaze went to the right where I'd heard him, and my mouth dried.

Another wolf, his coat just as black as the first, prowled toward me, staring at me with gleaming yellow

297

eyes. His lips pulled back, and he snarled. Freaking Midnight brothers!

"Not cool, guys!" My heart slammed against my ribs, pumping adrenaline through me.

'Mate. Shift.'

Did he put them up to this?

'Where are you?' I shouted at him, staring at the three black wolves before me.

My breaths grew shallow, and my wolf retreated until I couldn't feel her—only the strange panic emanating from her presence.

Oh, come on!

These creatures were *her* kind. Why did she tuck tail and retreat?

What was wrong with her?—with me?

I straightened, glaring at one wolf and then the other. "What do you want?" Waving my hands at them to shoo, I yelled, "Get out of here. This is *my* territory."

A fourth and final wolf approached from my left.

'Mate. Shift. Now.'

I froze. All four Midnight wolves were here, including my mate.

Holy Mother of Mages, this was confirmation that my mate was a Midnight prince.

I could feel his presence, his yearning to be with me. But ... which one was he?

The four black wolves advanced until they surrounded me.

"What are you doing?" I asked, my gaze darting

from one to the next, but the question was for my mate. "What is this?"

Instead of an answer, they snarled at me. All of them, in unison.

My heart jumped from panic to full-blown freakout. Would they attack me to force me to shift?

'Shift.' His word was a call to action, and I battled with the desire—almost a desperate need—to force my wolf out. But I couldn't.

'I can't.'

One of them lunged forward, jaws snapping, and I spun away, bumping into another one of the wolves.

"Sorry," I stammered, reaching out to pet the one I'd run into.

'Mate,' he growled, and the sound wound around my core. *'Shift.'*

Panting, I shook my head and begged, "Please. I *can't*. Don't do this to me."

Why couldn't he just understand—

One of the black wolves launched forward, teeth bared, and I stared, filled with disbelief.

No way would my mate ask his brothers to attack me. No way—

I yanked my arm back with a gasp.

"What the hell?" I screamed at them. He'd barely missed me. "Honor, I'm going to kick your ass!"

My mate snarled, and I jerked toward the sound. But instead of attacking me, he charged the animal who'd just lunged my way.

The two wolves snapped at one another, back and forth, and my adrenaline spiked. Crap. Crappity. Crap. Crap. Crap.

These two were brothers. They wouldn't hurt each other.

But I knew better.

Even the loyalty to clan or family would be overruled by the animal's instincts. I'd seen members of my pack, even siblings within our pack, fight. Even if my mate had asked his brothers, and they'd agreed ... all human promises could be forgotten by the wolf.

The snarl of the wolves tore through my entire being.

Could I do something with my magic to break up the fight? Maybe. But which one of them was which? And how much was too much. And—

Two of the wolves turned and then advanced on one.

'Mate. Help.'

His plea shot through me, and I clenched my fists.

Oh, hell no.

No sooner had the thought crossed my mind than my wolf snarled. Seeming to appear out of nowhere, she surged forward. Desperate to save our mate from a fight with his own brother, her instinct overwhelmed me. My body seized, and I pitched forward with a snarl, my bones crunching and rearranging as fur exploded from my skin.

I inhaled, a low guttural growl of warning, and then,

leaping forward on all fours, I sank my teeth into the nearest wolf's flank, not deep enough to cause serious injury but hard enough to be a warning.

The creature yipped in pain, trying to spin toward me, and created the perfect gap.

I released him and pushed through the space toward my mate.

His wolf crossed the space between us and nuzzled me.

'Mate. Strong.'

I inhaled, letting his scent fill me with comfort. He was safe.

He continued to nuzzle me, and suspicion trickled through me. I glanced behind me, and sure enough, the other three wolves were gone.

'You set me up.' I'd meant it to sound accusing, but honestly, I felt nothing but relief that he was okay.

'Mate. Learn. Shift. Safe.'

I knew what he was saying, and I nuzzled him back. While I might not shift in self-preservation, my wolf had no reservations when it came to protecting my mate. *'But I don't know if I can do it on my own.'*

'Practice.'

I snorted, the sound odd coming from a wolf, and then barked with laughter. *'Fine. I'll practice.'*

'Run?' he asked, his yellow eyes alight with enthusiasm.

How could I say no to that?

'One thing first. Thank you for the food.' Even if I didn't

know if it was Rage or Justice, I still appreciated the kindness. I leaned forward and sniffed his once-injured shoulder, but it smelled totally healed.

I didn't want to talk about the attack on the academy, how his mom was doing, why he wouldn't tell me who he was, or anything else. I'd save all that for Samhain in a few days when I could confront his human side. Right now, I wanted one last night with his wolf.

'Mate.' He nuzzled me again and then nipped at me playfully. *'Run.'*

He darted into the darkness, and I chased after him.

THE NEXT MORNING, I woke and ran through my usual routine. Hair in a messy low bun to cover my neck mark, ignore Nolan and hide my mate marks from him as I grabbed breakfast, and then time to head over to Nell.

After crossing the foyer of our dorm, I wrenched the door open and gasped, stumbling to a stop, face-to-back with Rage. Even before he turned, I knew who he was. How exactly? No clue.

More importantly, why was he here?

His black shirt hugged his broad shoulders, dipped around his biceps, and tapered at his waist, accentuating not only his physique but also his wealth. No way those shirts were standard issue.

Out of habit, I snaked my left hand behind my back

to hide my mate mark and then rolled my eyes. How ironic would that be? That I could be hiding my marks in front of my actual mate.

He pivoted and stared down at me, saying nothing.

I stared right back.

My breathing grew more shallow the longer we stood there, him exuding rugged sexiness like spilling a bottle of pheromones. I licked my lips, and his gaze dropped.

I needed out of here pronto or I'd forget how much I hated him. I did still hate him, right?

Yes! I hated all of them. A little. Every Midnight prince held the secret that could set me free. After last night's "training session," it was clear they all knew which one of them was my mate, and like a loyal band of siblings, they told me nothing. Which pissed me off.

"Can I help you with something, Rage?" I snarled.

He cocked his head to the side and narrowed his eyes. "Why are you mad?"

Glaring at him, I snapped, "I didn't say I was mad. I asked you if you needed something."

"But you're angry." He continued to stare down at me, and his expression shifted from scrutiny to pride as his chin jutted and nostrils flared. Crossing his arms over his chest, he filled the small portico, blocking my path. "Why won't you tell me why you're angry?" he asked.

"You already know." My gaze dropped to his fingers, bare of any marks. Of course.

When he said nothing, only swallowed hard, I pressed on. "It's just..."

I pursed my lips, stopping my pathetic plea. I wouldn't chase a mate who didn't want me. Either him or Justice, I wasn't going to beg. I was done and changing course. I wanted nothing more than to get away from here, away from his impenetrable gaze. "Why are you here, Rage?"

He shifted his body weight as if anticipating an attack. "I came to tell you thanks."

I was 71.5% sure what he meant, but that 28.5% wanted confirmation.

"Thanks for what?"

"For saving my mom." His voice grew softer as he continued. "The potion you got saved her life. She ... she's totally fine."

Relief washed through me. "Good. Your mom is cool. She's kind, and it's clear she cares about the students. All of us."

Rage tightened his jaw and swallowed hard. "What does that mean?"

"It means I didn't do it just for *you*, Rage." I leaned closer, and my voice grew sharp. "I did it for Honor and Noble and all of us at the school—but mostly ... I did it for her. Since your despicable, *lame-ass* uncle won't even fight to protect his own wife."

How could the king slink away in fear and leave his wife to be kidnapped and assaulted? I would never bow to that asshole. Ever.

His pulse feathered in his neck, and even if he didn't understand the insinuation, he knew I meant the dig to sting. Crouching to meet me at eye level, he snarled. "You have no idea—"

"Well, if I don't know something," I hissed. "It's only because no one bothered to clue me in. *You* treat me like a pariah—"

"Yeah. *That's* only because Crescent Clan doesn't have the best record for loyalty."

What. The. Hell? This again? My jaw dropped, and I sucked in a breath, trying to rein in my fury. He did *not* just say that.

"I am so over your ignorance. Stay right there!" I whirled back through the doorway and raced to my room, hands shaking. Grabbing the top yearbook, I flipped through the pages until I found one of the pictures of my uncle with his arm around Rage's dad. Then, I stormed back down the stairs, still incensed, through the foyer and out the door. Rage stood there, eyes glowing yellow. I reached out, slamming the thin volume of class pictures to Rage's chest, and growled. "You're the one who's been lied to. You're wrong about Crescent Clan, and as far as I see it, you've been wrong about me."

I shoved past him and stormed across the quad toward Harvest's dorm, hoping Nell would still be there to hide my mate marks.

If Rage was my mate, fate must *seriously* hate me.

Chapter 20

I WAS SHOCKED at how quickly school settled back into its normal, fun-filled routine ... with only one tiny exception. Well, maybe two.

First, the entire student body, save the Midnight princes, buzzed with excitement surrounding the upcoming Samhain ball. Apparently, it was printed on the school schedule and everything.

Second, the headmistress disappeared. Her office, once open to students, now remained closed—with guards outside. Guards with guns, tactical knives, and a few extra clips on their vests just in case. Apparently, the king was finally protecting her like a mate should.

I'd heard whisperings of retaliation, that the king had gone into the magic lands and slain some shifter packs in retribution for the island attack.

I still received packages from my mate, but after my fight with Rage, those lost their appeal. While Noble and Honor still said hi when our paths crossed, I kept things brief and ignored their appeals to hang out. I informed Honor our Saturday classes were over. Knowing the brothers had banded together to keep my mate a secret from me made me not want to deal with them anymore. Rage probably still thought my clan was traitorous and shady. *Whatever*.

It only took a day of stony-faced ignoring for the jokes in the cafeteria line to disappear. As well as the teasing. As for Justice, any time I caught him looking, his expression furrowed before he turned away.

And Rage … he lived up to his nickname. Whatever angst I'd hoped the picture would clear up, apparently it had done the opposite.

Well, fine. Screw them all! I was done.

Even my time with Kaja and the Harvest Clan sisters waned. Not that I blamed them. They probably needed time to heal after such a horrific trauma, almost losing their sister. I respected that, but I suddenly felt so alone. I worked, went to class, worked, and then went home to draw the covers over my head until morning.

I also focused on what I could do. Besides, far more important than a moody, distrustful werewolf, *or four*, was the mid-year exam that determined my future, the day after the Samhain ball. One way or another, I'd win the respect of my teachers and the other students—for me and my clan. My studies took on renewed purpose. I buried myself in my books. Every. Single. Day.

"Are you excited for Samhain tomorrow?" Kaja said, sliding onto the bench across from me in the cafeteria. Dinner was officially over, and I'd loaded my plate to the top, so hungry I couldn't wait to dig in.

Grinning at me from across the table, she practically bounced with energy. "Well? Are you?"

I pulled the hair-net off and shot it into the garbage. Tomorrow was Saturday, which meant the Samhain ball, and also, most likely, almost certainly, running into my mate. Something that no longer excited me. "Not really."

After a long guzzle of water, I bit into my burger, nearly groaning as the flavors hit my tongue. "But-this-is-so-good."

The words slurred together around my mouthful of food, and I swallowed and opened my eyes, only to flinch away from my BFF's proximity.

Kaja glared at me, not even six inches from my nose.

"What's wrong?" I asked, leaning back on the bench. I shoved cold tater tots into my mouth and chewed, waiting for her to spill the tea, but when she said nothing, I went back to the main course.

She shook her head and pointed at my burger.

I glanced down to see what she meant. But the burger looked fine to me—more than fine, really. "What's wrong with it?"

"Not the burger." She rolled her eyes until they nearly disappeared and then gave me a flat stare. "You."

"What did I do?" Besides me not inserting myself in her life every single waking moment, not much had changed.

She drummed her fingers against the Formica tabletop. "Just eat your burger, Nai. Then we can talk."

Her tone was light, but I had a bad feeling in the pit of my stomach. Did I do something wrong? Lately, it felt like I couldn't do anything right. The loneliness that had been eating away at me the past few days ramped up a notch. I quickly ate every bite on my plate before sighing with contentment. "That was a good burger."

"Yes, all three of them." She snorted and jerked her head toward the door.

The cafeteria was empty, save Kalama, but I wasn't about to argue our departure.

We stepped out into the cool air of autumn, and I chuckled. "All right, tell me what's up. I can deal now."

"That's just it," Kaja muttered, her expression tight. "I don't know what's up. You just don't seem like *you* anymore. You're a ghost, always studying, always busy. Ever since that night ... you don't come over anymore."

"Wait a minute. What do you mean, *that night*?" I tried to buy time while my brain assessed the situation. Was she mad? Hurt? How bad did I screw up? I'd just been trying to give them space.

"That night ... you know, the one where you saved my life by binding yourself to a dark mage with a blood debt *for a year*." The longer she spoke, the more her shoulders drooped. Finally, she offered me a small smile. "That one. You pulled away."

I cocked my head to the side and shook it. "You think *I've* pulled away? I thought no one wanted me around. Rage and the Midnight boys hate me because they think my uncle killed their dad. You almost died, so you probably want time with family. Nolan is demon-spawn, and I'm ... coping. Sort of."

She frowned and reached for my hand. "Nai, you used to come over all the time, and now? Only in the morning, and just enough time for Nell to cover your marks." She shook her head and swallowed hard. "Do you ... are you mad at me? I've been giving you space because I thought you were mad about the blood debt. That you regret it."

I shook my head, shocked she'd misunderstood, and tears blurred my vision. "No. Not at all. I could never regret saving you." I pulled her in for a sideways hug. "You're my BFF. You do know that the second F is for 'forever,' right?"

She sniffed, and the sound pulled at all the strings of my heart.

"We ... I-I thought ... I was afraid you'd resent me."

I chuckled, not because her pain was funny but because the whole misunderstanding was so crazy. Relief poured through me as I came to terms with my lame coping skills. I'd blocked everyone out because I was hurt, but maybe it was better to get it all out in the open.

"Nope." I popped the p. "I don't resent you one bit. I thought you and your sisters wanted or maybe needed time together to heal. Because—" I shrugged. "—the school doesn't offer therapy."

Kaja snickered. As she pulled me into a tight hug, she whispered, "You're certifiable. Also, you're my BFF too. And I want you around all the time."

On second thought, the alpha king could keep the money and get his own therapist. I had Kaja.

"Let's go order pizza," Kaja said, pulling me toward the Harvest dorm. "Nell and Rue will probably demand a sleepover too. Girl, don't ever think we need time away from you. As far as we're concerned, we're all part of the same pack."

Tears pricked my eyes again as we strode toward her dorm, each of us with an arm around the other. We walked through the door, and both Rue and Nell screamed and raced forward to greet me.

"Nai's back!"

Nell burst into laughter.

"I can't wait for us to all go to Samhain tomorrow," Rue said.

Oh, crap.

The ball was tomorrow, and I didn't have a dress.

∼

I STARED at the empty white dress box that lay at the

edge of Kaja's bed, the red silk ribbon now on the floor from when she'd torn it open for me.

I clutched the card against my chest and tried to rein in my breathing.

BEAUTIFUL MISS BLUE,

Wear this tonight so I can find you.

-Your Mate

"IT'S SOOO ROMANTIC," Kaja squealed.

I ran my fingertips over the dark blue silk where it faded to teal near the hem.

"It's psychotic," I replied.

Nell and Rue shared a worried glance, making me feel like I needed to explain.

I shook my head. "He's not proud to be my mate in real life, only in hidden corners and moonlight runs. I feel like a secret mistress."

Tears burned my eyes and clogged my throat. *Mother Mage, I care too much.* More than I'd allowed myself to believe.

Rage.

Justice.

They *knew* me.

I understood it wasn't ideal to have your mate be from another clan—it was a high crime, even—but then why bother with the beautiful dress? Why the freaking boxes of food? Why get all of the Midnight princes to help me shift? Why do all these things *and* still keep me in the dark?

I was done playing his games. From here forward, it needed to be all or nothing. So tonight, I was going to tell my green-eyed Midnight boy to choose. Either we were honest with each other, trusted each other, or … not. If he wouldn't share his identity, then I was done. I was Nai of Crescent Clan, and no one worth my time was ashamed to be with me.

"A girl in our pack found her fated mate last summer." Kaja's voice was small, and she offered me a tremulous smile. "I'd never seen anyone so blissful and euphoric. He was a few years older than her, and everyone wondered why he wouldn't pick a mate. I don't know if he knew and was waiting for her to grow up or what, but when she turned eighteen, he kissed her at her birthday party, and all these white butterflies descended onto her shoulders … it was *incredible*. They light each other up, and the coolest thing is they can speak to each other telepathically." She sighed and then added, "Our entire pack partied for three days and three nights straight; we were so happy for them."

Silence descended.

A wistful sense of melancholy settled in my chest, a dull ache of loss. I took a deep breath to dislodge the sensation then cleared my throat. "I'll never have that."

Kaja came over and wrapped her arms around me. "No, and I'm so sorry because you deserve it."

We hugged, and Nell and Rue murmured their agreement and then came up from behind and wrapped their arms around us, squishing me in the middle.

"You also deserve a trophy for being a badass fighter," Nell said.

Rue chimed in with her soft voice. "And for keeping your promises."

"Holy Mother Mage," Kaja quipped, rolling her eyes. "You'd better stop or she'll get a big head and make friends with Mallory, and then where will we be?"

I laughed. "No way that's going to happen."

Our group hug disbanded, and I glanced at each of the Harvest girls, my heart brimming with affection. "You guys are the best."

"You're pretty okay too." Kaja surveyed me in my blue ombre dress. "So, you ready to do this?"

Nell had once again dyed my hair blue, and a waterfall of ringlets fell down my back. Together with my curls, the off-the-shoulder sleeves hid my exposed elemental marks—better than if I'd planned it. The masks hid our clan marks, and for the first time since the ball at the beginning of the year, I asked Nell to leave my mate mark. I wanted Rage or Justice to see I wasn't ashamed to be bound to him. If he didn't feel the same, no more wood runs, no more masked balls—no more.

Reaching up, I pulled my white pearl and jeweled mask on and then headed out with the girls. Whatever we'd had was over. Time to break the news to my mate.

Midnight Kisses

. . .

THE ENTIRE ISLAND glowed with magic tonight. Lanterns and candles lit every pathway. Students and teachers, dressed to the nines, laughed and joked. *Everyone* was dressed up, even the guards. They stood like sentinels on the pathway, holding swords, in black masks and tuxedos.

After returning from Dark Row, Justice didn't ask again about the masquerade, didn't follow up to make sure I'd be here. He'd ghosted me, which only served to make tonight easier.

After giving a drop of blood to the masquerade-chalice to ensure I would not make out with Nolan, the masked-man magicked our voices, and then we stepped inside the atrium.

The ceiling had been retracted, revealing a sky filled with twinkling stars. Slow music played over a speaker system, and I scanned the crowd.

This party was bigger. Much bigger.

I started to count and realized this wasn't just students. With over two hundred people here, the packs must've sent in some of their members from the outskirts of the island.

"Our other siblings and packmates are here tonight too. Usually, Samhain isn't masquerade, but the princes made the rule. Now, I know why." Kaja winked.

The statement pricked my heart and filled me with fire. One of the Midnight princes was so ashamed of being my mate that he'd talked his brothers into making the ball masquerade so that he didn't have to be seen with me.

"I'm going to get mage wine!" Nell sauntered off, Rue in tow.

Kaja looped her arm through mine: "Wanna dance?"

I gave her a fake smile, trying to keep the depressing thoughts at bay. "Sure."

We wove through the crowded dance floor toward the center, and Kaja started to wave her arms, twisting to the beat. I swayed, trying to feign fun, but I couldn't get into it. When a guy stepped between us and asked her to dance, I gave her a genuine smile and thumbs-up.

"Find you later," I shouted and then fled, grateful to escape the dancefloor.

I needed air. Massive crowds of people and social niceties were not my things. Insincerity and politicking, also not my thing. Finding my way to the patio, I stepped out through the open doors and gulped in the crisp night air. Maybe Alpha Academy wasn't my thing, but I'd stick it out for my pack.

I felt him before I heard him, a presence at my back. "You came," he said.

It was him. He drew near, his proximity sending heat down my spine. The same way a magnet was drawn to its pair, I pivoted and faced him.

My mate.

I sucked in a breath, ready to tell him off, to cut him

off. I needed to say I couldn't do this, that I wouldn't. But then my gaze fell to his left hand.

Mate marks.

He'd kept them. On display, for all to see.

I was so stunned that when he reached for me, I let him. He gathered me into his arms, and then we were dancing. The melody filtered out through the roof and open doors, and he pressed his hand to my lower back, coaxing me closer. I nuzzled my head to his chest.

Home. He felt like Montana, like pack, like my future. Tears welled in my eyes because that felt like a lie. As long as he wouldn't tell me who he was, it was a lie. I wouldn't play these games. Not anymore.

Pulling back from his chest, I tilted my chin up to look him in the eye.

"This is the last time you will ever touch me. I can't do this." My voice shook, but I held strong. His eyes widened, but I rushed on, determined to finish my speech. "You've played with me. You're ashamed of me. Or you don't trust me. Either way, I don't deserve any of it."

I stepped away from him even though it was the hardest thing I'd ever done.

He stumbled forward, reaching for me, "I want to be with you, Nai, but—"

"But you're a Midnight prince, and your pack hates mine," I said, shaking my head.

I held his gaze. He stared at me, frozen in place, lips parted.

I exhaled and then continued in a whisper. "You're either Rage or Justice. I'm not sure which, but it doesn't really matter. If we can't be together, I need this to stop."

He shuddered, hands balled into fists, and his eyes flashed yellow.

For the first time, I retreated several steps back in fear.

Would he attack me? I scanned the darkness, but there was only us in this corner of the garden.

He shook his head and put his hands out, palms up. "My wolf is angry with me. It's trying to take over, but I'd never hurt you, Nai."

I crossed my arms across my chest. "You already have." My shoulders sagged with defeat. "We're done."

I turned to leave, ignoring him when he growled.

I heard him move, felt him crossing the space between us, and then he pulled me to him. My back to his chest, his arms encircled my waist. "You're wrong. We will never be done."

His warm breath caressed my neck, making my knees go weak. I could pull out of his grasp, but I didn't want to.

"You're mine," he said, his voice rough. His breath grew shallow, and his chest pressed into my back with every heave. "Mother Mage, I'm ... I'm so in love with you."

I gasped as the shock of his declaration ran through me, causing my heart to grow wings and take flight.

He ... *loved* me?

I spun in his arms and stared up at him.

"Being away from you is physically painful." He closed his eyes and sucked in a ragged breath. "You're all I think about. Everything I do is to protect you. The food boxes, meeting you for forest runs, making sure you got a healing serum, and running a perimeter around your dorm at night, Nai ... you're *everything* to me."

Whoa.

Whoa.

Whoa.

"But ... you've ignored me, been so cruel," I whimpered.

He frowned. "I tried to fight it. My human side tried to push you away. I thought if I was mean enough, if I could find enough reasons to hate you ... but I can't. I'm done fighting."

A single tear rolled down my cheek.

"Please..." he whispered.

I waited for him to finish his plea. Waited to know what he wanted so I could give it to him.

He opened his eyes, and his vibrant green gaze fell to mine. "Please, let me show you."

Really?

Stunned, I watched, lips parted, as he bowed his head and tugged his mask off.

He raised his chin, and tears burned my eyes.

Rage.

Holy Mother of Mages.

My mate was Rage.

"I wanted it to be you," I whispered, almost afraid to admit the truth. Raising up on my toes, I brushed my fingers over his lips and then swallowed. "I'm so glad it's you."

He growled, a low possessive sound that made desire flare within me. He gripped my hips and pulled me closer. "I need you."

Threading his fingers into my hair, Rage tilted my head to expose my neck. He traced his nose up the side where my pulse pounded, stopping only to nip at the tender flesh. "I'm sorry for what I said about your pack, about your uncle, about everything. I'm so sorry."

My breathing grew shallow as he continued his ministrations, kisses, and hot breaths against my skin. He grazed my skin with his teeth, and his hips moved.

I moaned, desperate for more. "Rage, please," I panted.

His warm tongue traced the outside of my ear, and then he sucked the fleshy part between his teeth. Every second was agony and pleasure.

"Rage..." Reaching into his jacket, I raked my nails down his back, and he groaned. Desire and need shot through me. "Kiss me."

His lips crashed against mine, and he nipped at my lower lip. I opened to him, and our tongues tangled. He brushed his fingertips over my skin ... up my arms, over my shoulder, and then the swell of my breast.

Midnight Kisses

I arched my back and clung to him as heat and magic buzzed under my skin.

Rage guided me backward until my back pressed against a wall. I tilted my head to give him better access. He pressed kisses down my neck then licked where he'd caressed seconds before. My mind clouded with lust, and I pulled him closer, desperate for more.

"I've missed you," he murmured against my breasts and then inhaled sharply. "Your smell." He moaned, and my desire became an inferno of need. "Nai," he huffed, kissing between my breasts as he fumbled with the corset clamps of my dress. "I love you."

"I love you too," I panted.

He kissed my shoulder, and I pushed his jacket off over his arms.

The first clasp on my dress released, but I was so lost in my lusty haze I didn't remember my marks until it was too late.

His body went rigid against mine, and then he pulled back, his gaze fixed on my chest. "What's that?"

Frick. Frick. Frick.

My fire mark. Right between my breasts where he had just been kissing.

I pushed him away. "Nothing."

He growled. "Don't lie to me."

Oh, no you did not. Lying was your middle name—it might still be.

I swallowed hard but said nothing.

He frowned, and his gaze darted deeper down into

321

my dress, where my water mark was.

I yanked the top part up and refastened the clasp.

"Nai..." His voice was low and tinged with panic. "How many marks do you have?"

"What does it matter?" I snapped defensively.

His eyes widened, and he swallowed hard.

"I see we're back to you not sharing things once again," I laughed, a sarcastic and biting sound. Then I spun and lifted my hair to show him the mark at the base of my neck. "There you go. Now you've seen them all."

I pivoted to face him again, but instead of a smug or haughty expression ... Rage looked terrified.

Not quite what I'd expected.

"What are you?" he whispered, his voice filled with awe and fear—his wide-eyed expression emphasizing his emotions.

His words slammed into me, shaking me to my core. *What* am I?

Not once had I seen the marks in that light ... in a way that made me *different*. How could he ask that? As if I were a ... *creature*, not a fellow wolf shifter and alpha heir.

Tears filled my eyes, blurring my vision, and I raced away from him, through the grass, and into the woods. The back of my heel snapped, but I didn't care. I needed to get the hell out of here.

"No!" Rage yelled after me. "I'm sorry!"

But this time, his apology came too late.

Chapter 21

THE MORNING SUNLIGHT filtered through the window, brushing against my skin like an unwanted lover. I wasn't ready for today. Or any day. How could this be reality?

Rage is my mate.

Hot tears pricked my eyelids, and I blinked them away. As I sat up, the memories of last night roiled through me, and my stomach clenched. That beautiful moment with Rage, *my mate*, dancing, kissing, *trusting* ... he confessed his love. We both wore our mate marks out and proud ... but then, all of it was destroyed because of these strange marks.

Even now, I heard his voice echoing in my mind.

What are you?

I stared at the elemental marks on my chest like hideous scars that declared me different. I didn't want them.

But what were these? None of the other students had them; my dad didn't have them.

I'm a freak.

After tying my hair into a top knot, I brushed my teeth and focused on the day ahead.

I needed to survive the midyear games tonight or I'd flunk out of Alpha Academy. If that happened, I wouldn't be allowed to lead Crescent Clan. Nolan would take over. None of that was an option.

I spat into the sink with an angry snarl.

Screw Rage.

Screw Nolan.

Screw these marks!

I dabbed some concealer over my mate mark just in case Nolan was in the kitchen. The last thing I needed was for him to know I was one-half of the fated mate-pair. My plan: breakfast, and then head over to Harvest Dorm to run drills with my friends for tonight.

I slipped into yoga pants before pulling on a tight tank top and my sneakers. Popping into the kitchen, I skidded to a stop. Yep. Nolan sat at the island, eating *my* food. His eyebrows dipped into a scowl when he spotted me.

"Think you're ready for tonight?" he growled.

I sighed. So not in the mood for his crap. I'd cried myself to sleep last night. Why couldn't I have a peaceful breakfast before fighting for my life in front of all the teachers?

"Absolutely." I gave him my back and opened a cupboard for oatmeal. "Are you?"

He hissed, a sharp intake of breath.

Ha! Maybe the universe had served him with a nick or cut to his hand. Total comeuppance.

But when I spun around, he stood inches from me, his face in front of mine. Glaring down on me, Nolan flared his nostrils, and his eyes were wide.

I jumped back, startled, and banged into the cabinet. Placing my hand over my chest, I tried to slow my thundering heart. "Geeze, psycho. You scared me!"

His eyes turned yellow as he slowly reached for me.

"What. Is. That?" He pointed toward my neck, curling his finger as if to touch the back.

Frick.

My mark. I'd forgotten about the one at the base of my neck and tied my hair too high.

I smacked his outstretched hand away then pulled my hair down, letting it cover my neck as I stepped past him. "Nell was practicing mark-forgery on me."

Was that a thing? I didn't know, but hopefully, he'd buy it.

He chuckled and shook his head. "You better be careful. If they catch you or her trying to pass for a high mage—that would only spell trouble."

My eyes widened, nearly falling out of my head, and my throat went dry. After forcing a swallow, I glanced over at him. "What do you mean?"

Nolan shook his head like I was an idiot. "See you tonight, *cousin*."

I sat at the island countertop, blinking at my cold oatmeal.

High mage? Why would he think that? Unless...

I swallowed, and a stone sank into my stomach.

Did the high mages have marks like these?

Just then, Kaja's voice rang in through the front hall. "Hello? It's unlocked. I'm coming in."

I pushed the freaky marks to the back of my mind. First things first. I needed to get through the midyear games. Tomorrow, I'd go back to the library and find something about these marks. Maybe the lady behind the black door could help me again.

"In here!" I shouted to my bestie.

Kaja popped into view, wearing a thick black swatch of paint under each eye like an American football player or a warrior going into battle.

I burst into laughter, all of my problems forgotten at the sight of her.

"Too much?" she asked, frowning.

Grinning, I shook my head. "No, it's perfect."

She placed her hands on her hips and narrowed her eyes. "Damn right. We're going to kick ass and take names."

I nodded, knowing how high the stakes were.

"Hey, I never found you last night. Why did you bail early?" she asked, sidling up next to me with a frown.

My eyes flicked to the hallway, and she gave me a

knowing look of understanding. Nolan could be listening.

"Let's go practice at my place," she said. "The games don't start until sundown. Plenty of time to chat about who you hooked up with."

I nodded and grabbed my cold oatmeal. Then, we shuffled over to Harvest Dorm.

This place was like my second home. The burnt orange curtains, Fiona with her face in a book, quiet Rue either reading or writing. Even the maid staff. Everyone knew me.

But this time was different.

As soon as we crossed the threshold, fear prickled my skin and charged the air. Nerves churned in my gut, and I froze.

"You need to look UP!" Fiona barked, standing over Nell, who lay on her back on the living room rug. "Your enemy can be in the trees, and you won't see them until it's too late."

Whoa.

The furniture was pushed to the walls, the coffee table gone; their entire living room had become a battleground. Fiona was graduating this year, so I knew she was taking it especially seriously.

Nell popped up and glared at her sister. "I've got it! I did this last year, remember?"

Fiona laughed, a harsh, brittle, mocking sound. "They grade first-years way easier than upperclassmen."

Ouch.

"I said I've got it." Nell turned, and her furrowed expression melted into a smile. "Oh, Nai is here. Hey, girl."

Nell broke away from her sister, shooting her a parting glare, seemingly grateful for the distraction my presence brought.

Fiona and Mele started to spar, ignoring me while Rue and Nell came over to greet me.

"Where did you go last night?" Nell asked.

Rue cocked her head to the side and added, "We were worried until we saw your broken heels at the back door of your dorm."

I took in a deep breath. I needed to get this part off my chest. "Rage is my mate. He confessed."

Jaws dropped, and silence descended on the entire group of girls as their eyes widened. I sucked in a breath, followed by another, and then finally, one by one, they recovered from the shock.

"I thought it was Justice," Rue said.

Nell grinned. "I knew it was Rage."

"Are you okay?" Kaja reached for me, her eyes narrowed.

I wanted to tell them more, about the marks, about his question: *What are you?* His words burned their way into my soul until I felt empty.

But if I told them now, I'd become an emotional wreck, and I needed to concentrate on tonight. First things first. I'd tell them everything tomorrow.

"I'm okay. But ... it didn't end well," I confessed.

Kaja pulled me in for a hug. Then Nell and Rue joined until we were all sandwiched together, and tears leaked from my eyes.

Fiona's voice shattered our love powwow.

"Nai, you're next!" she shouted.

We parted, and I wiped my eyes, nodding. I needed the distraction. The games were happening whether I was ready or not. I needed to win.

I strode over to the center of the carpet, and Fiona stared down on me, her eyes yellow.

"They will try to break you," she warned. "You'll be outnumbered. Nolan won't help you, so you have to be smarter."

Whoa.

Fiona was scary as hell, but this was how she showed love. She wanted us all at our best—even me. All the years I longed to have a sister, and now I did. Five of them. The Harvest girls were my pack.

I nodded, bringing my arms up into guard as I slid my weight back into a defensive stance.

Fiona assessed my stance, and then her gaze flicked behind me.

I spun.

Too late.

A duct-taped bag of flour slammed into my back, and I fell to my knees with a growl.

"You need to have eyes in the back of your head!" Fiona snarled. "Try again!"

I stood, readying my stance for another blow.

Thank the Mother Mage I had these girls.

Tonight would test everything within me, and may the healing mages have mercy on any wolf who got in my way.

~

"WELCOME, STUDENTS!" Headmistress Elaine stood in the clearing of the forest on the east side of campus, her voice amplified by magic.

She looked beautiful and healthy, and I couldn't help but feel a bit of personal pride at that.

"And welcome, clans and esteemed guests," she added.

Just like that, my confidence waned to almost nothing. Nerves churned in my gut as I scanned the crowd. Wolves from the outer fringes of the island sat in risers like an arena. Harvest Clan, Midnight, Daybreak, every one but mine. My gaze snagged on the High Mage Council, sitting high up on a platform stage with the alpha king among them. Why were they here?

Behind them, suspended in air, hung a huge hundred-foot white cloth as their backdrop. I smiled at the kind grandpa mage, and then the headmistress was talking again.

"At Alpha Prep, we pride ourselves on turning out the most dominant, battle-ready alpha for each clan."

The packs standing around the clearing roared their

approval as the students tipped their heads in pride toward their kin.

Nolan and I stood alone, no pack present to care.

"In an effort to hone our students' skills, we do twice-yearly practical exams." The headmistress turned to us. "This exam is a display of your elemental power. The power that separates you from the others in your pack, those who do not carry royal blood."

Another roar from the crowd. A row of guards approached us, started to hand out colored vests, and a stone sank in my stomach when I was handed a bright green vest, the same color as Nolan's.

"For this test, you will be paired on a team with the other heirs in your house," she said boldly.

Two. There were freaking two of us.

Midnight had *four*.

Harvest girls had *five*.

And Daybreak, even with the recent loss of their sister, had *three*.

We were totally outnumbered, and I was on freaking Nolan's team. My breath grew shallow as I considered our odds. Stab-me-in-the-back Nolan ... so not fair. But I remembered Nell saying they changed things up every year.

I felt Rage's gaze burning into me from a few feet away as he and the Midnight heirs put on their blue vests, but I wouldn't give him the satisfaction of looking. *Keep your head in the game, Nai.*

Four guards entered the field then, each holding a

colored flag, red, blue, yellow, and green, all colors that matched our vests.

"The midyear practical is Capture the Flag, magical version." The headmistress smiled, and again, the packs went wild. Nell and Fiona rolled out their necks, appearing seasoned, and even Nolan bounced on the tips of his toes.

I, however, stared into the air, stunned. How was I going to get anything done with Nolan on my team?

I don't know why I assumed they would scramble the teams evenly.

The guards disappeared then, running off into the forest to hide the flags.

"It's less about capturing the actual flags than it is about showcasing your skill while you defend your territory and seek out other teams' flags," said the headmistress.

Okay ... I exhaled with a modicum of relief. So ... even if our flag was taken, if I could show a little bit of good magic defending it, I shouldn't be kicked out.

"Now, listen carefully." Her voice dropped low in ominous warning. "The rules clearly state you cannot openly attack a fellow student without cause, but you *can* and *should* defend your territory, or life, by *any means necessary*."

What the what?

Nolan peered at me with a grin, saliva glittering on his teeth.

"We're on the same team," I hissed.

Creep.

"This battle-like scenario separates the weak from the strong." Her voice was hollow like maybe she didn't believe that line. She took a breath and then said, "So be careful, and let's have a clean game."

The crowd went wild, roaring and howling and stamping their feet.

A chill rolled through the night air, and I hugged my arms around my waist.

Father once told me Alpha Academy separated the alpha from the second in line. Getting in was easy—that was a birthright—but getting through four years here was what made one ready to lead a pack of animal shifters through any situation.

Now I understood.

This was what he trained me for. Every sparring session, every run through the woods, throwing knives, pinning Ellie to the ground until she'd submit, it was all to prepare me for this.

"We've stripped your beds and rubbed your scent around your pack's territory. You'll have to use your nose to scent out the other packs' borders. At the center of each territory is a flag, in plain sight—and ripe for the taking," she bellowed.

I jumped on the balls of my feet to dispel the nervous energy I was feeling.

"If at any time you fear for your life, shoot your colored flare gun into the air. If you do this, you'll forfeit and be out of the game." She paused, and I leaned forward in anticipation of her next words. "If you forfeit, you'll be expelled from the school as well. Banished. Never allowed to become the alpha of your clan."

Uh ... what?

A guard walked up with a green flare, and I glanced sideways to see what the others were doing.

Just as I thought.

One by one, they declined to take the flare gun.

Well, there was no way I was going home, forfeiting my place in my pack.

"No thanks," I muttered, and the guard nodded.

"A strong bunch this year!" the king yelled from the stage.

The crowd roared in approval.

Not one student took the flare. We were all in this to win. No matter what.

The headmistress chuckled nervously. "Okay, we have a network of night-vision cameras and spotlights throughout the entire game field. Your judges—" she pointed toward the king and five high mages on stage "—will be rating your magical ability the entire time. The game only ends when all four flags have been torn from their trees."

Lights flickered, and then the forest appeared on the white cloth behind the stage. It was a projector screen.

Oh, Mother Mage, please don't let me do anything stupid on live TV.

Dozens of little squares appeared, each one broadcasting a different patch of trees, and the four corners of the screen showed flags.

"You have sixty seconds to plan your strategy with your teammates. When the horn blows, the games begin, and I suggest you run to find your territory."

My stomach dropped as I turned to face Nolan. "Okay, here's what I think we should—"

"You think you're in charge?" Fury glittered in his eyes. "I don't answer to you."

"What's your deal, Nolan? We're supposed to be a team." When he said nothing, only sneered, I pressed on: "I know you and your mom have always hated me and my dad. But are you going to let jealousy screw up this game? Lose because of it?"

If he wanted to spend our sixty seconds together fighting, then so be it.

He shrugged. "I don't like people who are born into privilege. Status needs to be *earned*."

I laughed. As if his mother had ever challenged my father and won. "It *was* earned."

He nodded. "And tonight it will be again."

I glared at him, incensed at his stupidity, but before I could reply, I overheard Daybreak Clan next to us talking loudly.

"Let's take out the green flag first. There are only two of Crescent. They're weak."

Looking at Nolan, I raised my eyebrows. "We should both defend the flag first, let the teams come, and when they see we are united, they'll go for other flags, *and then* we can separate and go on the offense."

He laughed. "You do whatever you want. I'm going for Midnight's flag."

"Nolan!" I shouted. This idiot was going to screw this up for the both of us. How did he even make it through last year on his own? The only thing I could think of was that he was the only air element in the school. So he had an advantage with that.

Before I could say any more, Rage walked right up to me, stealing the breath from my lungs, and Nolan walked away.

"Nai, I need to talk to you." His voice was rough, and his eyes reflected remorse, but I shook my head. I couldn't do this right now.

"Go plan with your brothers." He had sixty seconds to plan with his brothers, and he was going to waste them on me? My voice held barely-contained fury as I met his gaze. "I'm not doing this right now."

The horn sounded, and before he could say anything, I took off after Nolan, running away from Rage, away from my mate problems, away from the marks.

Guilt twisted my stomach, and I glanced over my shoulder. I'd expected to see him tearing after me, but instead, he stood where I'd left him, head hanging low.

Pushing it from my mind, I hit the thick tree line. The second I dipped into the woods, Rage's scent washed over me. Less strong, I picked up the smell of other males: Honor, Noble, Justice. I noticed little strips of their bedsheets tied to trees. We were in Midnight territory.

A black Midnight wolf blasted past us, probably to make it to the center of the territory and protect their flag.

I couldn't tell them apart, except it wasn't Rage.

I veered right, and Nolan went left. Running to the edge of Midnight territory, I inhaled as I scented new fragrances.

Harvest.

Fiona's scent washed over me, and then Nell, Rue, and finally Kaja, the forest permeated with my bestie's vanilla and sage scent.

I pumped my legs hard, desperate to find our flag. I curved to the left, assuming the four territories were set up in a circle. My heart thundered against my ribs as I plowed through the woods. Relief washed over me as my own scent filtered past.

Crescent.

But I wasn't alone. Footsteps pounded behind me. I considered shifting, but it could take too long, and my elemental powers were more reliable, at least for me. And wasn't that the point of the game anyway? To show our elemental powers?

Where is that flag?!

I ran deeper into our territory, picking up both Nolan's and my scents. Twigs snapped behind me, but I didn't take the time to look. As much as I wanted it to be Nolan, I doubted it, especially considering his declaration to go on the offense and get other flags first. I wasn't going to stop until I found our flag.

My goal was to defend our flag the entire time, *alone* if necessary, just as I would defend my pack. I'd never leave my territory in a war, never abandon my people. Never be like the slimy alpha king.

The second I spied the lime green cloth whipping in the cold night air, I squealed in triumph. I crossed the last ten yards and, planting my feet at the base of the tree, spun to face my oncoming attacker.

Mallory.

Of course.

Heat rolled down my arms, but I pushed away my fire power. Mallory was a fire elemental too, so I'd fight her with water.

As the semester had progressed, I'd discovered my two forms of magic were like a tangled mass of yarn filling me. I needed to only tease what I needed from the bulk of energy. The power of cool water trickled down my arms like spring rain, and I grinned when Mallory launched a fireball.

The orange sphere sailed through the air in a clean arc, and I shot a stream of water to meet it.

The flame extinguished with a hiss of steam.

"Going to have to do better than that," I growled.

A twig snapped behind me, and my heart plummeted.

Mallory was the distraction.

Her brother and elder sister leapt out from the woods behind me and started climbing the tree, heading right for my flag.

Oh, hell no.

Spinning, I raised both hands and pushed fire through one and water through the other so the tree and flag wouldn't burn. The flames hit Sean, Mallory's brother, first, and he dropped to the ground with a thud, screaming as he rolled on the damp leaf litter. Heather fell next, coughing and sputtering like a drowned rat.

Roars from the crowd, distant but detectable, filtered through the trees, and I wondered if it was for me or in protest of Daybreak's failure.

My victory grin slid from my face as Mallory's hands clamped around my neck from behind, and I felt heat simmering under my skin as she squeezed off my air supply.

Dammit.

Sean and Heather climbed to their feet, both wearing matching, vicious sneers.

"Boil her blood," Sean snarled.

My skin prickled and blistered, and my mind raced.

Where the hell was Nolan? Didn't he want *us* to win? But I already knew the answer even if I'd hoped otherwise. *Nolan would never help me.*

Gasping, I reached for water and let the moisture in the air soothe my searing hot skin. I pushed against Mallory's magic with my own. I could take Mallory, but could I take her *and* protect our flag from her siblings?

The heat in my blood intensified as I started to panic.

Dig deeper, Nai.

Reaching up, I fumbled until I felt her pinkies. Taking them into my grasp, I yanked them away from her other fingers, snapping them backward.

Hard.

Lesson #1 from my father: Where the pinky goes, so does the body.

I felt her skin tear and the bone crunch as she released me with a sharp scream that rivaled a dying cat's.

A searing pain pulsed at my lower back. I'd just gained another mark.

Earth. It had to be. I now had all four elemental marks, but I didn't have time to dwell on it.

Sean leapt from halfway up the tree and landed before me. "I'm going to kill you for that!" Mallory bellowed with fury. They both advanced.

Crap.

I swallowed back my fear. One hundred percent I'd fight them as best I could. 99.9% certain their sister Heather would take our flag. Ten to one odds I'd get my alpha heir ass jumped by all three of them after they won.

But I was one hundred percent not prepared for the blur of black fur that arced through the air…

My jaw dropped as the Midnight wolf landed on Sean's back, knocking him to the ground. Snapping his jaws, the wolf tore into Sean's shoulder, and the young heir screamed.

Why was a Midnight wolf here?

A wolf who was *not* my mate—which meant this was one of his three brothers.

I spun as Rage, in human form, barreled down on Mallory, fire shooting from his hands like flamethrowers.

"Justice, the tree!" Rage barked at the black wolf.

Mallory ran off into the woods, clothes smoking, screaming. Sean fled next, in the fraction of time when Justice in wolf form shifted, and then a very exposed Justice stood and yanked the third Daybreak Clan member out of the tree.

Heather squealed as she fell to the ground, her thud accompanied by the snap of bone.

"You haven't won," she snarled as she limped off.

Maybe not, but then neither had she. My flag still stood; I was still in the games.

Justice raised his eyebrows and looked to Rage, who nodded. He shifted back into his wolf form before trotting off to protect his flag.

But Rage stayed.

He stepped in front of me, his green eyes simmering with emotion as he studied me. "So what's our plan?" he asked, his voice rough. "Defend until we show each clan they can't take us and then go flag hunting?"

He knew me so well. My throat tightened with unshed emotion. "Rage," I whispered, shaking my head, "this isn't your fight. Just … go. Your brothers—"

"My brothers understand my mate is more important than a stupid school test," he said, holding his hand up so that I could see the mate marks he clearly wore. "I'm not going anywhere."

My stomach tightened. I wasn't sure if the cameras in the woods had sound, or how clear the picture was, but Rage … with the king watching, Rage was showing off his mate marks. His courage shook me to the core. Now I understood how he carried his real name.

"I didn't mean to say that last night. To ask *what* you are…" He swallowed hard. "You're my mate. I love you. *That's* all that matters."

My lips parted in shock. What could I say? My emotions were more tangled than my magic, but under it all… "I lo—"

Nolan stepped into the clearing, and my voice disappeared.

The wind swirled around my cousin, and a wolf kept pace at his side.

A wolf?

I stiffened with recognition. The dark patches of fur, the menace in its gaze. That was the wolf who'd attacked me on the beach.

Rage stepped in front of me, squaring his shoulders, blocking my view.

"Nolan," Rage growled, "leave now, and I won't kill you."

Nolan barked a hard laugh, and the dappled golden wolf separated from my cousin, stalking the right perimeter as if to come up behind me. A twig snapped, and my attention jumped to the left.

Mallory and her siblings were back, and I was one hundred percent confident they weren't here to apologize.

Frick.

The odds were not in our favor, but that didn't mean they were working together. *Right?*

"Neutralize Rage, but don't kill him. Nai is mine," Nolan barked to Daybreak.

What. The. Hell? Daybreak and Nolan were working together? And how did Nolan hire a rogue to take me out? Who the hell was this wolf?

Wrath boiled under my skin. The commotion from the crowd rumbled through the trees.

No way was this legal! To bring a rogue wolf in to assassinate students? Where the hell was the king to protect his heir?

My mind spun, trying to make sense of all the implications of this betrayal.

"Stay human." Rage's advice barely registered before he shifted blindingly fast, the tatters of his clothing falling to the ground in his panic. As if I had a choice. My wolf was so far away at this moment I couldn't feel her, just the low buzzing of magic under

343

my skin. He stepped in front of me, hackles raised as he faced our enemies. Tipping his head back, he howled a long deep call for his brothers.

Nolan threw his arm out and shot a burst of wind at a tree.

My initial gloat at his terrible aim turned to dread as a camera fell to the earth with a crash. He'd not been aiming for me. Whatever his plans were, he didn't want it televised.

"Nolan, you coward," I shouted. "You want to be alpha, fight me fairly!"

This was not how alpha status fights were done.

He just grinned.

Still tracking the rogue wolf, I spun and shot a fireball at the animal, but it splashed into the forest as he deftly rolled away.

"What's in this for you?" I yelled at Nolan. "Seems like a lot of risk just for alpha status."

The ground rolled beneath our feet, and my gaze darted to Sean, an earth elemental. Rage licked my hand and then broke away from me to take on Mallory and her siblings.

I understood. There were too many of them; we needed to keep them busy until Justice, Noble, and Honor got here.

Okay. I could do this.

New plan: keep my cousin talking while taking out the rogue wolf.

"You can't believe the pack will follow you after

they know of your betrayal," I shouted across the clearing.

Nolan barked another laugh, this one closer than the last.

"After I kill you, then I'll fight your dad. Once I win and your family is eliminated, Crescent gets to come back to Alpha Island with me as their alpha."

My shock turned to sickening understanding.

The alpha king was in on this. He was the only one who could lift the banishment.

All of this: the attacks, Nolan's ferocity toward me, it was all driven by the king. It had to be. Nolan couldn't afford an assassin. I had no idea when he'd seen the mate mark or if this was something more, but—

"Nai! Look out!" Kaja screamed, her voice deep in the trees.

I spun as the rogue charged. I had no time to think, not even to act, only *react*.

Raising my hands, I produced fire in my left and water in my right, and then I shot a torrent of steam at his face; so hot his fur, and then skin, and finally his muscles melted ... right off the bone.

Oh mage.

Bile rose in my throat as the wolf dropped to the ground, thrashing and writhing in pain.

I...

I forced a swallow and pulled. I couldn't even say what I pulled at, only that I felt a surge of power course through me. I grabbed hold of it and doused the rogue with a final burst of steam, and then he stilled.

Horrified, I gulped and turned, facing Nolan once again.

The wind picked up; the trees creaked with the force of his power, and branches snapped. The gale-force slammed into me, lifting me up into the air. I lurched from the ground with a scream on my lips as Nolan's wind power took hold of me. Up, up I went—and then the wind disappeared.

Gravity hurled me toward the earth, past a blur of trees, and pain seared through my right side as a branch sliced into me. I flailed, arms and legs waving as I pummeled toward the ground.

Suddenly, a soft force of magic slowed my fall, cushioning me. I landed hard enough to have the air knocked out of me. But gulping with relief, I tasted ash in the air as I climbed to my feet—

To the tortured cry of Rage's wolf.

My attention shot to the sound.

Mallory and Heather were shooting fire at my mate, and Sean was staring at the dirt where a gaping hole was inching closed around the lower half of Rage's wolf. My mate scratched and tried to climb out, but it was too late. He was trapped, being buried alive.

Something deep down inside of me, something dark and wild snapped. The tangled mess of my magic swelled, coursing through me so quickly I gasped.

My mate was in danger.

My mate.

"Stop!" I shouted, flinging my arms back to propel me forward. I flew up as if the wind were carrying me, skimming the ground as I sailed across the clearing like a freaking witch on a broomstick. I landed next to Rage, and the earth shook. Trees uprooted around Rage as he was propelled up from the packed soil and freed.

Mallory punched her brother in the arm.

"It's not me," he said, backing away from where Rage's wolf now stood, whole, on solid ground.

No. Not Sean at all.

I didn't know *how*... I didn't know *why*... but I knew. This was one hundred percent me.

I could feel it.

I could feel ... *everything*.

The line where the mulch met the soil as well as the soil content, how much iron it had, where the vein of quartz crystal ran through the shale, deep into the sedimentary rock. I could feel the tree roots snaking through the earth, and below the stone, all the way down to the magma at the core of the planet ... I felt it *all*. The earth, the air, the moisture and humidity, and the heat. I was one with everything around me, even the ethers. I felt the stars, their burning hot gasses, and something blissful just beyond where this world ended. I floated over Rage, my feet skimming his fur, and all three Daybreak Clan took a step back, eyes wide with fear.

Inhaling through my nose and breathing through

my mouth, I released a cooling mist to douse the fire still licking Rage's wolf; his fur sizzled as the burns cooled.

Instead of bringing me relief, my anger spiked at the audacity of their clan—at the betrayal of my cousin and, most of all, at the treachery of the alpha king. Filled with power and indignation, I turned just as Nolan lunged for me.

Instead of modulating the power I held, I lashed out … with all of it.

Whip-like tendrils of blue light burst from my fingers, and at the same time, Nolan released the knife in his hand, sending it right for me.

Knife. When did he get that?

I exhaled a sharp breath and tilted my head, sending a gust of wind to throw the knife out of my way. The blue light from my fingertips wrapped around Nolan like bands of silk. The magic caught Sean as well, the little threads of energy twisting tight like magical string. When I felt the urge to tug, I yanked my hands apart, telling the power what it should do.

Because no one, *ever*, would harm my mate and live to tell about it. The entire realm needed to know what would happen if they dared try. The bands sliced through Nolan and Sean like a hot knife through butter. Their bodies fell to the ground in pieces of flesh and droplets of blood, and gasps rang throughout the entire forest.

"High crime!" the king's voice came from somewhere far off in the woods, startling me.

Holy. Frickin'. Mage. My feet slammed to the ground as my power waned. He'd seen me rip Nolan apart through the opening in the trees, and now he came with a pack of guards, headed my way.

"High crime!" a dozen more voices took up his pronouncement, and the guards voiced their agreement, the thudding of their feet coming at us from the woods.

Was killing Nolan a high crime? Frick.

I dropped to the ground and buried my hands in Rage's singed fur.

"Rage, they're coming for us." Fear and confusion stole my confidence, and the magic left me. I looked up. Kaja stared at me, her jaw unhinged. Mallory and Heather were gone.

The three remaining Midnight brothers stepped out from behind my best friend, in their human form, all of them wearing the same look of shock.

"It's you," Justice said, his voice hoarse. "You're the high crime."

What did that mean? I gulped, and tears burned my eyes. Blinking to clear them, I felt the tears drip onto Rage's wolf as I looked down at him. "What am I?"

Rage's yellow eyes pierced my soul, holding me captive. He bared his teeth, but without a growl or snarl, I didn't understand. I frowned, but before I could ask *why* he looked like he wanted to rip my head off ... he *bit* me.

As soon as his teeth broke my skin, his wolf's voice filled my mind. *'I am your shield. Any harm that comes to you will first pass through me.'*

Gone was the short beast like speech of his wolf. This was ... magic, a spell, a ... *shield* spell. Dizziness rocked me, and I swayed.

Why would Rage be my shield unless...

The truth hit me like a ton of bricks.

The marks.

What Nolan said about *pretending* to be a high mage.

Was I ... the high crime my clan was banished for?

That was impossible, right?

My uncle had committed the high crime.

My breathing grew shallow.

Was it *me*?

Justice, Honor, and Noble appeared before me, all in their black wolf forms. One by one, they tore at my flesh with their teeth until my blood soaked their gums.

'I am your shield. Any harm that comes to you will first pass through me,' Justice said in my mind.

'I am your shield,' Noble said. *'Any harm that comes to you will first pass through me.'*

And then Honor pledged, *'I am your shield. Any harm that comes to you, will first pass through me.'*

Four shields.

All four Midnight brothers had just pledged and sacrificed *their* life before mine.

I stood, lips parted and speechless, when the king entered the grove. His guards flanked him, and the high mages arrived with their shields.

The king's eyes widened when he saw the four Midnight wolves around me, and his face paled.

"Get away from her," he growled, his dark hair flying free of his gel as he shook his head. "Get away from her, now!"

The high mages wore equally repulsed expressions of disgust like I was the scum of the earth—all except one.

The nice old dude with gray hair and silver cloak stared at me, but when he caught my gaze, he turned away. Was he upset or hiding something?

"I thought you took care of this problem two decades ago," Kian growled at the king.

The alpha king sneered. "I took care of her wolf-father. You assured me the pregnancy hadn't come to term before you exterminated the mother."

Holy. Mother. Mage.

What were they saying?

"She is a *shifter* high crime," Kian snapped. "The responsibility falls at your feet, Declan, not mine."

My jaw hit the ground, and my entire world tilted.

I blinked, barely seeing the students and pack members gathering around, but I could feel the crowd pushing into the small clearing. What would they do? I could only imagine the picture we made, a small pack of black wolves surrounding a bleeding girl.

The wolves perked up, and I followed their gazes to their mother. The headmistress entered the clearing just as the king pointed at me and declared, "Nai, of Crescent Clan, is a foul perversion of the highest order. Half shifter, half high mage."

Everyone gasped. Even me.

My mother was ... a high mage?

I glanced at the only nice high mage I knew, but his attention remained fixed on the other high mages.

"The sentence for this crime is death," Kian roared.

The king flicked his head to the royal guards, and they advanced.

Oh, hell no!

I thrust my arms out, and a gust of wind blew outward, knocking the guards back.

The alpha king clenched his jaw, the anger turning his face purple, and he drew his sword. Like Rage, the alpha king's element was fire, and he pointed his blade at me, flames dancing down the sides to the tip.

Heat pricked my skin, and a hot searing pain ripped through my body as he tried, no doubt, to ignite me. I sucked in a deep breath to cool his magic, and then it was gone.

As I exhaled, relieved, I heard a whimper. My gaze shot to the wolves, and I gasped in horror as realization dawned.

The scent of burning flesh confirmed my fear.

Honor, the smallest of the wolves, let out a cry, and smoke curled in the air. He was my shield. The last to take the oath, he would be the first to fall if…

"No!" I screamed, desperate to help my friend. "Please, stop, he's—"

The rest of my plea died in my throat as Honor's fur burst into flames. He collapsed to the ground, writhing as blood oozed from his eyes, nose, and mouth.

Time slowed to a crawl.

Howls of agony rose up from the three Midnight wolves, and shock ripped through me. I fell to my knees, water gushing from my palms to douse the fire. Tears streamed down my cheeks, and my whole body shook.

"Honor … no."

Honor's mother screamed. Her loud wail of anguish tore through the night, mourning for a loss that could never be replaced.

Rage snarled and stalked toward the king, head low and hackles raised, and the alpha king staggered backward.

The coward.

"Shields?" the king gasped. "You idiots!"

I crawled to where Honor's wolf had fallen and gathered him up in my arms. Rocking him back and forth, I sobbed.

No.

No.

No.

Not him.

Not sweet Honor.

Not for me.

The loss cracked open inside of me like a cavern swallowing me whole. There was a gaping space in my heart…

He was gone, melted from the inside out by his own alpha, his uncle, his king.

The grief clamped my throat, and I released a guttural wail.

Then I felt it. A slice of breathtaking pain as another mark branded me. This one at the top of my head. The searing pain crawled down my spine, and my vision disappeared with an explosion of white-hot agony.

A fifth mark? How? What?

When I opened my eyes, I knew what the fifth element was. The one no one spoke about, the one no one at school had. My gaze shot to the silver-cloaked mage, and he offered me a sad smile. And then he pointed…

At Honor's ghost.

He stood over me, watching as I held his dead wolf, with a frown on his lips.

My eyes filled with fresh tears, and I scrambled to my feet.

"No," I gasped. "Please … come back."

"*Oh, Nai,*" he said, his voice a mere echo of its normal strength. "*It doesn't work like that.*"

He leaned forward, and I felt a whisper of a kiss against my forehead.

"*I'll miss you,*" he said. *"And my brothers and Mom, but I have no regrets."*

He turned and strode away, walking without his limp, right to where his grieving mother pounded her fists on the forest floor. He paused there, bent down, and tried to give her a hug, but his arms went right through her. He straightened and squared his shoulders, turning to meet my watery gaze. *"Make sure you tell them that and that I love them—and when Mom is ready, tell her too."*

I stood there, numb with grief and shock, but nodded, unsure of what else I could do, then glanced at the old high mage, the one with the silver cloak, the one who must be the master of the element of spirit.

He merely pointed for me to keep watching.

Almost as if everyone had been frozen and then thawed, a cacophony of wailing and yelling erupted.

The headmistress leapt to her feet and launched herself at the king. "How could you!"

Four guards struggled to pull her off, and Honor blew her a kiss before he walked into the trees toward a blinding white light.

"Honor, no!" I stood, dropping his wolf's body to the ground with a sickening thud and moved to go after him, to beg him to stay. Maybe I could stop him...

"You've been living on borrowed time," Kian growled, stepping toward me. "That ends now."

There was so much commotion, the students backing into the trees averting their gaze, uncomfortable with death, the king and his wife fighting in the woods, the guards holding her back. Rage at the edge ready to rip his uncle's head off. Justice and Noble nuzzling Honor's dead wolf with their noses as if they could revive him.

Kian's lip curled with disgust. "High crimes deserve their fate. You're an abomination. Half wolf, half high mage."

That might even be true, but if I let Kian hurt me, then he'd hurt the Midnight boys. One by one, they would fall, and I wouldn't let that happen.

The silver high mage stepped in front of Kian and held up his hands. "Kian, you're being hasty. Think! You'd wipe out all the Midnight royal heirs to kill her? She has *three* shields." He indicated the congealing bite marks on my arms. "What would that do to the shifter-mage peace accord?"

Kaja's sister, shield to the high mage of spirit, pulled her sword.

"I don't care about the accord!" Kian bellowed. "I want her dead!"

Wow.

Probably not the best time to tell him, but I wished he was dead too.

I glanced at the Midnight princes, debating my next step, when I felt a presence in my mind.

'*Run,*' the silver-cloaked mage said. '*Go to the mortal*

realm, and hide until I get word to you.'

I gulped and noticed Rage, Justice, and Noble all stood erect as if they'd been given orders too.

'Mate. Run. Protect,' Rage said, nuzzling my leg.

Kaja ran into the space, screaming, "I'm on fire! My blood is boiling. No! Aggghhh! Get out of here!"

I frowned because she looked fine…

"Flee!" Kaja bellowed, dropping to the ground. Her gaze hit mine, and she screamed, "Now! My blood!"

The students all screamed, creating a massive distraction.

The mage must've told her something too. Why was he helping me? I didn't have time to figure it out.

With one last glance at my bestie, I took in the hellacious ending of the midyear games and then raced off into the forest, my clothes falling in tatters as my wolf rose to the surface. Three black Midnight wolves kept pace next to me. I knew now why my wolf always retreated in danger. She knew my magic was there this whole time, that I was more powerful in human form. Not human … high mage.

My mind reeled as we ran. I was the high crime. I was … interbred between two races.

And Honor was gone.

The ache in my chest deepened, and I knew all of us grieved as our paws pounded the forest floor. I wasn't sure which of the boys howled first, but eventually, one by one, we tipped our heads back and yowled when the grief became too much. But as Justice, Rage, and Noble each pressed against me, I knew no matter what, we were in this together.

Rage moved our little pack to where we could catch a boat back to the shore and the portal into the mortal world. But I diverted to the right where the boats went to Dark Row.

'No. Mate. This way,' Rage growled.

I shook my head, weaving in and out of the bushes, only one thing on my mind.

The boys sidled up next to me, and I looked at each one of them. *'No. This way. We're going to bring Honor back from the dead.'*

I knew a certain dark mage who'd bragged about knowing the keeper of souls. I didn't even want to know what the cost was for bringing someone back from the realm of the dead. I'd have to negotiate better this time. Either way, I'd pay the price. No matter the cost.

Honor would not be taken from us.

Not tonight.

And *definitely* not like this.

Preorder book two!

Enjoying this series? Preorder book two here on amazon. Authors note: We will be pulling that date WAY in closer.

Midnight Kisses

Acknowledgments

A huge thank you to our families for dealing with the late night tippy tapping on the keyboard while we wrote this story. To our ARC team and reader groups, thank you so much for your enthusiasm for this series! We heart you. Lee and Dawn, our editors, this book would not be polished without you. Thank you to all our readers who help us get to follow our dream every day!

Also by Raye Wagner

Visit Raye's amazon page to see all of her books.

www.RayeWagner.com

Also by Leia Stone

Visit Leia's amazon page to see all of her books.

www.leiastone.com

Printed in Great Britain
by Amazon